2805

THE POELLENBERG INHERITANCE

by Evelyn Anthony

Evelyn Anthony

To my dear friend
Jenniver White,
with love

1

It took fifteen minutes exactly to walk from his apartment in the Avenida de Infanta to the corner of the Calle Royale to buy the papers; in winter, even when the weather was bitterly cold and there was snow on the streets of Madrid, he came to the store at the same time, collected the English, French and German newspapers, and went home to spend the afternoon reading them. He never bothered with the Italian press. They had turned coward during the war and joined the Allies. He had never forgiven them. It was May and the sunshine lit the city; in a few more weeks the temperature would rise and the atmosphere would become stifling. By the end of June he went away to the Costa Del Sol for a two-week holdiday. He had been in Switzerland for ten years, living a miserable existence in near poverty, unable to work at anything but the most menial jobs, supported by funds from the organization which had helped him escape. Then he was found a job in Spain, and life improved gradually, as the risk of discovery subsided and he applied his ability to the engineering work in which he was engaged. Now, twenty-five years after his flight from Germany, he was a well-paid executive with the original company, living in a flat in Madrid. In Spain he was known as Paul Weiss. He had very few friends

—one Spanish family whom he sometimes visited, and two German couples, both expatriate but much younger than he. He maintained no link with the past now except one. The apartment was on the third floor of a modern block; he disdained the elevator and always used the stairs. All his life he had emphasized physical fitness. He never lost an opportunity to take exercise. Inside his flat he went into the kitchen and made some coffee; this he brought into the small living room and settled down to read the papers during the four-hour siesta which closed everything in Spain from two till six.

The idea of wasting an afternoon sleeping was too ridiculous to be considered. He began with the French papers first, reading every item; occasionally he exclaimed under his breath. Then the English papers followed. On the inside page of the *Daily Express*, he saw the report of the divorce and the photograph. He read it carefully the first and then the second time. He folded the paper back and stared at the photograph. James Stanley's wife wins divorce. He would never have read the item except at a glance, because scandals didn't interest him, but the face in the photograph was large and clear, taken from a studio portrait. It was his own face, and the face of his mother and a sister who had been killed in a bombing raid during the war. Paula Stanley was granted a decree nisi on account of her husband's adultery with a Mrs. Fiona Harper. Then the account of the proceedings followed, and a long write-up about her husband and his career as a racing driver. He had the name that made news. James Stanley, the hero of the international circuits, wealthy amateur who challenged the world's professionals at the world's most dangerous sport. There was a photograph of him, too, taken beside a low-slung racing car, one arm flung across the body, the other cradling a large silver cup. The face was indistinct, and the caption mentioned some triumph at Le Mans. He picked up his coffee and tried to drink it. Then he read the story again. The racing driver and his exploits occupied nine-tenths of the report. The few facts given about his wife were bald and vaguely unsympathetic. She was twenty-eight. He had a pencil out by now, and he was underlining sections. The age was right. There were no children of the marriage, and her address was given in full. She was formerly Paula Ridgeway, and the marriage had lasted for five years. Ridgeway. That was the right name, too. The name of the man his wife had married after the war. The organization had kept him informed of his family's situation during the immediate period of Germany's defeat. He had heard about the confiscation of everything and the occupation of his home by British staff officers. And then his wife's remarriage. To a Major Ridgeway. They had left Germany, taking his daughter with them, and until that afternoon twenty-five years later, he had never heard of them again. He went to the desk, a functional piece of furniture where he kept his files and business correspondence for work at home, and cut out the article and the photograph. Inside his breast pocket he carried a wallet, and in the wallet was a small yellowed snapshot. Everything else which identified him had been destroyed. This one photograph he had kept. It had traveled through the nightmare of the Russian retreat with him; he had taken it out, with fingers so stiff with cold that they could hardly hold it, and looked at it and kissed it. It showed a little girl, a leggy child of three years old, dressed in a conventional party dress with a lace collar, her brown hair tied back with a bow, looking self-consciously into the camera lens. It was frayed around the edges, and a crack ran diagonally across it. He laid it beside the newspaper photograph; the resemblance was slight, probably only visible to someone who was looking for it; he recognized that. But the family likeness in the woman was unmistakable. It was a Bronsart face, high cheekboned, light-eyed, with hair that grew back from a wide forehead, exactly as his own had done. He stood back from the desk. After twenty-five years. After resigning himself to a permanent loss, to taking out his treasured memory, faded like the little snapshot, and contenting himself with that, the impossible had happened. He had found his daughter again. And the dream he had dreamed for her in the last year before disaster overwhelmed his country could now be transformed into reality. Love, as he often said, died quickly enough between men and women. Marriage was a convenience and sentiment a trap. But the love of a father for his child transcended everything. That, and his love for his country, were what distinguished human emotion from the weak and the carnal. He had never loved Paula's mother; he had adored his child with single-minded passion, with tenderness, with fanatical pride. She was his flesh, his blood; she had his eyes, so distinctively blue that they had hindered his escape; she aroused in him a protectiveness normally found in women toward their young. She was the only human being with whom his emotions had ever been involved. Because of her, he sat down again and made the first telephone call to Switzerland in five years. It was only to be used in emergency. He knew it still operated because any change would have been notified. He knew who would answer, because they had served together and fought together, and in the end through the offices of this one man he had escaped. He asked for the number and waited. When the call came through, he said only one sentence. "This is the general. I am flying to Switzerland tomorrow; meet me at Zurich Airport between six and seven. I need your help."

Paula Stanley was in the bath when the telephone rang. Since she had left her husband, she lived alone; she waited, hoping the caller would ring off, but the bell persisted. She got out of the hot water, wrapped a towel around herself, and went through to the bedroom. Her feet left wet marks on the carpet, and she looked down and grimaced. James, her husband, had always been untidy. He threw his clothes on the floor, dropped his ashes indiscriminately, flung his papers into the corner when he had finished reading them, and refused to submit to any kind of domestic routine. All his concentration and discipline had gone into his racing career. Perhaps it was the very carelessness with which he approached ordinary life which had attracted her when they first met. He hadn't given a damn about anything. He was deliberately unconventional. He spent money on nonsense and forgot about mundane demands like electricity bills; he would stay up all night going from one nightclub to the next, picking up friends and strangers on the way, surrounded by admiring spongers, dragging Paula, bewildered and impressed, along with him. Her own life had always been rigid; it was governed by routine since her childhood, by a strict boarding school and a mother whose principal dislike was being asked for anything or expected to do anything connected with her daughter. Paula had lived within narrow confines. Meeting a man like James Stanley was like being permanently drunk. The inhibitions vanished, the obligations of normality disintegrated, and there was a frightening sense of liberation. But it hadn't lasted. The euphoria was temporary; the liberty became, after marriage, a worse constriction of freedom than she had ever known. He declined all responsibilities; he picked up the details of their married life and dropped them into her lap, with the injunction to take care of it because he couldn't be distracted when he was racing. The fact that girls and drink and disorder weren't considered distractions made no impression as an argument. When Paula remonstrated, he simply disappeared. His cars were his life; the excitement, the concentration, the publicity and adulation were all that mattered to James. She had often wondered why he married her at all. She had refused to go to bed with him when they first met; she was too ashamed of her own inexperience to admit that at twenty-three she was still a virgin, and the existence of such a freak never suggested itself to him. He had wanted her and been unable to get her. So, typically impulsive and irresponsible, he had asked her to marry him, and in a public blaze of newspaper headlines, and screaming fans, they had rushed to the registry office and out again. Sexually, it had not been a success. Paula didn't know exactly when he had begun his infidelities, but an instinct that shrank from being hurt insisted that she ask no questions and investigate nothing, however flimsy his excuses. And so for five years they had lived, James projecting his free-wheeling image for the imitation of his fans, both on and off the racing track, and Paula waited uncertainly for something to happen. When it did, it was typical of her husband. He had begun a publicized affair with one woman and confessed, in a burst of boyish candor, that he was in love with another. One was a close friend of Paula's, who had twice accompanied them on holiday, but the object of his immediate affections was unknown, one of the crowd of speed-mad girls who surrounded the racing heroes. Paula had packed her suitcase the same day and moved out. Their divorce had been granted only a month ago.

She put the receiver to her ear.

"Hello?"

"Is that Mrs. Stanley?" It was a man's voice, with a foreign accent.

"Yes, speaking. Who is that?"

"My name is Black. But you don't know me. I would like to come and see you."

Paula hesitated. It was five thirty, and she was getting ready to go down to her mother's for the weekend.

"Why do you want to see me?" she asked. "What can I do for you?"

"I just want to come and talk to you," the voice said. "Don't be alarmed, Mrs. Stanley. I am not a crank. I have something very important to tell you. Something which is to your advantage."

"What do you mean? Are you a solicitor?" Which she realized at once was immaterial because there was no one to die and leave her money. Her mother was her only relative.

"No, Mrs. Stanley. I am not a solicitor. I am a friend of your father's. When can I come?"

"What do you mean, a friend of my father's—my father is dead."

"I know that; does the name Poellenberg mean anything to you?"

"Not a thing. I've never heard of it." For a moment she was tempted to hang up on him. The towel was slipping and she was cold.

"Let me come to see you and I will explain," the voice said. "But don't mention it to anyone. Don't mention Poellenberg. Can I come to see you tomorrow morning?"

"No," Paula said. "I'm going away for the weekend. Why mustn't I mention this to anyone—what's all the mystery about, Mr. Black?"

"I will explain when I see you," he said. "I will explain everything then, but you will have to trust me. On Monday morning, at ten o'clock."

"I go to my office at ten," she said. "Wait a minute, let me think—why don't you come there? About eleven thirty?"

"Will we be able to speak in private?"

"Certainly. Nobody will disturb me. One moment, tell me one thing—you say you're a friend of my father's—"

"I will come to your office on Monday at half past eleven," the voice cut in. "I know the address. Good-bye, Mrs. Stanley. I look forward to meeting you."

The line clicked and then buzzed clear. He had rung off. Paula put the phone down and stood shivering, holding the towel around her. Of course she wasn't afraid. That was what James always said about her—"Nothing would scare you, sweetheart; you're a real tough little Hun." It was a remark that wounded, assuming as it did, that she was able to take care of herself, and consequently he was free of obligation. Even if he was right, that epithet—Hun—always rubbed raw. It was not as if she had been to Germany since her childhood or even spoke the language. James had made the accident of blood into a genetic crime. She had been born in Germany, but she left it as a child, and the Englishman her mother married had adopted her legally and given her his name. Paula went back and let the tepid water out of the bath. She dried herself and stood for a moment before the mirror, examining the naked body for defects. There were none visible; she was young, firm, slenderly built, with an attractive face framed in smooth brown hair. Only the eyes were different. They were blue, but with an extraordinary depth of color. She went back into her bedroom and dressed in trousers, sweater, and jacket. Her weekend case was packed. She looked at the telephone again. What an extraordinary call. A complete stranger ringing out of the unknown, claiming to have news of great importance for her, claiming to have known the dead father she could not remember. It was odd, but Paula realized suddenly that this was what had made her agree to a meeting, not the curiosity aroused by his talk of something much to her advantage, not the natural courtesy which prompted her to agree rather than decline. He had known her father. Who was he, this Mr. Black, with an accent that came from her own unknown homeland across the Rhine? The voice was that of an old man, and if he knew her father the general, then he must be well into his sixties. She locked the flat door behind her and went into her car. As it started up, her thoughts were far away from the teeming traffic that choked her route out through the city of London, through the East End and on to the Newmarket road. She knew the route by heart; she had traveled down to her stepfather's house in Essex for the last ten years, ever since she had left home at twenty to live and work in London alone. Alone. It was the operative word to describe the best part of her life. Five years of that dismal marriage, after a childhood which was spent playing gooseberry to two adults who only really wanted to be left alone with each other. Now that she was truly independent, free of family ties and without James to nag her about neglecting them so he could go off on his own, Paula paid infrequent visits to the house in Essex. They didn't miss her when she stayed away. They were pleased to see her in a distant way, and kind, prepared to let her share their warmth and smugness in each other's company. The result was to drive her out of the house as quickly as good manners would permit.

But her mother was sixty, although she didn't look it, and sometimes Paula's conscience jabbed. On those occasions she gave up her weekend with friends in London or declined another invitation to go away, and invited herself down to the farm.

It was a handsome lath and plaster Essex house, sixteenth century in the most part, with an eighteenth-century wing, which her stepfather's ancestor had built on.

Brigadier Gerald Ridgeway, D.S.O., M.C. She could remember that rosy-complexioned face, with the brisk little gingery mustache and the hearty voice, bending over her from what seemed a gigantic height. He used to smell of leather and some kind of cologne. He had always been kind, but it was a stiff, withdrawn relationship, with bouts of false bonhomie which embarrassed Paula even when she was very young indeed. Children have an instinct for what is assumed, and she knew instinctively that the new man with her mother didn't really love her.

So there was no relationship; she didn't hate him as she might have done if his attitude toward her had been more positive. She accepted him as part of her life and accepted also that she had lost her mother to him as inevitably as if her mother had died, like the general. She didn't remember the general. She knew he was dead, and her mother had answered her questions about him with obvious resentment at being expected to explain. Paula hadn't pursued the subject. Her mother indicated her displeasure, and Paula, even though nearly grown up, withdrew from the contest.

The man called Black knew her father. She was clear of the traffic and beyond the bottleneck at Epping; Paula pressed down on the accelerator and the little car gathered speed. And he had insisted upon secrecy; what was the name he had mentioned—Poellenberg. Paula shrugged as she drove. It meant nothing to her. What was it, a name, a place—what was its significance? In an hour and a half she had turned into the drive and pulled up at the entrance. It was June, and the front of the low-built house was covered with a blaze of yellow climbing roses. The brigadier was a keen gardener; he had interested her mother in the art, and Paula remembered her astonishment at seeing that elegant figure down on its knees with a garden trowel, grubbing in a flower bed.

Two black Labradors came bounding out of the front door, barking and leaping up to welcome her. Dogs, roses, the Women's Institute, a distinguished retired soldier as her adoring husband—this was the role in which her mother had elected to live out the rest of her life. She came through the door after the Labradors, a tall, thin woman in muted tweeds, old but still beautiful with the agelessness of fine aristocratic bone structure, the blue eyes filled with vitality.

They were not the same color as Paula's; that astonishing blue was the general's legacy.

"Paula, dear—" She gave her daughter a light kiss on the cheek. "You're early; did you have a good journey down?"

"Rather a lot of traffic," Paula said. "How are you, mother? You're looking very well."

"I am, dear. But your poor father's got a cold. Come inside, and push those naughty dogs down; they're ruining your clothes."

She always referred to the brigadier as "your father." It was quite unself-conscious; Paula was sure her mother would have been horrified to know how deeply she resented it.

Inside, the house was furnished with comfort and elegance. They spent their time in a small paneled study which was filled with her stepfather's collection of military books; the pictures and furniture were exactly in character with the owner. Very English, slightly shabby, valuable and understated. There was nothing in this country gentleman's home to remind Paula of the dimly remembered gilt and stucco palace where she had been born and lived until the age of four. That was a confused and fading memory, unaided by photographs or any of the normal souvenirs of another life. It was as if her mother had decided to erase the first thirty years before she had met and married Gerald Ridgeway.

She had succeeded in what she set out to do, as indeed she succeeded in everything. A German-born baroness, a widow of a man who had risen to the rank of general fighting the Allies, she now played a leading part in the village social life, was looked up to and respected by everybody. She had succeeded as an army officer's wife under the most difficult postwar conditions. Even her husband's ultra-Conservative military family had ended by accepting the beautiful young German into their circle.

Paula was offered a drink, and she sat down; one of the Labradors had settled beside her and was pressed against her knee. It should have made her feel at home, relaxed, and at ease in the warm, reassuring room, her mother sitting opposite, talking pleasantly about the latest village news, the dusk deepening outside. Instead its effect upon Paula was to make her feel strange and isolated from it all. It was not part of her, however much it had been superimposed upon her. Unlike her mother, she had not adopted the protective coloring of an alien country and an alien culture. As a result she had no country and no affiliations, but it was not possible to miss what one had never known. Or at least it was difficult to blame the sense of restlessness and vacuity upon that deprivation. If Paula was unhappy, she did not know whom to blame or how to define what she needed. She was merely aware of a condition within herself, which had always existed. This she accepted.

"If you don't mind, dear," Mrs. Ridgeway said, "I've made your father stay in bed; I don't want him to take any risks with that cold. The last one was on his chest. It made him quite ill."

"Of course I don't mind," Paula said. "I'll go up and say hello to him later. By the way, mother, I'm glad we're on our own tonight. I want to talk to you."

"Oh? What about?" There was the same guarded look on her mother's face, an instant letting down of shutters, whenever Paula attempted any intimacy.

"I hope there's no more trouble with James."

"It's nothing to do with James," Paula said.

"You know we were very upset about that," her mother said. "It's such a final step, breaking up a marriage."

"Sleeping with my best friend was a pretty final step," Paula said. "Not to mention the little bird he wanted to marry. I suppose I might have taken one of them, but I'm sorry, mother, both was just too much. Besides, we weren't in love with each other. It was bound to come sooner or later."

"I could never imagine leaving my husband," Mrs. Ridgeway said. "Whatever he did."

"But he didn't do anything, did he?" Paula countered. "He's adored you all your married life, so how would you know what you'd do if you had a rotten husband, for instance."

The beautiful, aging face was like a mask. The coldness struck at Paula suddenly and made her angry. How would her mother know anything about the problems of being married to a man who neglected you, avoided responsibility, and made love only when he felt like it? Her mother had been loved and spoiled by one man with an obsessive passion for her. All they had ever wanted was to be alone together, to share their bed and their life without the encumbrance of a child, who seemed always standing in the shadows, looking on.

"Anyway, I don't want to talk about James. I had a very curious telephone call tonight. A man rang up and said his name was Black and he was a friend of my father. He asked to see me."

Now there was a faint color in the face opposite her; it tinged the fine white skin with pink, as if her mother were blushing. Paula saw the expression change from impassive disapproval to outright alarm. The mouth opened for a second; she thought her mother was going to say something. Then the moment passed. Now it really was a mask; the color was fading, leaving the face a gray pallor, and the eyes were bright with wariness, watching her daughter like an intruding stranger.

"I don't understand." The voice was cold, angry. "I know no one connected with us called Black. It sounds like a practical joke."

"It wasn't," Paula insisted. "I'm quite sure it was perfectly genuine. Mr. Black. He sounded German. Mother, please don't go out of the room; I want to ask you about this!"

"There is nothing to ask." Mrs. Ridgeway was standing, poised to walk out. "I advise you to have nothing to do with this man, whoever he is. I know your father would say the same."

Now Paula was standing, too. "He's not my father. He's your husband, but he's nothing to me. Let's leave him out of it for once. I want to talk about my *real* father. Don't walk out on me, mother. What are you afraid of?"

"I refuse to be bullied," her mother said. "I have nothing to discuss with you about your father. He was killed in Russia, and you never even knew him. I suspect you've been building up some fiction about him in your mind. My advice to you is not to make a fool of yourself. As for Mr. Black, it's probably a hoax or else some unpleasant creature with a kink about telephoning women on their own. I think you'd be extremely foolish to have anything to do with it. That's all I have to say."

"He mentioned something," Paula said. "Poellenberg. That was what he said. He asked me if I knew what it meant. By the look on your face, mother, it seems to mean something to you."

"I'm going upstairs," her mother said. "I'm going to your father."

"Stop calling him my father." Paula burst out with it, the suppressed anger of a lifetime exploding in that angry cry. "He's my bloody stepfather and I didn't choose him! Go up to him and leave me. That's what you've always done!"

She dropped back into the chair and began to cry. Immediately the Labrador leaned its black muzzle on her knee. She heard the door close as her mother left the room.

There was a long silence. One of the dogs moved around the room and then resumed its place by its mistress' empty chair. Paula cried for some time. It was a luxury in which she had refused to indulge, even when her marriage disintegrated. She had been unable to feel pain in such clear definition as she did at that moment, sitting alone in the study where she had grown up and always felt a stranger. After a time she became calm. Her head ached and her eyes were swollen-lidded and sore. She looked around her and fought down a sudden impulse to run out of the room and the house and drive straight back to her flat in London. In the quiet she could hear sounds above; boards were creaking as if someone were walking up and down, but the house was built with the solidity of centuries and no voices could be heard. They must be talking up there, her mother and the brigadier. He would be in their double bed, nursing his cold; Paula could imagine him in a dressing gown with a silk handkerchief tucked into the neck. She had never hated him. At that moment it was her mother she hated with all the bitterness of a rejected child. She had dismissed Paula all her life, turning aside her quest for affection as she had done her questions. She had dismissed her father as if Paula had no right to think of him at all, as if his death were a reason for complete oblivion. It was as if he had never walked the earth, married her, slept with her, and produced a child.

Damn her. Damn them both. She heard herself say the words aloud. She had an identity of her own, and her father was part of that identity. They had no right to deny him to her. But the expression on her mother's face was frigid with resistance. It was as if Paula had brought up some forbidden subject, something which was under an unspoken ban. She had denied knowing Black, and Paula had believed her. But the peculiar name—Poellenberg—that had meant something to her. It was as if her daughter had suddenly struck her in the face. It was useless to go upstairs and demand to be answered. If she faced her mother and stepfather, they would combine together as they always had, and she would retire from them in defeat.

They didn't want to discuss her father. The general, Paul Bronsart, dead and buried in the Russian wastes around Stalingrad; they had laid his ghost and enjoyed their own association without any sense of guilt, so long as he and what he represented were effaced from human memory. It was such a pity she had been born, she thought angrily. That must have made it difficult for her mother to forget that she was the widow of a distinguished German soldier, who had fraternized with the invader within months of his death. They had been living in their old house in the Platzburg outside Munich when the Allied forces entered the city and the company commander billeted himself and six of his officers in their home. Paula had heard the story from her mother in snatches over the years, a sentence here and there, and once a sentimental recital of how the brigadier, then a young major, had discovered the mistress of the mansion living in the freezing attics with a sick little girl. It had all been very touching, and Paula remembered how they had reached across and held hands while they talked about it. Her mother had married him and fled the ruins of Germany and the past to make a new life for herself, cocooned by the adoration of her English husband. It might have made it easier for Paula to understand if she had seen some sign that the brigadier had been duped, that her mother had used him in order to escape the disaster of defeat. But it was not so. They were inseparable, smug, completely wrapped up in each other. The inference was very plain. Whatever her father was like, his wife couldn't have cared for him at all.

Paula got up and lit a cigarette. She felt tired and angry, trapped in the house at least for that evening, a criminal waiting in the room below while her mother stayed upstairs to be comforted. The clock in the hall outside struck eight o'clock, and at the last chime the door opened and her mother stood there.

"Aren't you coming for dinner? We're waiting."

He must have got up and come down to support her. Two against one again.

"I'm not hungry," Paula said. "I've got a headache, I think I'll just go to bed, if you don't mind."

Mrs. Ridgeway came into the room. Her daughter noticed that she had changed out of her tweeds into a long black skirt and blouse. She looked very pale and handsome.

"Paula, you've been crying! I haven't seen you cry since you were a child. Do come and have some dinner with us. Do let us forget this stupid quarrel." She came and put a hand on Paula's arm. She looked concerned.

"I don't want to quarrel," Paula said. "I'm sorry I swore at you, mother."

"That's all right dear. Just promise me you'll forget all about that telephone call. Have nothing to do with it. It will be better for all of us."

"Why? Can you just answer me that? Why will it be better?"

"Because there's nothing to be gained by bringing up the past." The look was firm, determined to overcome resistance. She had made her gesture and now she was demanding her price. Surrender. Now do what I want and forget the whole thing.

Paula shrugged and stubbed out the cigarette. Her step-father detested anyone smoking during meals. "That's not much of an answer, mother. But I can see it's the only one you're going to give me, so don't let's argue. I'll have dinner and then I will go to bed early." She opened the door and her mother went ahead of her without answering. Paula heard her stepfather coughing in the dining room.

Nothing was mentioned during the next day. Paula slept late, then drove her mother to the village for some shopping. Everything seemed normal and peaceful. The brigadier had been friendly and in good spirits the night before, but Paula was not deceived. All was not what it appeared. In spite of the people invited to drinks, the determined bonhomie of her stepfather, who was thick and spluttering with his cold, and the grim dignity of her mother, Paula knew that their calm was a façade. Their glances at each other were apprehensive, their attitude tense and worried. The telephone call was never mentioned again. It was tacitly understood that she would do as her mother wanted and ignore the caller. But they weren't sure of this, and that was what disturbed them. Paula spun out the day and a half till she could leave with decency. At the door they came out to say good-bye, accompanied by the dogs. It occurred to Paula that only the animals were sorry to see her go.

"Good-bye, dear." Her mother brushed her cold lips against her face.

"Good-bye, Paula." Gerald Ridgeway had his arm linked with his wife's; he smiled at her and waved. There was a strained, unhappy look around his mouth under the ginger mustache. His hair was white and growing back from his forehead. He looked miserable and unwell. She got into the car, wound down the window, and waved to them both. "Good-bye, thanks for the weekend; it was a lovely rest. Take care of yourself, Gerald, don't stay out in the cold."

All the clichés of departure, the trite little phrases of farewell expected from a stranger. It was the coldest leavetaking she could remember, and it suddenly hurt so much she couldn't wait to start the car and drive away from them.

And then it didn't seem to matter. The next day was Monday, and her appointment with Black was only a few hours away. For the first time she would be able to discover something about the other half of herself. She had forgotten that the caller had something important to tell her; she had forgotten about Poellenberg, that mysterious word which had drained the blood from her mother's face till she looked like a corpse. Paula wasn't thinking of anything but the excitement of discovery and the hunger to know, so that if Providence were merciful, she would be able to love, even if it were a memory passed on to her at second hand.

Eric Fisher's plane landed at Munich Airport at three thirty. It was a warm afternoon, and the sun beat down upon the tarmac, making him sweat after the air-conditioned aircraft. Fisher was used to flying; he regarded it as a good opportunity to sleep. He was bored by the routine, the pre-lunch snacks, the trolley with rattling drinks, the bland hostesses who looked so unreal he was tempted to put it to the test by pinching a round bottom in a tight skirt.

So he settled into his seat, even for a short trip like the flight from London to Munich, and went straight to sleep till they landed.

He knew Munich slightly and was looking forward to spending a day and a night there, revisiting old places known from the early days of the Cold War, when he had been a journalist. He supposed that his business could be accomplished within a couple of hours and that he would have the rest of the time free. The clients were paying all expenses, and he had booked himself into the Hoffburger, which was the city's best hotel. Outside customs, he paused. He was expecting to be met. A man in dark-brown chauffeur's livery came toward him and gave a military salute. Fisher noticed with surprise that he wore old-fashioned leather boots and polished leggings.

"Herr Fisher?"

"Yes."

"Her Highness' car is just outside. Your bag if you please. Follow me this way, sir."

With pleasure, Fisher thought, threading a way through the crowd. Nothing so crummy as a common taxi or hired car. Her Highness' very own awaited. He grinned, enjoying himself. This was the sort of client he preferred. The car was an enormous Mercedes, shining black with silver-gray upholstery and a large elaborate coat of arms painted on the doors. He got into the back seat; he felt tempted to give a regal wave to the porters left outside on the pavement.

The drive took thirty-five minutes; Fisher timed it, just for something to do. Scenery didn't interest him. He took a case of cigarettes out of his pocket and lit one. The glass screen separating his compartment from the front slid down; without turning his head the chauffeur spoke.

"Excuse me, Herr Fisher, but Her Highness dislikes cigarette smoke in the car. Would you mind not smoking? I am very sorry, but her orders are strict."

"Anything you say." Fisher stubbed the cigarette out. Her Highness sounded as if she might be hell on wheels. But then money, rank, and power seldom improved human nature. Especially when they were inherited along with an armament empire in a country where feudality was deeply ingrained in the people. The Germans had a passion for rank and authority. He could tell that the chauffeur despised him because he was casually dressed and his attitude was like his clothes.

With a different breed of passenger he wouldn't have mentioned the no-smoking rule. He'd have cleaned and aired the car and never said a word. Fisher knew his Germans. They were the only race in the world he really disliked. He spoke the language fluently, as he did French and Italian. He liked to think of himself as completely unacademic, but he despised the English attitude which refused to learn any language on the assumption that if you shouted, foreigners understood. He had worked as correspondent for a major midlands newspaper for five years, and then he had met Dunston, who was working for Interpol on a smuggling ring which was spiriting gold out of Western Europe into the East in return for a supply of pure opium. It had been a nasty case, with several murders and an abduction thrown in; Fisher joined the hunt on behalf of his newspaper, and by the time it was over and the ring dispersed, he and the man from Interpol had become good friends. It was Dunston who contacted him a year later and put a proposition to him over drinks in London. Dunston had left Interpol and set upon his own as a private detective. He had the skill and the police contacts, but he needed a partner. Fisher had impressed him. He was, Dunston said, a natural bloodhound. And one of the best sources of information in the world was the press, to which he had entrée. To start with, the money wouldn't amount to much, but if they were successful, the sky could be the limit in fees.

Fisher had no dependents; both his parents were dead, and he had no intention of getting married. He could take the chance and see what happened. Within six years the Dunston Fisher Agency was the biggest private investigating service in Europe, with offices in every capital and a staff of a hundred operators. Now Dunston sat in the head office in London, and Fisher only undertook the biggest assignments, where the fees ran into thousands just as a retainer. The letter from the Princess Margaret Von Hessel had been addressed to Dunston, but Dunston was on holiday in Portugal. A check for a thousand pounds had been enclosed with the letter as an inducement to take the case without delaying. Fisher had cabled back immediately, saying he was coming in his partner's place, and before he left for Germany, he had investigated the family. The name was famous enough. Steel, coal, armaments, property—millions and millions before both wars and a new fortune made since the end of the last. Blood which could be traced to the Bavarian kings and to several European Royal families now dispossessed or extinct. A title granted by Frederick the Great. Castles in Germany, a vast property in East Prussia which the Communists had overrun, a villa at Cap Ferrat which had not been used for twenty years. A passion for the vicious concentration camp dog, the Doberman pinscher. And at its head the princess, age seventy-six, the mother of two sons. Widowed in the last war when her husband died of a heart attack. Even before he arrived at the house itself, Fisher was expecting something formidable.

The car turned in through wrought-iron gates, surmounted by the heraldic boar which was the Von Hessel crest. The house was enormous—a square, stuccoed building, painted pale washed pink. Flowers were growing in ornamental tubs all around, and there was a paved courtyard big enough to have taken half a dozen of the Mercedes. Trees enclosed the garden, which stretched out on either side; the whole place gave an illusion of being in the depth of the countryside instead of within five miles of Munich's center.

He got out, and the chauffeur preceded him. A butler in uniform, brass-buttoned tailcoat, white cotton gloves, opened the front door, took his hat away, and made a small bow, asking him to follow. The main hall of the house was like a church. It was dominated by a huge, hideous Victorian stained-glass window at one end; the ceiling disappeared upward in painted clouds and bibulous fauns pursuing naked nymphs. The smell of flowers was overpowering; there were huge bowls and urns filled with them, and it gave the hall a funereal atmosphere. The furniture was heavy mahogany, massively carved, upholstered in velvet. A ten-foot carved gilt mirror gave Fisher a sudden glimpse of himself, standing dwarfed and uncertain in the ugly, overpowering surroundings with the light from the stained-glass window making bloody patterns over him.

"This way, please," the butler said. He opened a door and Fisher blinked. It was like walking into the sunlight. The room was large and painted white. The colors were yellow and green, and the sunshine poured into it from three floor-length windows. Three people waited for him like figures in a stage set; the center one was sitting, very upright, her back to the light, holding a cane in one hand. Behind her two other figures were silhouetted, standing sentinel on either side of the sofa where she sat.

"Your Highnesses, Herr Fisher." He heard the butler's voice and then the click of the door closing. He walked forward into the room, across an Aubusson carpet covered in green and golden flowers woven in garlands from the center, and stopped in front of the sofa. The Princess Von Hessel held out her hand, palm downwards. Fisher looked her in the eye and shook her hand firmly.

"How do you do, Mr. Fisher. Let me present my sons."

Seventy. She looked about fifty; there wasn't a white hair

on her head, and the face was like a predator bird's—beaked nose, taut skin, dark eyes bright and unblinking, with a yellow circle around the iris. Formidable wasn't the word. But he hadn't kissed her hand. He felt comforted by that.

"My eldest son, Prince Heinrich. My second son Prince Philip. Please sit down."

He took his eyes off the woman and examined the two sons. The younger attracted his attention first because he was an extremely handsome man in his late thirties, and very blond. He looked out of place beside the South German darkness of his mother and his elder brother. The elder was very like the princess. He had the same birdlike face, but the sharp lines of character and pride were blurred, the contours sagged, and the dark eyes were sunk in puffs of flesh. He stood very upright, shoulders well back and one hand with a big gold-crested ring on the last finger, rested on the back of the sofa.

"Did you have a good journey?" That was the younger son, Philip.

"Fine thanks." They were all speaking English. Fisher would have preferred to converse in German, but there seemed no way of changing over. He decided to take the initiative before the old woman did. He suspected that the sons were not expected to contribute much.

"You didn't say very much about this investigation in your letter, Princess." He had no intention of calling her Your Highness, like a bloody footman. His hostility was rising with every minute. He resented the imperious stare, the arrogant look which was quite unself-conscious. "You mentioned the recovery of some property, but that's all."

"I thought it best to wait until you were here and we could discuss the details privately. I believe one should keep these things out of correspondence, Mr. Fisher. As a family, we have learned to be cautious."

"Would you like to give me the details now?" Fisher suggested. He was in need of a cigarette, but he remembered the chauffeur's warning. The inhibition made him even more irritable than the deprivation. Who the hell did she think she was, that he couldn't have a cigarette when he wanted one—

"As you know . . ." The princess began what he suspected was a prepared speech. She had folded her hands and settled in her seat. He recognized the symptoms of rehearsal. "As you know, the Nazis conducted a systematic policy of looting art treasures during the war. They confiscated pictures, jewelry, *objets d'art*, and every kind of valuable; I had the misfortune to go to Göring's house and see the result of this disgraceful pillage for myself. The houses of all the high-ranking Nazi officials were stocked with other people's property. They stole from some of my dearest friends in France, for example. The property was recovered after the war and returned to them in a deplorable state. It was in Berlin and the house was shelled by the Russians. There was a magnificent Titian which was ripped to pieces by shrapnel. It was very sad."

Fisher sat still. It was going to be a long speech. Her eldest son shifted his position behind the sofa. Fisher noticed that he gripped the back of it so hard that his knuckles were taut against the skin. Unrelaxed, that was Prince Heinrich. Finding it a strain standing at attention like a dutiful soldier behind the general's chair. . . .

"All this you know Mr. Fisher, as I said before. What you probably don't know is that these creatures stole equally from their fellow Germans. There are many old families in this country who were looted as if they were enemies. A lorry with S.S. troopers just pulled up outside the door and loaded everything from a list which had probably been made when some senior official was a guest in the house. It was infamous, and I could quote you several cases."

"And is that what happened to you?" Fisher interrupted. He wasn't interested in the vicissitudes suffered by those who wined and dined the members of the Nazi hierarchy. The woes of the aristocracy seldom moved him to compassion.

"No, it was not," she answered. "We were too important to be treated in that way. My husband had a certain amount of influence with people like Göring, for instance. He was a dreadful gangster, but he had come from a gentle family and it was possible to trust his word. We were not harmed in any way."

"But something was stolen from you."

"Yes. Stolen. Taken out of Schloss Wurzen, our home in the Rhineland. I must tell you, Mr. Fisher, I had given up any hope of recovering it until I read this in the newspaper. Philip, get the cutting of the *Allgemeine Zeitung*, will you? It is in the second drawer of my bureau, on the left."

Fisher watched the son move across the room. By contrast with the rigid figure of his elder brother, he was pleasant to watch. He walked like a human being. He even looked across at Fisher and smiled as he handed his mother a newspaper cutting. She held it out and Fisher took it. He read it quickly; he showed no sign of surprise. Impassivity was part of the job. But if this was tied in with the princess' desire to recover her stolen property, that thousand-pound check was just confetti. He gave it back to her.

"It's only a report," he said. "There've been a lot like it."

"Not for this man," she said. "He's been accounted dead since 1945. Believe me, Mr. Fisher, we made our own inquiries after the war, and they all said the same. Dead. Positively identified and buried. Now this report says he was seen in Paris, walking down a street in broad daylight."

"I presume this means he's the thief," Fisher said.

"It does." She nodded. The eyes reminded him of something, but he couldn't think what. Some kind of bird. And certainly no domestic pet. It was the circle of yellow around the dark-brown iris. "He stole the Poellenberg Salt from us, Mr. Fisher. It's never been found, and if he's alive, he's the only person who knows where it is hidden. That is why I've sent for you. I want you to find him."

2

Mr. Black was a small man. Paula was behind her desk when he was shown in, and she was surprised to find that he was a head shorter than she was. She had expected someone tall.

But Black was slight and small-boned; he took off a dark felt hat, and his hair was completely white, brushed right back from a wide forehead. It was a Slavic face, high cheek-boned, with heavy-lidded gray eyes and a narrow mouth.

Paula held out her hand and he made a little bow and kissed it. It was not a real kiss, just an upper-class German gesture in which the lips never made contact.

"How do you do, Mr. Black," she said. "Please come and sit down."

"How do you do, Mrs. Stanley. Thank you. Over here?"

She pointed to one of the two modern armchairs which furnished her office. It was a cheerful room, the walls covered with Paula's own fabric designs. This room and what it represented was a very important part of her life. During the latter part of her marriage to James, her career as a designer had provided refuge and self-respect. In this sphere she had succeeded.

"What can I do for you?" she said. "Have a cigarette?"

"No, thank you, I don't smoke. Mrs. Stanley, I have something very important to tell you, but I think I should explain myself a little first."

"You said something on the phone," Paula said. "You mentioned knowing my father. I'd like you to tell me about him. Please."

"What do you want to know?" he asked her. "I served under him for three years and I was also his friend. And his devoted admirer. He was a great man, Mrs. Stanley. I hope you realize that." The gray eyes were dilated; his stare made her uncomfortable. "A very great man. I was with him and I know. You resemble him very much, did you know that?"

"No," Paula said slowly. "I didn't know."

"You have his eyes," Black said. "The moment I came into the room and saw you, it was like seeing the general again. He was very proud of you; he carried a photograph of you in his wallet. He used to show it around. He didn't mind that you were not a son. You don't remember him, do you?"

"No," she said. "I was too small. I haven't even a photograph of him. I don't even know what he looked like."

"Ah," he said slowly. "Your mother married again, didn't she—to an English officer? Yes, I heard about it. She would prefer to forget the general then. You didn't tell her I had telephoned, did you?"

"Yes," Paula admitted. It seemed pointless to lie. There was a fanatical look about him which disturbed her. For a small man, white-haired and frail, he was rather frightening. She had never met anyone like him before, and she couldn't have described why she was afraid. Then he smiled, and his face became gentle again. "I am not criticizing her—please don't misunderstand. She was always charming to me," he said. "Things were very difficult after the war. We had to survive as best we could. It's a pity you don't remember your father. He was very fond of you. Very fond."

"I didn't know that," Paula said. "I've never been told anything about him."

"He loved you," Black said. He leaned a little forward in his chair, his hands clasped tightly together on his knees. "He loved you as no man has ever loved a child. He told me in the last months before the end, that if he was killed, his only regret would be leaving you. He felt your mother would be able to take care of herself."

"She did," Paula said. She was surprised by the sensation of bitterness. "She married and got out."

"She was very fortunate. Most of the prominent families lost everything, apart from the unlucky ones in the East, who were taken away by the Russians and never seen again. Many of us committed suicide. I chose to live, Mrs. Stanley. And I have a question to ask you. A very important question."

"What is it?" The pale eyes were glittering at her. It struck Paula suddenly that what made the little man frightening was the unhinged expression which came and went in his eyes. She found herself gripping the arms of her chair. "What question, Mr. Black?"

"Would you like your father to be alive or dead?"

"There is no question of what I would like," she said. Now she was frightened. He looked completely crazy. "My father has been dead for twenty-five years. He was killed in Russia."

"A lot of people were said to have been killed in Russia." He smiled and his look was sly. "Or in Berlin during the final Russian advance. But supposing he had escaped, by some miracle—how would you feel, Mrs. Stanley?"

"I don't know," Paula said. "I'm sorry, I can't take any of this seriously. I know my father is dead, and that's all there is to it." She raised her wrist and looked at her watch. "Mr. Black, I have an appointment in a few minutes—"

"I understand," he said. "You want to get rid of me. Very well, Mrs. Stanley. But I promised your father I would give you a message, and I must keep my word. The general's money and properties were confiscated after the war. He guessed this would happen; he guessed we would be defeated. So he put something away for you, Mrs. Stanley. Something very, very precious. Does the name Poellenberg mean anything to you?"

"No," Paula said. "Nothing. I've never heard of it."

"In the sixteenth century," Mr. Black said, "there was a Count von Poellenberg who married a niece of the Medicis. They were married in Florence, and part of the bride's dowry was at the wedding feast. Benvenuto Cellini had made it. It was the wonder of the city, Mrs. Stanley. A salt, a marvel made of solid gold and covered with jewels, made by the greatest goldsmith the world has ever seen. A huge ornament, so heavy it took a man to lift it. And it was known afterward as the Poellenberg Salt. For four hundred years it was one of the treasures of Germany. Then during the war it was given to your father."

"Given?"

"Given," Black repeated. He said the word with emphasis. "The general accepted it as a gift. He had done the owners a favor, and they wanted to show their gratitude. They knew he was a man of taste, a connoiseur. They gave him the Poellenberg Salt. And he bequeathes it to you."

"I don't believe you," she said. "I don't believe any of this. Either you're trying to hoax me, Mr. Black, or you should see a doctor."

He got out of his chair. He looked at her, and there was something cold and authoritative about him, an echo of the past when he had been a young man, serving her father. If that too were not a madman's lie.

"You don't believe me?"

"No, I'm afraid I don't. The whole story is too fantastic. I don't know why you've come here, and I shall not take it any further if you'll please leave now. If you bother me again with this sort of thing, Mr. Black, I shall go to the police."

"I told the general this might be your reaction." The little man stood up. His expression was contemptuous. "He believed in your love for him, more than he trusted me. He wouldn't tell me where the Salt was hidden. But he gave me this clue to give you. Paris, twenty-fifth June, 1944. Tante Ambrosine and her nephew Jacquot. If you want the Poellenberg Salt, without your father, then you will have to solve this little riddle. If you want both of them, then you can get in touch through me. I will telephone once more. I leave the day after tomorrow."

"I don't believe you." Paula got up. "I think you're mentally unbalanced, coming here with a story like this. There's no such thing as a Poellenberg Salt, and all that nonsense about a riddle and my father being alive. If he was alive, he would have come to find me himself!"

"You don't know very much about him, do you, Mrs. Stanley? You can believe me or not, as you like. But I have told the truth. Think about it. You may change your mind. Good morning."

His heels came together with a click, and he bowed. Before Paula could move he had gone out of the office.

The reference room at the British Museum smelled of must. The attendant in his dark-green overall shook his head. "Never heard of it, miss. Look in the section on Cellini; you'll find a book listing all his known works; some of 'em are illustrated. Then there's the European Treasures, the History of Gold and Silverwork, Art Treasures of the Renaissance. Try Cellini first; if it's a major piece by him, it ought to be in there." Paula got out two volumes and sat down at one of the long reference tables. A scattered group of students and two elderly men were reading and making notes. It was her lunch time, and she had been telling herself all the way from her office, what a fool she was being, and that she ought to have gone for a walk instead of wasting a lovely summer's day on a wild goose chase to prove a harmless lunatic in the wrong. Of course Black was an eccentric; perhaps he had known her father or been in the army with him. That part

she was inclined to believe, probably, as she suspected afterward, because she wanted to believe it, she wanted to hear
about her father, whereas she didn't in the least want to hear
about a hidden treasure made by Benvenuto Cellini, which
was obviously a figment of the old man's sick imagination.
She was disappointed and angry, and she assured herself
that she was setting out to prove that the whole story was
nonsense. There would be no Poellenberg Salt, made of gold
and covered with jewels. It was just fantasy.

It was illustrated in the last third of the book on Cellini's
work. It was photographed in color, detailed as being thirty-
six inches high, set with a hundred and eighteen diamonds,
eighty-three rubies, a hundred and five sapphires, and twenty-
five Baroque pearls of large size. Brought to the Poellenberg
family as part of Adela de Medici's dowry. Now in the possession of the Prince of Von Hessel at Schloss Wurzen in the
Rhineland. Paula sat looking at it.

All right. There was a Poellenberg Salt. That part was true.
But it belonged to a prince, not to her father. Then she turned
to the front of the book. It was dated from before the war.
Black must have seen it somewhere, perhaps in a museum or
in a magazine illustration, and woven the whole crazy story
around it. Just because one thing was true, it lent no credence
to the rest. Of course the Salt was still in the possession of
the Bavarian prince. Von Hessel. She had remembered the
name. What she really needed was an up-to-date book on
Cellini, not something written forty years ago. Something
which could identify and place the Salt in its present ownership. She put the book back and began to search among the
shelves. Then she chided herself for being ridiculous. She was
behaving as if there might possibly be something in the old
man's fairy story. She looked at her watch and told herself it
was late and she had to go.

But toward the end of the shelf there was a recent volume
on Great Art Treasures of Europe. She took it down and

turned to the index. Poellenberg, page 187. It was illustrated again, gleaming and glittering in color. The figures of nymphs and centaurs intertwined around a rock basin hollowed out of solid gold to take the salt. A massive collection of gems glittered around the base and in the leaves of a spreading golden tree which surmounted the whole.

The figures were so beautifully molded that they could have moved. There was a paragraph written under the photograph, giving the same history as the book on Cellini but in less detail. The Salt had passed into the possession of the Von Hessels through marriage with a Poellenberg, who was the last surviving member of the ancient family in 1693. The last sentence seemed to enlarge before her as she started reading. "Tragically the Poellenberg Salt was among the art treasures looted by the Nazis during the war and its whereabouts have never been discovered." Paula shut the book and put it back on the shelf. It was heavy and her arm ached. He must have read about that, too. She walked out of the room; the attendant called softly after her—"Find anything, miss?"

"Yes, thank you," Paula said. Outside, it was sunny and warm; she had left her car around the corner of Bedford Square. She walked toward it slowly. It was all lies. The man was mad, unbalanced. He had looked mad at times during that meeting. Then why had the name Poellenberg upset her mother? She had been hiding away from that question because it somehow made sense of what Black had said. Her mother had heard of it and not just casually as a national possession.

Looted by the Nazis during the war. Given, the sinister little man had said, biting on the word. Given out of gratitude. If you want to find it, go to Paris, ask for somebody called Tante Ambrosine and her nephew Jacquot. June, 1944.

What had her father done? Had he really owned the Salt and hidden it? Was there any use asking her mother, trying to force the forbidden subject out into free discussion? Paula started the car and swung out into the traffic. Just supposing it were true—just suppose for a moment that strange visitor that morning was telling the simple truth, that her father was still alive and had hidden a priceless art treasure. . . . At first it had all seemed to be nonsense; fantasy was the word which described it. But now there was enough truth to cast credibility upon the rest. She didn't even know where to find Black. And her mother wouldn't help. Why would it be better to leave the past alone? Paula had demanded that over the weekend, and the answer came back to her. Because there was nothing to be gained from it. Now she saw that answer for what it was; not only a cliché but a lie. If there was nothing to be gained, perhaps there was something to be lost. Lost to her and the brigadier and their cozy life from which the general's daughter had always been excluded. Just supposing the most important part of Black's story were a fact and not the delusion she had first believed it—supposing her father was not dead, supposing he was only missing and her mother had lied, contracting a bigamous marriage. . . .

No wonder she wouldn't want the matter raised, no wonder she preferred to keep consistent silence about the past. Now some of it was beginning to make sense. If Black was really telling the truth. What a fool she had been to dismiss him. How hasty and arrogant to call him a liar or a madman and let him go with nothing but that flimsy promise to contact her once more before he left. Back in her office, Paula tried to work, but concentration was impossible. The facts she had read about the Poellenberg Salt chased around her brain. It had been looted by the Nazis. That part did not accord with Black, who insisted that it was a gift. And her father was an army general, not a Nazi. Perhaps this cast doubts on Black's story—perhaps she was building insane hopes upon something which was only a delusion after all. By five o'clock her head was aching, and she had wasted the afternoon; everything she had done would have to be thrown away. She had a date for dinner that evening; the prospect of making conversation with the pleasant but unimportant man who had invited her, was only one degree better than spending the evening alone waiting for the hours to pass until Black might telephone her again. If he didn't, she would be left with an insoluble mystery which could never be answered. Tante Ambrosine and her nephew Jacquot. It sounded like a nursery rhyme. And a rhyme which she would never try to solve in terms of any hidden treasure. Because from the confusion and doubt which had assailed her, one salient fact had emerged, taking precedence over everything else. If any part of Black's story was true, then the only thing which mattered was the possibility of coming face to face with her father at last.

"I wish you wouldn't go to London." Mrs. Ridgeway had never nagged or frustrated her husband when he wanted to do something. Only her intense concern for his health would have made her repeat herself so often during the morning. He still had the cough, and he looked pale and puffy under the eyes. He had made up his mind to go to London and see Paula and nothing she could say would stop him.

"Your cold is so bad. That trip on Monday morning made it worse," she said. "You know the doctor told you to stay in bed; going on a train journey could make you very ill! Why must you go up again?"

"I'm much better," the brigadier said. "The pain's gone and those pills have done the trick. Don't fuss about me, darling, it's not necessary. What's much more important is to stop this damned nonsense with Paula. I know you haven't had a night's sleep since she came down."

"You won't be able to do anything," his wife said. "I tried, I appealed to her to leave it alone, but she's determined. She wants to dig up the past. And she'll be more sorry than anyone else when it all comes to light!" Her husband came and put his arm around her. He kissed the pale brow and held her close to him.

"Not as sorry as you and I," he said gently. "We have everything to lose. Your peace of mind, your happiness—that's what matters to me, nothing else. I couldn't give a tinker's curse for myself, but I can't bear to see you unhappy. I never could, you know that. And I know what this means to you. We've made our lives, my darling, and nobody's going to come in and start ruining our last years on any pretext. I like Paula; she's a good girl. I think she's messed up her life, leaving James and going off on her own, but that's her business. The general and everything connected with him is *our* business—I'm going to see her and make her drop it. And don't you worry. Promise me, you won't worry."

"I'll try," his wife said. "But it's like a nightmare. After all these years—why should anyone contact her, why should anyone even mention the Poellenberg Salt!"

"That's what I'll find out," the brigadier said. His breath caught and he coughed. "I'll go and see Paula, and I'll even frighten her if I have to. But I promise you, sweetheart, you won't have to worry. Now I must go or I'll miss the train. I'll be back after tea." He kissed her again, and she went to the car to see him drive away. He was a gentle man; his gentleness had attracted her from the first—that odd mixture of diffidence and kindliness which she knew now was so typically English.

The general was not a gentle type; diffidence was not within his comprehension. Fanatical, disciplined, courageous, and completely without feeling as far as she could ascertain in the thirteen years they had been married. He had behaved with scrupulous correctness toward her and complete indifference. They had existed together rather than lived. He had made love to her in the beginning to satisfy his impulses and then to beget children. He had not been cruel or unduly inconsiderate, but only after she had been married for some

months to Gerald Ridgeway, had she realized what this relationship could mean between two people. The general had
wanted sons; she had borne him one daughter. The only in-
consistent thing she had ever known about him was his reaction to the child and its sex. She had expected disappointment
and reproaches. Instead he had astounded her by his attach-
ment to the little girl. He was a grim, forbidding man of
whom she had always been fundamentally afraid. She hadn't
been sure whether the sight of him cradling the baby and
crooning to it repelled her or increased her nervousness toward him. But unconsciously something jealous and primeval
stirred in her nature, some buried instinct of resentment for
the response called forth by another female to the male upon
whom she had made no sentimental impression at all. She had
hated the child and suppressed the hatred, as she had done
with her feeling for her husband, which had begun by being
love. When they married, he was young and splendid, with a
glamor peculiar to the elite of the day. He was a handsome
man who attracted women, all the more because of his cool,
unapproachable attitude toward them. To the masochistic
yearnings of her women friends he was a godlike challenge.
To his wife he was a ruthless, cold-hearted stranger with
whom she was forced to share her life. She had ended by hat-
ing him and she hated his child because he loved it so ex-
travagantly, and as it grew it was the carbon copy of him.
She turned back into the house and sighed. Gerald's chest
was still infected. He had gone to London to a club committee meeting on Monday. He should never have got out of bed
and gone a second time to see Paula; she shouldn't have
rushed upstairs that first night when Paula told her about
Black and burdened him with everything. But the habit of
dependence upon him was too strong. She relied upon him
for everything, and he had never disappointed her. She loved
him with the single-minded intensity of an obsessional and
introverted personality, to whom emotional security has fi-

nally been given. She would have done anything in the world for Gerald Ridgeway, and he would have equally done anything for her.

The room in the cheap hotel where Black was staying was in darkness when he opened the door. He never left a light on; for twenty-five years he had lived on the pittance allotted him, scraping a casual living here and there, doing odd menial jobs and moving on. He had lived like a nomad, always alone, collecting a monthly pension from the fund, which kept him at subsistance level. In return he acted as telephone liaison for others like himself. Often in the early years he had debated whether life was worth living under these conditions. As he had told Paula, many of his comrades had chosen to die rather than suffer the consequences of defeat. But Black had an instinct for survival. Hope persisted in him, though he had long since forgotten in what or for what. Merely to wake and see the sun, to move about freely in the world. This was enough, and the years had dimmed and distorted his memories. Now he lived with them and through them, withdrawing a little more each day from the present and its realities into that golden past when he and his kind had possessed the world. It was a world in which beautiful women moved, suave and smiling, hanging on the arms of men in uniform; where champagne was drunk and music played. The houses were palaces, the beds were thrones, the cars were huge and sleek, with outriders. It was a soldier's paradise, and even the destruction of the enemy with its attendant horrors, had a Wagnerian magnificence that made it poetry to watch so many dying, by the light of such a fire.

He had spent the day in St. James's Park, feeding the birds. He had bought himself some sandwiches and sat by the water's edge, throwing crumbs to the sparrows and coaxing them onto his hand. A group of children had surrounded him, watching, delighted. Black liked children; he gave them pieces of bread and showed them how to hold it still to tempt the fluttering assault of the sparrows. He smiled and talked a little to them, enjoying his day in the sunshine. He had been married, with a son and daughter. Both were dead. His daughter had been killed in an air raid on the Berlin hospital where she was nursing, and his son had died in Poland. He had divorced his wife in the early part of the war, and even now he never thought about her. After the last child she had been sterilized, and it was impossible for Black to remain married to her. It set a bad example to the younger officers. She had taken his decision very badly, especially since the court awarded him the custody of both their children, and he decided it was better if she did not contact them. There had been great bitterness and reproach on her side.

He had forgotten about his dead son and daughter now. So many had died. So much had dissolved in ash and disintegrated in blast. He had dozed in the sunshine on his seat. He had kept his promise; it made him happy to think that after all these years, he had been able to be of service to the general.

The resemblance between father and daughter was extraordinary. She had the same blue eyes, so bright and piercing. The women used to go mad about the general because of those eyes. But he was a handsome man, with a natural swagger to him, which caught the onlooker's attention. No matter who he was with, the general always stood out. Truly, Black had loved him. There was nobody he admired more. The general had befriended him, taken him into his confidence. They had fought in the last campaign in Russia together, when the Red wave crashed against them and rolled on toward the fatherland. There had been death and destruction during those last months. Black had a dream even now, where he walked through a passage and the walls were built of the dead. It wasn't a nightmare which frightened him. It was just a dream. He had lived through the reality and emerged sane, determined, and skillful enough to survive. The years of exile had unhinged him a little; the loneliness taught him to converse aloud with himself; people in the streets stared after him because he was in earnest conversation as he walked along. He had admired the general's daughter. She had spirit, like her father. She had received him well and heard him calmly, until she spoiled it all at the end by refusing to believe and telling him he ought to see a doctor. He had recognized the general immediately at Zurich Airport; he was older and his hair was completely white, but he carried himself with the same upright arrogance— he stood unbent by the years. When he took off the tinted glasses for a moment, his remarkable eyes were as blue as Schwarz remembered. He was not a homosexual, but he admitted to himself that there was something stronger than normal junior officers' allegiance in his attitude toward the general. It had always been so; he had conceived an almost adolescent hero-worship for the man when he began to serve as ADC. The general personified the ideological ideal by which Schwarz lived; all Germans ought to look and act as he did. Schwarz had followed him like a dog, and the general had honored him with his confidence and occasional marks which might be broadly interpreted as friendship. And he had got the general out when the war was ending, because he had been chosen by the organization as one of its key men. He had taken the general out through Germany and into Switzerland and then been ordered to leave him alone and vanish out of sight himself. Since he had never disobeyed an order, Schwarz had done what he was told. Twice in the twenty odd years that followed, he had spoken to the general; on both occasions it was to request fresh papers and a new place to live. Schwarz had procured the papers and made the arrangements. He had seen and heard nothing of the general since then, and as he had aged and the number of men living in disguise were diminishing through old age and death, he had less to do for the organization. Time had weakened him and shifted his mental equilibrium until it was delicately balanced.

He lived now for the simple pleasures of existing, like spending the day in the park in London and feeding the birds, with English children hanging around his knee. His meeting with the general had induced a powerful upsurge of old feelings; he had shaken his hand and wiped tears from his eyes. They had gone to have a meal together, and to Schwarz it was like a dream in which the past had swung back as if time were a pendulum. He had listened to the general and promised to do as he asked.

He accepted the general's money, which was a generous amount, and repeated the curious clue which he was to give the general's daughter. He had sensed, although he was too proud to put it into words, that what the general really wanted was for him to establish a contact between him and his daughter. But even if she rejected him, as in fact she appeared to have done, his love for her had provided the means of her finding the Poellenberg Salt. Schwarz had seen it once; it was the most beautiful thing he had ever imagined. Too beautiful, too rich with jewels and gold. The possession of such a thing would be beyond him. He would have melted it down and taken out the priceless stones. Only a man of the general's stature could have owned such an object. He understood that the general hadn't trusted him with a plain message; he accepted that caution. He hoped, because he knew it was what the general also wanted, that the girl would come out on the side of her father and ask to be taken to him direct. He hoped, but without much conviction. The idea of her disappointing her father made Schwarz angry. He would telephone her the next day before he left. He hadn't delayed after he left her office. He had sent the general a telegram. "Contact has been made and your instructions carried out."

The general had flown to Paris and remained there, waiting. He wanted to be near in case his daughter came. It had seemed an unnecessary risk, but then Schwarz didn't dare to argue. Paris was closer than Switzerland. Closer to what— Schwarz put the thought away from him. The Poellenberg Salt was not his concern. Had the general told him to go and recover it, he would have done so without any thought of personal gain. He opened the door and switched on the light. There was a gas ring and a gas fire; he filled a tin kettle and put it on to heat for some coffee. He had just made himself a large mug when he heard somebody knocking gently on the door.

"Heinrich, open the door." The princess banged on the panel of the door with the handle of a stick. She rapped once, twice, in a sharp staccato. "Open the door! I know what you're doing!"

There was a shuffling sound from the other side of it, a heavy lurch against the wood, and the noise of a key being clumsily twisted the wrong way. When the door did open, Henry, Prince Von Hessel, stood leaning on the door jamb. His mother walked past him and turned around.

"Close that and get out of sight. I don't want a servant to walk by and see you in that disgusting state!"

"I am not in a disgusting state," her son said. "I am a little drunk, but that is all. You knew I would be, mother, why did you come in?"

"Because I want to talk to you," she said. "Go and sit down before you fall over."

She herself went and sat stiffly in an armchair; she was a woman who had never slouched in her life. She looked at her eldest son with a mixture of distaste and despair. "Couldn't you have waited till that detective was out of the house? Couldn't you control yourself for just one day and night?"

"I didn't have to be there," Prince Heinrich said reasonably. He made his way across the room, picking a path across the carpet with great care, as if it were strewn with rocks. He sat down on the end of his bed and slumped.

"This business is nothing to do with me. I've told you; I'll have no part in it."

"You had a part in it," she said fiercely. "If it weren't for you—ach, what is the use of reproaching you? What is the use of talking to you at all?"

"Don't let me keep you, mother. I shall not be down to dinner."

She looked at him. "Philip could search this room. We could smash every bottle you've got hidden."

"You could have me committed," he said. "That would be more sensible. If you take my bottles away, mother, I only get more. Why can't you leave me to get drunk in peace? It isn't much to ask. I don't bother you; I keep to myself."

"Except when you're driving." The princess' voice rose. "Then you take your car and kill some wretched child, and who has to pay the parents and silence the police? Your family! Always your family—"

"You didn't want the scandal," he said. He shrugged. "I don't even remember an accident."

"How could you? You were unconscious over the wheel, stinking of brandy; Philip could hardly get you out of the car."

"Being a Von Hessel has its uses." He laughed at her, his mouth wide in a drunken grin, his eyes narrow and taunting. "There's nothing we can't buy, is there? Even the parents were calling you Highness and bowing and scraping when you paid them off! Go down and deal with your detective, mother. Get Philip to impress him. I don't matter, so long as you have Philip."

"If he sees you drunk," the princess said, "if he asks questions or gets curious, this whole thing could blow up in our faces. I saw him watching you in the drawing room. You were swaying on your feet; I could feel it!"

He shrugged again, spreading his hands. "If you say so. Why don't you leave it alone? Why try to dig the dead out of their graves? It's a mistake, and you'll be sorry. You and my brother, who is always right, of course. But not this time. This time it's a mistake."

"I'm not digging the dead out; I'm trying to make sure they're still buried. If he's dead, then we can rest in peace. If he's alive—"

"Yes," her son said. The drunken grin was a leer now. There was hatred in the look he gave her. She didn't see it; her own gaze was distant, fiercely concentrated upon something else. "Yes, suppose that newspaper was right. What are you going to do about it, mother? You can't buy *him* off. He has the Salt. What are you going to do then?"

The princess turned around to him; slowly she rose from the chair, supporting herself on the cane. "I am going to get it back," she said. "That's all I will say. I want you to stay here and not come down tonight. Fisher is with your brother in the library, looking at some of our records. He mustn't see you, and I want the key of your room. Give it to me."

"It's in the lock. Take it, mother. Lock me up like a naughty boy. I'm in my fifty-second year, but you can lock me in my room if you like. I have a bottle to occupy me, and I shall not batter the door down to get out."

"Make sure you don't," his mother said. "Finish your bottle. I don't care what you do so long as the world never knows what you are."

She took the key and went out. He heard her turn it and saw the handle move from the other side. He opened the cupboard beside the bed and took a full bottle of cognac from the chamber pot compartment. There was an empty bottle standing at the back of the recess. He poured some into his water glass and raised it to the door. "Prosit, mother," he said. "Let's hope he really is alive. By God, he'll be a match for you!"

Fisher caught the early morning plane. He had paid off his taxi cab and was walking through to the departure lounge when he felt a touch on his arm. He turned and saw Prince Philip Von Hessel.

"Good morning." He looked very handsome and agreeable; he had a charming, frank smile. In spite of his disinclination to unbend toward any of them, Fisher had found himself liking the younger son. "I hoped I'd be able to catch you. Have we time for a cup of coffee?"

Fisher looked at his watch. "I should think so. Let's go through to the lounge." People turned to look after them, and Fisher knew it was the other man who was attracting their attention. He was very tall, and he moved with purpose, fast but without hurrying. The majority of people traveling slouched and scurried, anxious about the time, about their luggage, about the flight. This superior German wouldn't be discountenanced by anything. Fisher followed and let him order. The smile was still there, but a shade less bright. Perhaps, Fisher thought, he's not quite as invulnerable as he appears. Something has brought him here at this God-awful hour, and it's not to have coffee and wave me good-bye.

"I wanted to talk to you alone," the prince said. "That's why I came."

"Go ahead." Fisher offered him a cigarette.

"Do you think it's possible this man is still alive?"

"I don't know. I shouldn't have said so; your mother seemed certain you had covered all angles after the war, but a lot of them did slip through. I couldn't answer that till I've done some digging around myself. What do you think?"

"I think we should drop the whole business." The prince leaned forward. "So does my brother. The Poellenberg Salt has gone forever. It's a terrible loss, but compared to other people we were lucky. We have survived."

"That's putting it mildly," Fisher said. Philip Von Hessel laughed.

"My mother is a very determined woman. When my father died during the war, she ran the complete business—the factories, the estates, everything. She's remarkable; we owe everything to her. But this time, Herr Fisher, I think she's going too far. She has an obsession about the Salt. She wants it back; I know her—I know how tenacious she is. She'd accepted its loss as a fact, and then she saw that newspaper with the report of him being seen in Paris, and the whole thing was reopened. It's become an obsession."

"What are you trying to say, Prince?" Fisher finished his coffee. There was an announcement over the tannoy.

"I'm trying to suggest that you cut this investigation short. Your fee will be met, Herr Fisher. You won't lose by it. Humor my mother for a time, but don't take this assignment seriously. It's a waste of time. He is dead. That report from Paris was just nonsense, I'm convinced of it. Would you do that?"

Fisher stood up. "No," he said. "One thing is essential in my kind of business, Prince Philip, and that's integrity to the employer. Your mother engaged us to find this man if he's alive and to get back the Poellenberg Salt. And that is what I'm going to try to do. If he is dead and that report was nonsense, then you've nothing to worry about. That was my flight. I've got to go. Thanks for the coffee."

The prince stood up. "It was my pleasure. Good-bye—have a good journey."

Fisher went through to the departure lounge to board his plane. The Von Hessels thought he was returning to England. In fact, he was on his way to the Interpol headquarters at Bonn. That was the place to make inquiries about General Paul Heinrich Bronsart. They would have the complete dossier on him there.

Three days later Fisher walked into Paula Stanley's office.

He had a preference for blondes; redheads he avoided—he disliked the freckles and the temperament that went with the hair; brunettes he could take or leave.

He was unprepared for the combination of her coloring and her astonishing eyes. It gave him a shock because his photographic mind registered instantly that they were listed among the general's distinguishing marks. She got up and came to shake hands with him. He caught a drift of expensive scent; she had a firm grip, which he liked. Limp handshakes from either sex always repelled him. Pretty. Very pretty indeed, smartly dressed, upper class, didn't look German, but on closer inspection wasn't typically English either. He sat down in the same chair once taken by Black and produced his cigarette case. He had given the name of a French manufacturing company when he made the appointment. People were none too pleased to give interviews to private detectives. He was prepared to be thrown out when he revealed himself.

"What can I do for you, Mr. Fisher?" A pleasant voice, an attractive smile. It would very soon be wiped away when he produced his identification card. There was no point in wasting time. He walked over and put the agency wallet on her desk. His photograph was on it.

"I'm sorry, Mrs. Stanley. I'm here under false pretenses. I'm from the Dunston Fisher Investigating Agency. I'm making inquiries for a client, and I hoped you might be able to help."

Paula looked up at him. "You said you were from Levée Frères," she said. "If this is the normal way of getting in to see people, Mr. Fisher, I don't think much of it."

"I'm sorry," he apologized. "But you wouldn't have given me an appointment otherwise. People are very cagey with investigators. It makes our life that much more difficult."

"I feel very sorry for you," she said coldly. "Now either

you can tell me very quickly what you want or you can leave. I have exactly five minutes to spare."

"Make it ten." Fisher grinned at her. "And stop looking so angry. It won't take very long, and it might even interest you. You're General Paul Bronsart's daughter, aren't you?"

"Yes." By God, he said to himself, that had hit her where it hurt.

"I plan to talk to your mother, but since you're in London, I thought I'd come and see you first."

"Why?" Paula kept her voice calm; she put her hands below the level of the desk. The man had sharp eyes; they ranged over everything, noting detail, storing it away. She didn't know why she was nervous or why he mustn't see it. "I never knew my father. He was killed in the war. What is the inquiry about?"

Fisher made a snap decision. His friend at Interpol Bonn had emphasized this point. "If the bastard is alive, and coming out of cover, he'll go to the daughter if he goes to anyone. The mother's remarried; he won't contact her. The daughter could be the key. If there's anything in it at all. . . ."

"The inquiry," Fisher said, "is on behalf of German clients, and I'm not allowed to give their name. They want to trace your father."

"But I told you," Paula said, "he's dead. He was killed in Russia in 1944."

"Mrs. Stanley"—Fisher got up—"I don't want to raise any hopes on your part, but it's just remotely possible that he's alive. Would you let me give you lunch and I can tell you about it? It's a long story, and you have only five minutes."

An hour later, they were sitting side by side at the Caprice. It was Fisher's favorite restaurant; he was well known there and was given a banquette table, close to a large party, where a famous theatrical knight was holding court. It gave Paula something to look at; the first few moments when they met in the bar had been difficult. Fisher had tried talking, but she found herself unable to make casual conversation.

"Marvelous-looking man, isn't he?" Fisher said. "I saw him play Othello, and it was the greatest thing I've ever seen on the stage. Did you see it?"

"Yes," Paula said. She and James had gone. She remembered that they had enjoyed the evening. She hadn't thought of James for a long time. She wished desperately that he were with her now. There was something about this man sitting beside her which made her uncomfortable. He was tough. That was it; she recognized the elusive quality for what it was. He had nice manners, he was attractive in a rough-hewn way, he had authority and a sense of humor, but he was fundamentally a rough, tough man from a completely different world. Nothing in existence would have persuaded her to lunch with him except that one phrase: "It's just possible he's still alive."

She had got over the initial shock; her hands were quite steady. She lit cigarettes and the lighter flame didn't tremble; she ordered a Tom Collins before lunch and watched the famous actor giving a private performance for the benefit of the restaurant. Fisher sat beside her, drinking Scotch and soda, letting her take time to relax. She looked white and strained, and he felt rather sorry for her. He wondered exactly how much she knew about her father, and felt instinctively that from the way she talked it was the minimum. Killed in Russia in 1944. Full stop. He had spent two hours reading through the file at Bonn, making notes, reading back into the past, looking at old photographs.

Many of them showed the father of the girl whose elbow was touching his at that moment. A good-looking, impressive man, splendidly uniformed. Was it possible she knew anything beyond the simple fact of a soldier father killed in battle —he didn't think so. He gave her the menu and suggested the restaurant's speciality.

"Would you like to eat first?" he said. "And then we can get down to business. There's no reason not to enjoy a good lunch."

"I'm not very hungry," Paula said. "I'd rather talk now. Please tell me, Mr. Fisher, what is this all about?"

"Can I ask you a couple of questions first? I'm not being difficult, but it will help me to explain if I know how much you're in the picture. Your mother has remarried, hasn't she?"

"Yes—soon after the war ended. She married an English-man called Ridgeway; he was billeted in our house. I can just remember him—I was about three and a half at the time. I never knew my father; he was away fighting."

"Did your mother talk about him to you—what did she tell you about him?"

"Practically nothing," Paula said. "She's not a confiding type of person. You'll see that when you try asking her questions yourself."

"If you can help me enough I may not have to bother her," Fisher said.

"I hope you won't," she answered. "It'll upset her very much. She never wants to discuss my father. I think she'd rather pretend he never existed at all. Anyway that's the atti-tude she's always taken with me."

"So she told you nothing; he was a general in the German army and he was killed. On the retreat from Stalingrad, I believe."

"If you say so." Paula lit another cigarette; she had chain-smoked since they sat down.

"You don't like your mother much, do you?" Fisher said suddenly.

"That's a very personal remark."

"I'm sorry. It wasn't relevant—just an observation. So that's all you know? Nothing about his war record, who his friends were, any family left living?"

"No, nothing." She hesitated. It was humiliating to admit

such total ignorance. He wanted information from her; she wanted to get it back. She had never wanted anything so much in her life as what this stranger might be able to give her. "Wait a minute, I do know of somebody. There was an officer who served under him in the German army. He called himself Black."

"Black?" Fisher said. "Black. That's funny. He had an *aide de camp* whose name was Albrecht Schwarz. How do you know this?"

"Because this man Black came to see me last week," Paula said.

Fisher didn't twitch a muscle. He even sipped at his drink before he said anything.

"Black came to see you? Here in England?"

Albrecht Schwarz, Anglicized to Black. There was a companion file on him, twice as thick as the general's. He was marked disappeared, presumed killed in Berlin during the Russian bombardment of the city. Schwarz. Jesus Christ. He changed his mind and finished the Scotch. He looked into her face. It was pale but innocent. There was nothing in those beautiful blue eyes.

"Yes, he came to the office. Actually I thought he was a bit eccentric."

Eccentric. Oh, just possibly, Fisher said to himself. Just possibly he had bad dreams at night. "Why did he come to see you?"

"Just to introduce himself."

That was a lie, and Fisher knew it because she glanced away and wouldn't look at him. He wished for a moment that he were still a journalist. What a trail this could turn out to be. Albrecht Schwarz turning up in England. If he had come through alive—

The first course came. Paula began to eat it; she felt taut and unhungry. He had ordered a good wine and she drank some.

"Did he talk about your father?"

"Yes. He said what a wonderful person he was." Paula spoke quietly, more for her own benefit than for Fisher's. "He said he carried a photograph of me in his wallet. You may think this silly, Mr. Fisher, but I was rather touched by the idea."

"I don't think it's silly at all. Was that all? There wasn't any hint that his death wasn't certain—that he might have got away?"

"Yes, there was, as a matter of fact. But the man was eccentric, as I said. I didn't really believe him."

"I see. Where is this Mr. Black, or Schwarz? I ought to go and see him."

"I don't know," Paula said. "He just came into my office and then walked out again. He didn't leave any address, and I forgot to ask him. I told you, he was a little—odd, I can't explain it. He said he would ring me again, but I've heard nothing from him since. To be honest, I rather doubted that he knew my father at all, he seemed so strange. Rather a frightening little man."

"Little?" Fisher prompted. There was a photograph of the general reviewing an armored corps, with Schwarz walking behind him.

"Yes, quite short. About five feet six, I should think."

"That tallies," Fisher said. "If I got a photograph for you you'd recognize him, wouldn't you—even though it was taken years ago?"

"Oh, I should think so. He had a rather distinctive face. You could advertise for him."

"Yes," he said. "Yes, I suppose I could." The idea made him smile in irony. He had already been advertised for, but the man had no sense of propriety. He had just kept quiet and never answered. He was really feeling sorry for Paula Stanley now. The trouble was that his excitement kept getting in the way. "Here, have some more wine. Is there any-

thing else you can think of? Anything to help me? You've
been marvelous so far."

"Nothing," Paula said. "Do you mind if I don't finish this—
I'm really not hungry. It was delicious, but I just can't man-
age any more. Now it's your turn, Mr. Fisher. I want to know
everything; I want to know exactly why you said my father
might be alive."

He faced the anxious look and thought how pretty she was
when she was worried.

"Two months ago there was a newspaper report in Germany that he'd been seen in Paris. It appeared in the *Allgemeine Zeitung*, and was reprinted in all the major European
newspapers through A.P. My clients saw it and wanted an
investigation."

"Seen in Paris? But that's impossible! That could mean
Black was right!"

"It certainly could," Fisher agreed. "It seemed pretty defi-
nite. It has to be looked into; anyway that's what I'm being
paid for."

"Who said they saw him in Paris? And who is employing
you?"

He had the photostat copy of the original cutting in his
briefcase. It was a Frenchwoman who had made the claim.
And she insisted that she knew. She recognized the general;
she knew him by the eyes.

"Somebody said they knew him during the Occupation
and that he was walking down a Paris street. They tried to
catch up with him, but he disappeared in the crowd. As for
the second question, I can't answer that. Not without the
client's permission." He couldn't quite imagine the princess
giving it. He had promised to go back in a month and make
a personal report on his progress. He was looking forward to
seeing the younger son's face when he heard this latest development.

Why in hell had he been so anxious to have the affair

dropped cold? And why hadn't the eldest, the heir and head of the family, said one bloody word during the interview, except shift from foot to foot and hold onto the back of the sofa as if he were frightened of falling over? Fisher had been too busy in Bonn to ask the questions with any view to finding an answer. Now they came back to him, prompted by Paula's question. He felt awkward at holding out on her, but as he had said to the smiling, persuasive prince when he tried to double-cross his mother, in his business, integrity to the client was all important. It was the profession's one claim to respectability.

"Mr. Fisher, you know some of the details about my father. Would you tell me about him—everything you know? I'd be very grateful."

Fisher signaled the waiter. "Nothing else?"

Paula shook her head. "No thanks. Just coffee."

"Two black coffees. When you say everything I know, you don't want a history from start to finish, do you—I mean you know all that of course. You want to know where he was killed. If he was."

She wanted to hear it all, but shame prevented her from asking. Shame at not knowing. She felt like a foundling. More and more she judged her mother for that damnable reticence which had closed her out. James always said she was uptight and disoriented. He liked long, medical-sounding words, and the description irritated her. But if what he said was true, she knew who to blame for it.

"Just the end," she said. "Where it was and how it was supposed to have happened."

"In a village outside Cracow, during the final German retreat in 1944. Let me light that for you. You're smoking like a chimney, Mrs. Stanley. Don't you know it's bad for you? Anyway, your father's H.Q. was in this place; it has a hopeless name I couldn't begin to pronounce, but he and his staff were there, including our friend Schwarz, or Black. He had taken up quarters in the police station, some kind of brick-built house. These Polish places were pretty small and primitive, and most of them had been occupied and fought over before during the original campaign. I imagine conditions were pretty rough at the time; the Russians were chasing hell out of the German army, and the fighting was not exactly Queensberry rules.

"Anyway on November twenty-third, a massive Russian bombardment began over the area. The house where your father was living was hit, and everyone in it was killed. Apparently a body was found wearing his decorations but otherwise unidentifiable. Half a dozen survivors of the battle swore that the general had been in the house in conference with his staff at the time. Nobody got out alive. The bodies were buried on the spot. Your mother must have been notified of his death in action. I can't understand why she wouldn't tell you this."

Paula ignored the question. "One thing puzzles me," she said.

"What's that?"

"Why was anything reported in all the papers? Why should anyone bother about whether my father was alive or not after all these years? It seems very odd."

"He was a very important man," Fisher said. "He had the Knights Cross of the Iron Cross, and every other decoration you can think of; he was one of Germany's glamor soldiers." He had a mental picture of the faded photograph in the Bonn file. The hard, clean-cut face under the distinctive peaked cap, the pattern of gold braid and the unmistakable lightning flashes on the collar. He must have looked pretty good in his prime, perfect specimen of the Wagnerian superman. He smiled at Paula.

"There's nothing more intriguing than the dead coming back to life," he said kindly. "Naturally it aroused interest."

"Do you believe it, Mr. Fisher?" she asked him. "Do you think it's possible?"

"You'd like it to be, wouldn't you?"

"Wouldn't you—if you had never known one of your parents?"

"I don't know," Fisher said. "I didn't know either of mine very well. They died when I was in my teens. But I made out. I should think you have too. I wouldn't let it worry you. If I find anything out, I'll let you know, just privately, between friends."

"That's very kind of you," Paula said. In spite of her first reaction she was beginning to like him. He looked different when he smiled; she felt that he was not normally as nice as he was being to her. "Will you promise?"

"If you'll have dinner with me this week," Fisher said, "I'll give you a full report. Just in case you want me before, here's my address, and you can get a message to me at this number. It's a calling service. How about Thursday for dinner? I thought I might motor down and see your mother and stepfather on Wednesday. Can I come and pick you up at about eight?"

"I haven't said I'd go," Paula said. "This isn't more investigating, is it? I've nothing more to tell you."

"No, this is strictly pleasure from my point of view." Fisher paid the bill. "And as I said, I'll give you a progress report— free. I usually charge blood money for this sort of thing. You will have dinner, won't you?"

"All right. I live at Twenty-eight Charlton Square. Flat Two. I warn you, you won't get anything out of my mother and stepfather. I tried to bring it up not long ago, and I got absolutely nowhere."

"Perhaps I'm a little tougher to deal with than you," he said pleasantly. "Anyway, we'll see. Come on, I'll put you in a taxi. Are you going back to your office?"

They stood outside on the warm pavement; the sky was clouding over with the advent of a summer shower of rain.

"Yes, of course. I have to do some work." She held out her hand. "Good-bye—thank you for lunch."

"I have to do some work, too," Fisher replied. He liked the way she did her hair; it curled around her head, not too short, but soft and casual, taking its own shape. He had never liked brown hair before. But with those eyes, she couldn't fail. "See you Thursday," he said. He helped her into a cab and, turning, walked back down the street to find his car.

He wondered what the mother would be like. He had seen her in one of the photographs, too—a tall, very good-looking woman, with blond hair plaited around her head, fox furs trailing around her shoulders, shaking hands with her husband's boss, the general beside her.

He wondered about the English husband. What kind of man had he been to pick her up and take her on, knowing what he must have known? Perhaps there was a beautiful love story being lived out in the serenity of the Essex countryside. Perhaps the attractive girl he had just left was the changeling, cursed with her heredity, even though she didn't know it. Fisher doubted that. Blood wasn't thicker than water; heredity without environment didn't make sense to him. What did make sense was the appearance of a man who was obviously the general's ADC, a man accounted dead for twenty odd years, and his contacting of Paula Stanley with hints that the general was still alive. He would wire Bonn for a photocopy of Schwarz's picture just to confirm it, but the coincidence was already too close. Schwarz had been Anglicized to Black; he had claimed to have served under the general, to have known him personally.

Why had he contacted Paula Stanley? Why, after all these years, had the little bastard risked disclosing himself? Just to effect a reunion—to drop hints and test her reaction? It sounded unlikely, flimsy. She had described him as odd, eccentric. Maybe this would account for the inexplicable lack of caution. But nothing would persuade Fisher that he had found her and introduced himself without a purpose. And whatever the purpose was, she hadn't told Fisher about it. His invitation to dinner was not entirely motivated by her attractiveness. There was something he had to know, and somehow he had to make her tell him. Seeing the parents was a formality he couldn't afford to neglect, but if there was a lead anywhere, and he had begun to feel a strange conviction that there was, then it would be found through Paula Stanley.

3

"I tried to telephone your office, my dear, but you hadn't come back from lunch. So I thought I'd just pop around."

Paula had opened the flat door and found her stepfather standing there. He looked embarrassed and then cheerful. He had a permanent air of bonhomie which Paula found extremely depressing. "What a nice surprise, Gerald. Come in and have a drink." He had sat in the little drawing room, made exactly the same soothing remarks about the decorations as he had on his last visit, and fidgeted until she could have screamed at him to get to the point and stop going around in circles of small talk. When it came out, it was unusually simple, as if the effort to approach her with tact had exhausted him.

"I had to come and see you, Paula. Your mother's very worried."

"Oh? I'm sorry to hear that. What about?" She knew before he said it. She knew exactly what was worrying her mother and why the brigadier had left his comfortable nest in Essex and made the trip to London. He wanted to know about Black.

"She's not been sleeping," he explained. "I made her go to

the doctor yesterday. You told her something that upset her. Something to do with your father."

"That's right, I did. I said a friend of his had asked to see me. She didn't want me to; we had a row about it last week-end. I know she told you about it, Gerald. She's never kept anything secret from you. And you want to know what I did, isn't that it?"

"Yes, put like that, I suppose it is." The false cheerfulness had been sloughed off; he looked like a worried old man, deep creases between his brows, a resentful expression on his face. "What did you do, Paula? Did you take your mother's advice? Or did you see this man?"

"I saw him," Paula said, "last Monday, in my office. We talked about my father, and he told me quite a lot about him."

"Oh, Christ"—the brigadier put his head in his hands—"why couldn't you have left it alone? If you knew what an agony your mother's gone through—"

"I don't know anything about my mother," she said coldly. "She's never confided in me. She's never talked to me or told me anything. She's kept me at a distance all my life. And why do you say Christ like that? Why shouldn't I hear about my father!"

His face had reddened; he straightened up in his chair and glared at her.

"Because of what it means to her! She deserves to be left in peace now. Don't you realize how old she is?"

"What's that got to do with it? It's not as if she loved my father! She's never cared for anyone but you. Don't tell me she can't stand the painful memories—it's over twenty-five years ago. I'm sorry, Gerald, but I have a right to know about the other side of my family."

"Even at her expense?"

"But why should it be at her expense?" Paula demanded. "What is there to hide?" He didn't answer. He heaved himself out of the chair and faced her.

"Paula, if I asked you to drop this and not ask questions, would you do it?"

"No, Gerald, I wouldn't. I'm sorry. Give me a reason, one reason why and I might listen. But I'm not making an arbitrary promise to anyone."

"I can't understand you," the brigadier said. "We did our best for you. Your mother—"

"I don't want to talk about mother," Paula said. "You did your best for me, Gerald, and I appreciate it. I wasn't your child. You haven't had a visitor by any chance?"

"What do you mean—what kind of visitor?"

"A private detective. If you and mother don't like the past being dug up, then I'm afraid you're not going to like this. There's been a report that my father was seen in Paris. He may be alive, after all." To her surprise there was no reaction of astonishment or alarm. He looked at her and nodded.

"We saw it," he said. "But, thank God, it wasn't true."

"My God!" Paula said. "It didn't occur to either of you to mention this to me? It was only my father who might have come back, that's all! I can excuse you, Gerald, but I'll never forgive her. How could she have hidden it from me? How could she have been so cruel!"

"How much did this man Black tell you about him?" It was an unexpected question.

"He said he was a wonderful person, that he loved me very much. Oh," she said bitterly, "I know what the trouble is— I've always known. Father was a Nazi general—he fought for Hitler—and you and she don't want it mentioned. You're smug and English, and it wouldn't look good at the Women's Institute if it got around she was the widow of one of those Nazi beasts we heard so much about. I've been stuffed full of atrocities and concentration camps! I knew what a bloody Hun was before I was old enough to realize I was one myself. Mother's a coward; she doesn't want to own up to her country or to me! That's why she's never liked me; I tied her to father and to Germany. Without me, she could have been just Mrs. bloody Gerald Ridgeway."

"You don't know what you're talking about." Her step-father had drawn himself up; she had never seen him look so angry. "And don't you dare speak about your mother like that! I hope you'll never have to know what she went through, but you're too prejudiced against her to appreciate it if you did. I'm going home now.

"Any detective who comes near my house will be told to clear off pretty quickly. If he's chasing that story about your father being seen in Paris, he's wasting his time. He's dead, Paula, and all I can tell you is to be thankful for it!"

He walked out of the room, and she heard her front door bang. She sat down and lit a cigarette. Her eyes filled with tears. It was the first quarrel she had ever had with her step-father. God, how she envied that relationship! That close protective unity that existed between them, impenetrable from outside. He wasn't a cruel man or remotely unfair, but he was incapable of seeing her point of view, of appreciating anything but the feelings of his wife. Paula had said the un-spoken grievances of years. She had brought the sense of shame and difference endured through her adolescence into the open. She had grown up to realize that she was a member of a race whose crimes against humanity were an outrage to civilized societies everywhere. The marauding hordes of twelfth-century Mongolia were likened to her people. Geno-cide. Ten million Jews. Two million gypsies. Men and women and children being mowed down in France, Italy, Poland, the Low Countries. Horror piled upon horror. Names associated with unspeakable infamy. Dachau. Belsen. Buchenwald. Her name had been changed to Ridgeway when she was a child. So nobody would know what she was—a German and the child of a German general.

The only person who could have assuaged that awful lone-liness and calmed the sense of guilt was her mother. And she had brought down a curtain of silence that nothing Paula did had been able to tear open. She went and poured herself a drink, which was unusual. Normally she never drank alone. She brushed her hair and powdered her face; it was pale and her eyes looked tired. All her life she had been looking at that face reflected in mirrors without being able to identify it to herself. James had accused her of being a stranger; he was probably right. She had never come out of the inner shell into the cold winds of the world. It must have made her uncomfortable to live with. For the first time she understood why he had been unfaithful. Her best friend was a warm, affectionate woman, not particularly pretty but with an attractive laugh. James had liked her and the inevitable happened. She didn't know about the younger girl and she didn't care. She brushed her hair again and thought suddenly that she had forgiven James. She was quite calm about it; she poured another drink and sat down by the telephone to ring him up and tell him so when the front doorbell rang. Paula looked at her watch. It was nine o'clock. She had forgotten about dinner; she had forgotten about everything in her immersion in the past. When she opened the door, she found Fisher outside.

"It's not Thursday," she said. "You're two days early."

"Let me come in," he said. "I came right around when I saw the papers."

"What papers?" She walked after him down the hall; her own newspaper was still in the downstairs lobby. She had forgotten to collect it.

In the sitting room Fisher waited; she came toward him. "It's Black," he said. "So I came around."

The newspaper was in his hand. She took it from him. The black headline faded out of focus. There was a photograph of a face she knew, a face with high cheekbones and eyes fixed in a narrow stare. Then the heading came at her again: MURDERED MAN IDENTIFIED AS WAR CRIMINAL.

Fisher let her read, watching her face. He had been shaken himself when he opened the paper in a pub outside Shepherd's Market. It was an old haunt, and he was meeting a friend from his journalist days. He left the pub without leaving a message. It wasn't just the picture and the discovery that Albrecht Schwarz had been found murdered, his head beaten in. It was the story printed underneath.

Paula suddenly began to read aloud.

"Albrecht Schwarz, alias Black, alias Winter, resident in Switzerland with a Swiss passport for the past fifteen years, was one of the small band of notorious war criminals wanted for multiple murder in the Ukraine and for his part in the infamous massacre of the population of the Polish village of Darienne during the German withdrawal in 1944." She lowered the paper and looked at Fisher. She seemed dazed. "Come and sit down and I'll get you a drink," Fisher said. She didn't move. She was reading the paper again, her lips moving silently. He found the whisky and poured a stiff measure. The soda syphon hissed; it was empty. It suddenly occurred to Fisher that empty syphons and a lack of things like tonic water or matches were hallmarks of women who lived alone. Fisher swore and decided she might as well have the drink straight. He gave her the glass and made her sit beside him.

"You look very white," he said suddenly. "This has been quite a shock to you."

"I can't believe it," Paula said. "He was sitting in my office —a funny little old man with white hair. I thought he was crazy; I still think so! Mr. Fisher, I don't understand what's happening. I've just had my stepfather up here, shouting at me because I'd seen Black, telling me I was hurting my mother and hadn't any right to go digging up the past. Why haven't I? If my father is alive, why can't I find him?"

"Hadn't you better ask yourself why he hasn't come forward?" Fisher said gently. "Why did he have to send Black, or Schwarz—why's he been lying low for all these years?"

Paula put down the glass. "What do you mean? Are you trying to tell me he's done something criminal?"

"I don't know," Fisher said. "Interpol has a record of him,

as they did everybody on the top Nazi level. Your father wasn't in the Wehrmacht. He was a general in the S.S."

"Why didn't you tell me?" Paula asked.

"Because my job was to get information out of you," Fisher said. "And anyway you seemed so keen on the idea of him, I didn't want to point it out. Look, I've got an idea. Have you eaten dinner yet?"

"No." Paula shook her head. "And after this I'm not hungry."

"You never are," Fisher remarked. He patted her hand suddenly and grinned. "The time I took you out to lunch you left everything on the plate. I'm going to take you out tonight, Mrs. Stanley, and if you don't want to eat, you don't have to. And you don't have to talk about any of this either. This is going to be strictly pleasure and not business. Go and get a coat and put some powder on your nose."

"I don't want to go anywhere," Paula said. "If you want a drink, I can give it to you here."

"I can't do without soda," Fisher insisted. "And you're fresh out of it. Go and get that coat. Hurry up."

He lit a cigarette while he waited for her. She looked shaken, and he was quite certain that if he took her at her word, she would sit in the flat alone and cry after he had left. And that wasn't going to happen. Fisher didn't know why it shouldn't; he just didn't like the idea. He felt like an evening out; he had nothing to celebrate—rather the murder of Schwarz was a first-class check to his investigations. So he might as well celebrate that. But what he really wanted was to get Paula Stanley out of the flat. When she came back into the room, he got up.

"You look terrific," he said. "And that's how you're going to feel in a little while from now. I know just the place for both of us tonight. Come on."

They drove into the center of London, down past the Houses of Parliament, where a light burned in the clock tower of Big Ben to show that the House was sitting, on down Whitehall and around Trafalgar Square, where Nelson surveyed the city from his column and the pigeons roosted peacefully on the official buildings in spite of all efforts to dislodge them. The fountains shot water jets into a graceful arc, and the tourists wandered around the basins and clustered on the steps, enjoying the warmth of the evening. Up Piccadilly, past the Circus with its neon lights and sad little groups of addicts already assembling in a queue at the all-night chemist for their supplies.

They swung into Berkeley Square.

"Where are we going?" Paula asked.

"Annabel's," Fisher answered. "Soft lights, very loud music, and plenty to look at." He gave the car key to the doorman. "Put it somewhere for me, will you."

The doorman saluted and smiled. Fisher had a very big expense account on his company. He could afford the best nightclub in London. Paula had never been there. Better-class nightclubs were not James' idea of fun, and professionally she didn't move in that kind of circle.

The men who took her out were the type who chose discreet, folksy little places where the food was good. They went into the bar, which was exactly like the study in a rich man's country house. The walls were covered with sporting cartoons, prints, and pictures of considerable merit. There was an open fire with an old-fashioned wire guard in front of it, leather sofas, and a specially woven tartan carpet. A few yards beyond, the restaurant was a dark cavern filled with music. It was still early for the club, and there were very few people there. By eleven it was packed like a rush-hour train.

Fisher didn't take her to the bar; it was too public. People sat there in order to be seen as well as to see. They went straight to their table, and he made Paula sit facing the room.

He ordered champagne for them both. He reached over and held her hand. It was cold.

"I can't go on calling you Mrs. Stanley," he said. "It seems indecent in a place like this. My name is Eric."

"Call me Paula." She looked down at her hand in his. He had strong hands, with thick powerful wrists where dark hairs grew. His hand was warm and it gripped.

"Why did you bring me here?"

"To take you out of yourself. Drink up. Don't you like it?"

"Yes. Why are you doing all this for me? Why should you bother?"

"You've got a thing about this, haven't you?" Fisher said. He was leaning close to her; he could smell her scent, and her hand was warmer.

"Why shouldn't someone care about you? You must have had a lot of men."

"One husband," she said, "who left me for another woman. Two other women to be honest. He said I wasn't much good at it."

"Good at what? Sex? Or being married? They're not the same thing, I understand."

"Good at either," Paula answered. She drank some of the champagne. "I was too reserved. Too wrapped up in myself. I thought he was hell, too, so I suppose it was equal. And you're wrong about the men. The only ones who ever fell for me were thoroughly offbeat."

"I've never liked conventional women," Fisher said. "Maybe that's why I've never married. Apart from leading a slightly disorganized life."

"Why did you choose it—nobody ever meets a private detective."

"Now, now," Fisher said. "We're not all sleazy little men in macs, poking into hotel bedrooms. We have a very big agency. We deal with all sorts of problems."

Like missing Nazi treasure. Odd items like a Benvenuto Cellini masterpiece worth millions. Things like that. He looked down at her and smiled.

"You're feeling better, aren't you? Not quite so shaken."

"Not quite." He felt the hand inside his give a slight pressure. It roused a pang of excitement in him.

"Tell me some more about yourself. You're a bachelor and a detective. Were you in the police?"

"I was a journalist," he said, "for about five years. It was great fun, lots of travel, quite a bit of excitement. Then I met this chap called Dunston; he was in Interpol. We worked on a gold smuggling racket together in East Berlin, and we liked each other very much. He's not like me, much more of a solid type. Wife and three children. I didn't see him for quite a time, then one day he looked me up. He'd left Interpol and started his own investigating service. He asked me to join him. He thought I had a talent for it. So I did and here I am. More champagne?"

"I couldn't," she protested.

"Oh, yes you could. It won't hurt you. Anything more you want to know about me?"

"I can't think of anything. Except what you won't tell me. Why you're looking for my father and who's employing you."

"I tell you what," Fisher said cheerfully, "you tell me why Schwarz really came to see you, and I'll answer your questions. Now I am going to take you for a dance. We came here to forget about all that."

She got up as he did. "I can't forget it, Eric. I can't think of anything else."

"You *are* going to forget about it. Just for tonight. Tomorrow I shall bully the hell out of you to get the answers, but not tonight. This is a nice slow tune. Come on."

Paula didn't dance with him; she clung. His arm supported her; his body warmed hers as he pressed her against him. The dance floor was small, and it was full of people twined around each other. Some of the couples jigged and gesticulated; the discothèque switched from the slow beat to a fast rhythm, played at ear-splitting pitch.

Fisher ignored the tempo and went on holding her against him. She didn't respond to his pressure; his intention had been to cushion her against the shock, and he had succeeded. Too bloody well, he thought, and permitted a laugh at his own expense. She was extraordinarily attractive; he had known many women who could claim to be more beautiful or more obviously sexy, but Paula Stanley was having a profound effect upon him. The fact that she was completely unaware of it, and was doing nothing to contribute to it, made Fisher even more disturbed. She rested her head on his shoulder and danced with her eyes closed.

Fisher made an effort. "Back to the table," he said. "I'm thirsty." The club was now uncomfortably full; beautiful women in expensive evening dresses, smart young girls in velvet dungarees and pure silk shirts, escorts of all ages came drifting through to dance. Fisher settled behind his table and took hold of Paula's hand.

"You are feeling better, aren't you?"

"Better or high, I'm not sure which," she said. "Did I thank you for doing this for me?"

"You did," Fisher said. "This is about the fourth time. And I'm not going to repeat it again, but it's a pleasure. Drink up."

"If I do," she said, "I'll go to sleep."

"That won't matter," Fisher said. "You'll feel pretty nasty in the morning, but the worst will be over by then. One more dance to keep your eyes open, and then I'll take you home."

As soon as he met her, Fisher had decided that she had the most unusual eyes he had ever seen.

The color was indescribable; it was the vulnerable expression in them which was worrying him. She looked as if she were easy to hurt. Fisher wasn't used to this after a life spent in the company of assorted female toughs, good for a screw, a booze-up, and a laugh. Paula Stanley was not his type at all.

He spent another fifteen minutes holding her tight on the

floor and wishing rather hazily that he could go to bed with her, and then he drove her home.

Outside her flat he stopped, leaned across, and opened the car door.

"I'm not being a gentleman and seeing you in," he said, "because I'm a bit high myself, and I can't promise to behave unless you get out pretty quickly."

Paula turned to him. "If you want to come up with me, you can. I don't mind."

"Thanks." Fisher bowed his head. "Thanks very much. But I don't go for the lamb to the slaughter routine. You're not fit for anything but a good night's sleep. Ask me up another time and you'll be surprised what happens to you!"

"You can phone me tomorrow," Paula said. She slid out of the car and stood on the pavement. In spite of what he had said, Fisher got out with her.

"Have you got your keys?"

"Yes. I shall not go into the office. And I'll answer whatever you like if you call me tomorrow. I owe you that for what you've done tonight. Good night, Eric. And thanks again."

He watched her go through the front door; he waited in the car until he saw the light in her window go on.

She had asked him up and he had refused. He couldn't believe it. He had spent the evening wanting her so much it hurt, and then behaved like a gentleman. Something very suspect, he decided, very odd indeed, was happening to him in his old age.

Margaret Von Hessel was alone with her younger son. They were drinking coffee in the enormous conservatory that ran down the south side of the house. Every variety of hot-house plant was growing around them; the princess could remember exactly the same atmosphere in her grandmother's day. Heat, a humid closeness, and the pervading smell of tropical scents. She sat in a tall wicker chair, and her son

Philip arranged the cushions behind her. She looked up at him and patted his hand. He reminded her so much of her side of the family. Whereas her son Heinrich was a pure Von Hessel of the Wurzen branch. Weak, degenerate, a drunkard, useless to God or man.

Women and gambling had been the old prince's occupations; his great empire ran itself—wealth bred wealth without his making any effort! And he had married more. Margaret was his second cousin. She had not loved the prince; love was not part of the settlement. But fidelity in public, above all, the maintenance of the family's image were duties which the young princess fulfilled from the start of her marriage. She had been a handsome girl, tall and well-developed in the style which her generation admired. She was a most envied young woman in her own circle.

The prince was young, and his appearance was distinguished; if he showed little humor or animation, this was not regarded as a cause for criticism. Pride and their past sat like a mantle on the shoulders of the Von Hessel family.

His wife was treated with the awe accorded minor royalty; her jewels, clothes, and cars, her villa in France where King Edward VII had frequently stayed, the Grimm's fairy tale Schloss on top of a mountain, the Berlin townhouse, shooting lodges, and art treasures which would have graced any museum in the world—all these things were part of Margaret's daily life. Living with a man who contracted a venereal disease within a year of their wedding, who spent every night gambling with his friends or dining with any one of his many mistresses, was the hidden part of her existence.

She had borne the humiliation, the disgust he inspired in her, and the loneliness of her youth with silent fortitude. She was a Von Hessel, and eight hundred years of tradition helped sustain her. She occupied herself with charities, with taking a personal interest in the running of her houses, and with compiling a detailed inventory of the treasures in the

family's possession. And that was when her passion for the
Poellenberg Salt developed. They spent part of every year at
the Schloss Wurzen, a dark medieval castle built by an ancestor in the thirteenth century and extensively modernized
by her husband's grandfather. The Salt was displayed in the
main dining hall. It was not protected; it stood on the enormous oak table exactly as it had for hundreds of years, shining
with ineffable beauty in the dark, lofty hall, its magnificent
jewels like beacons when the lights were lit. Margaret could
look at it for hours, absorbed in the poetic lines of its figures,
touching the tremulous golden leaves of the central tree with
a finger to make the branches move. There was a ruby as big
as a large pebble; she loved to stare into its heart, where a
tiny reflection of her own face was discernible. It was said
to have belonged to Lorenzo the Magnificent. The faces of
the nymphs fascinated her equally; there was a sly sensu-
ality in the golden eyes and around the curving lips, more
subtle than the sexual leering of the muscular male figures.
It seemed impossible, but every female face was different.
The master had painted portraits in metal, each a distinctive
likeness to a real woman. Margaret loved the Salt; her feeling
toward it was so personal that she resented anybody even
touching it. It was as if the whole unbelievable creation had
been made for her alone, for another bride to look at and
fondle, after Eleanor de Medici who had been dead for five
hundred years. Her husband found this obsession with an inanimate object quite abnormal, and he said as much. The
exquisite beauty of form, the harmony in the jewels which
prevented so much opulence from ever being vulgar—none of
this appealed to him. He preferred flesh and blood women
to the cold nakedness of golden nymphs. But if it amused his
wife to gloat, then he had no objection. He objected very seldom to anything she did. She had borne him one son, and he
forgot her existence thereafter. She could spend what she
wished, travel where she chose, surround herself with her own

friends and amusements, while he enjoyed life in his own way. He took no interest in his son either; that was the mother's province.

And as the boy grew up, Margaret detected the same traits in him as in his father. He was stupid; even as a baby he lacked initiative, being content to sit and play with his own fists, sucking and chewing until his nurse put him into gloves. His eyes had the Von Hessel glaze of indifference to life. He made little progress at lessons. His tutors said frankly he was bored. At school he showed an aptitude for sport, and being who he was, his academic failings were overlooked. He was a failure whose family name protected him, and nothing his mother could say or do could light any gleam of ambition or enthusiasm in him. The more she criticized the less he reacted. He was found dead drunk in his room at the age of fourteen. He was a member of the Hitler Youth, which his father had insisted he become with the idea that the discipline would do him good. Margaret had objected bitterly, but there was nothing she could do. Her husband had to be obeyed. He talked of discipline, when what he meant was politics. They were immensely powerful and unbelievably rich, but even so they didn't dare to flout the growing power of the dictator who controlled the country. Friendship with the Nazi hierarchy wasn't required of people like them; but it was unwise to deviate in public. So Henry was enrolled in the Hitler Jugend and dressed up in the uniform. After a year he was privately expelled for being drunk. He was sent to a clinic in Austria under another name, surrounded by servants and a bodyguard to keep away the curious. He came back apparently cured, but within six months the bouts began again. He smashed the furniture in his room, and there was a short spell in a nursing home before another cure was tried, this time in Switzerland. It was the beginning of a pattern which was repeated over the next ten years. He grew up with his public Von Hessel image; a typical German aristocrat, heir to an immense empire of armaments, steel, coal, and allied industries, one of the most eligible bachelors in the world. Henry showed no interest in women. He had a permanent, passionate love affair with alcohol, and his world was bounded by the possibility and availability of drink. There was no contact between him and his father, who quite calmly declared him useless and gave no more thought to him. His only concern was to prevent the secret being known, to protect the family name. All the influence which his wealth could harness was employed to keep Henry's misdemeanors out of the newspapers. There was gossip among their friends. His frequent absences caused a rumor that he was subject to mental breakdown. He was said to be a homosexual because there were no women in his life. When war broke out, he was eighteen. The prince made him a director of the armament factory in the Ruhr, and he was exempted from military service. It was the only time in their long married life that Margaret had felt sorry for her husband. They spent the evening together, which was a rare occurrence, and he said quite simply that it was the most miserable day of his life.

"My son isn't even fit to serve his fatherland. He has to hide while his friends go out to fight. And he's the last of us. Our family dies with a drunken degenerate who can't be trusted not to disgrace himself and us. Which is my fault, not yours. We must have more children."

His wife had suspected his sterility, when he ceased to cohabit with her. His syphilis was cured, but its aftereffects were permanent. There had been nothing she could say, yet he seemed to expect an answer. The silence had grown between them. Finally it was the prince who broke it. "If you found a lover, I should not object, provided he was of our blood. I thought I should tell you this. Now I'm going to bed."

And two years later, in 1942, her son Philip, the child of her one love affair was born. She had met his father during a visit to Berlin. He was a Luftwaffe pilot, seven years younger than herself, a gay and charming young man, the son of her own second cousin. They shared the same Von Hessel blood, the same traditions. Together they would keep the line unsullied.

She had known he would be killed; there was a sense of impermanence about him which broke her heart. The child she carried was born after his death in action over the English Channel. It was baptized in the chapel at Schloss Wurzen in the font where ten generations of the family had been christened.

Philip Friedhrich Augustus Franz, Prince Von Hessel, the bastard son of a dead man. The princess stood in the chapel and accepted the congratulations of their friends. Her husband stood beside her. Nothing was ever said between them; it was never acknowledged that Philip was not his child. But he was content—the family had a second heir; the name would continue in spite of Heinrich. And by the same unspoken attitude he let his wife understand that there must be no more lovers.

"Philip," Margaret said, "I know I'm right. What that Englishman said on the telephone convinces me that we are getting near."

"Did you know there was a daughter?" Philip asked.

"Yes," his mother said. "There was one child, I had forgotten what the sex was. It was clever of Fisher to make contact with her so quickly. He says he's sure she knows something but that unless he reveals our interest in the case she won't tell him what it is. I gave my permission, my son, because we have to know what Schwarz came to tell her. Fisher agreed with me."

"Mother," Philip said, "mother, is there any use trying to persuade you to call a halt, even now? You know how I feel about it; you know what Henry feels."

"Henry has no right to feel anything," she said angrily.

"If it wasn't for him, we wouldn't have lost the Salt."

"One man is dead," her son said slowly. "Beaten to death, after all these years. Who killed him? Is there any connection between his death and that report about Bronsart being seen in Paris—mother, I think we're opening up something that should never be disturbed at all! Supposing that he is alive—now that we know Schwarz escaped and stayed in hiding all those years, it's possible that Bronsart did the same. And if he's coming into the open, moving around where he could be recognized, he's certain to be caught. If he comes to trial, the whole story could come out! Please, mother darling." He reached out and held her hand. There was a deep love and a close sympathy between them. "Please stop while there's still time. Forget the Salt. Other people lost great treasures; what does it matter now, beside the other risk!"

"It matters to me." The proud eyes blazed in memory. "It matters to me that one of the most beautiful objects in the world was taken from us by a ruthless parvenu, seized and hidden so that he could creep out one day and claim it. No, Philip, I'm going to get it back! If he lives, and I believe he does, he'll lead us to it. And it's coming back to the place where it belongs. It's ours, my son. One day it will be yours; you know that. You know that you'll own everything, be responsible for all our interests. The Poellenberg Salt belongs to you."

"And Heinrich?" her son asked quietly. "You talk as if he didn't exist. I wish you wouldn't."

"You have a kind heart," she said. "You find something to pity about him. I find nothing. There is no excuse for what he became. He's a degenerate; he had no will, no feelings, no interest in anything but lying in a coma of drink. He's my son, but the day he dies, I shall not shed a tear. Also he hates you, Philip. You know he does."

"That's because you've always loved me," he said. "And you've showed it. I don't blame him."

"He'll die," the princess said. "His liver is rotted; his health is getting worse every time he has a severe bout. One day he just won't recover. The doctors have made this clear to me for some time. And when that comes, you will be the head of the family, and I can retire and become an old woman, doing gros point in my armchair." She squeezed his hand and smiled. The memory of his father was very clear. Whenever Philip laughed, it was as if the man she loved had come back from the grave. It would all be his. Millions, power, prestige, a great future in Germany already counting high in the councils of the world which it had almost conquered. And the Salt belonged to him.

"If Bronsart lives," she said suddenly, "we will have our treasure back. If he died in the retreat, then it is lost to us. So it rests with fate, my son. Fate will decide what happens next."

"It wasn't fate that killed Schwarz," her son said.

"No," she agreed. "It could have been a thief that he disturbed, the papers said so. It could have been a quarrel. Or it could have been the general, come back to close his mouth. That, my darling, is what I think, and what I believe Fisher thinks also. Now we have to wait and see what comes from the daughter. Just imagine being the child of such a man! Come, it's time we went inside. I have to telephone about the extension to the Verbegen plant."

"I have the most terrible hangover," Paula said into the telephone. "Otherwise, I'm all right. How about you?"

Fisher sounded cheerful. "I'm fine. You said you weren't working today. How about lunch?"

"I've changed my mind." Paula spoke with her eyes closed. Her head was pounding. "I have some things to do, and I've got to get some letters written and sent off. I could have dinner this evening, or better still, come here and I'll cook something. We've got to talk."

"You haven't changed your mind about that then," Fisher said. "I'm glad. We need each other in this. Anyway at the moment I need you, and I can give you the information you wanted. Shall I come at about eight?"

"Make it seven thirty. I'll get my own back on you and give you a drink." She sounded as if she were smiling. He was sorry she refused an earlier meeting. He was anxious to get on and get the information; he had spoken to the princess at eight o'clock that morning and extracted permission to reveal her identity and the purpose of his inquiry. He was impatient to get on with his investigation, to start on a serious hunt for Bronsart, but no action was possible without exhausting Paula as a source. Another reason, which in the prosaic morning light he wasn't so eager to recognize, was a desire to see her again.

Her father was a Nazi general, a member of the infamous black uniformed murder squads which had spread Hitler's terror throughout Europe. No wonder the mother had played it down. Fisher could see her point. But it had been a cruel and selfish attitude to take in regard to her daughter. Some hint should have been given, some warning that her father was not the hero figure that the girl had obviously tried to create out of nothing. Besides, the mother had been married to him. She knew what he was and what he was doing. The wives of all the top men were singing the same song after the war. We didn't know, we weren't told, our place was in the home. Fisher called that excuse a lot of balls. Their estates were staffed by foreign slave labor, their homes were filled with other people's treasures, the furs and jewels that arrived back from France and the Low Countries were the property of captured Jews who'd tried to buy their lives. Fisher had no sympathy for Mrs. Ridgeway. She had bailed out after the war, with a well-heeled Englishman as a protector. If he felt sorry for anyone, it was Paula, who had been left as an appendage all her life.

He felt a vindictive impulse to go down to Essex that day and stir the pair of them up. Why should the girl be the only one to answer questions?

"I'm going down to pay your mother a visit," he said. "I'll tell you about it tonight."

"She must have seen it in the papers," Paula said. "I expect she's terrified she'll be connected with it."

"Why the hell should she be?" He said it irritably. "She's Mrs. Ridgeway; that is all anyone knows about her. She can go on hiding. Black's murder was on TV last night, on the news. So she can't frig about pretending she doesn't know anything to me."

"You'd be surprised," Paula said. "You don't know my mother. She never even telephoned me."

"To hell," he said. "What do you care? I phoned you, didn't I? Don't be greedy, wanting all the attention. You go and take something for that hangover, and I'll be with you at seven thirty. And don't work too hard today."

"I won't," Paula promised. "I feel so awful, I can't. I haven't thanked you for last night. It was very kind of you. I would have gone mad if I'd been alone here."

"We'll do it again," he said. "I liked it, too."

She put down the telephone and got out of bed. Her headache was a dull pain that throbbed; aspirins would stop it. She made herself tea and took two tablets.

The night before seemed very distant and unreal. She couldn't believe that she had invited him up. She must have been drunk. She had never asked a man up to her flat after two meetings in her life. Since parting from her husband, she had not spent a night with any man, or thought of doing so.

But this rather ugly man had woken something in her. In spite of the feeling of malaise it was still there. It was like having something to hold onto when one was swimming in a limitless sea. There was a man, and contact had been made between them. Only a transitory contact, a brief meeting, but for the moment it was enough. She went into the sitting room; the paper with Black's photograph was lying on the floor. She picked it up and read the inside story. Her father was an S.S. general. She had never been able to picture him in detail; she had no photograph, no mementos to prove that he had ever existed. But out of her imagination she had fashioned an image, faceless but identifiable; because it was a soldier, it wore the German general's uniform she had once found in a reference book of uniforms she had consulted as a girl. It had her bright blue eyes because her mother had once remarked on them to Gerald Ridgeway, and Paula had been listening. "Of course she has his eyes. That makes her look like him." And Paula had examined herself in the glass afterward and tried to visualize him as a man. The image was a shadow, but she borrowed for it from books and things she heard over the years. The German army weren't responsible for the atrocities. They were gentlemen. The best fighting soldiers in the world. The old officer caste hated the Nazis. Her father had been a man like those men, who were spoken of with respect by their enemies. She could be proud of him in secret. Even though her mother was so patently ashamed.

She bathed and dressed; she felt numbed. One part of her had spoken to Fisher with every appearance of normality; she had smiled and made a joke, responded to his determined cheerfulness, even looked forward to seeing him that night.

But apart from this there was a cold, suspended personality, almost a second entity, watching the other going through the motions as if it were a stranger. And now, with the paper in her hand, the two sides fused, and she thought with little surprise that she was no longer Paula Ridgeway but Paula Bronsart.

She had an identity at last. Not the competent divorcée with a career of her own and an independent life, with a mother and stepfather safely in the background, but a German living in an alien country. The shadow had a substance;

there was the smell of fire and death, the echo of a brazen trumpet in a vast arena where the people gathered to pay homage. Reality had come with knowledge. And now she had to live with it and with herself. She went to the outer hall, her bag and gloves in her hand, and paused before the mirror on the wall. She looked like him. There was no likeness to her aristocratic mother whose background really was the conservative old German army. She was Paul Bronsart's daughter; whatever he had been, she was part of it. A phrase returned to her. Flesh of my flesh, bone of my bone. He had taken her photograph in his hands and shown it to Black, to others. He had established a bond between himself and the child who had never known him, and it had stretched from the past, holding her to his memory. Whatever he had done and whatever he was as a human being, nothing could separate them. He had put something away for her, planning for the years ahead long after his death. If he was dead and not, like Black, in hiding somewhere and about to come out. He had hidden one of the greatest art treasures in the world so that she might have the evidence of his paternal love. But she didn't want the Poellenberg Salt. Paula opened the front door and stepped out. She didn't want his treasure. If it were within human possibility, regardless of the past, she knew what she really wanted was to find him.

Paula's mother was crying. She sat on the chintz sofa in the pleasant sitting room, with her husband's arms around her, weeping. "Don't, darling"—he kept repeating it—"don't upset yourself! After what I said to him he won't come back!"

It had been an ugly interview. Fisher's attitude was aggressive from the start. He hadn't made an appointment; he had just called, finding the brigadier out and his wife in the garden. There was nothing Mrs. Ridgeway could do but ask him inside, and there the ruthless cross-examination had begun. She wasn't as tough a proposition as Fisher had imagined. But then she wasn't dealing with her own daughter, he reminded himself. He had thrown the paper with Black's photograph in front of her and asked her to identify it as her first husband's ADC.

She had been shocked and pale, but she kept her head. She had tried to lie, but at the first denial Fisher sprang. "In March, 1938, you married Colonel Paul Heinrich Bronsart of the Fourth Division Waffen S.S. at the town hall in Potsdam; the wedding reception was at your father's home, Shrievenburg; you had four hundred guests and you spent your honeymoon in Denmark. Shall I go on or would you be kind enough to answer my questions now?" She had given in then. Nothing about her reminded him of Paula and he was relieved. It was Albrecht Schwarz, and he had served as ADC to her husband.

"You knew he was coming to see your daughter, didn't you?"

"I would prefer not to say any more till my husband gets back."

"You knew an ex-Nazi war criminal was on the loose and prowling around your daughter, and you never said a word about it? You never even warned her—didn't you think it might be dangerous?"

"I begged her not to see him." She had spoken with sudden passion, and Fisher knew there wouldn't be any more stalling till the brigadier's return.

"She refused to listen to either of us. She's extremely obstinate; there was nothing I could do to stop her!"

"Except tell her the truth." Fisher sneered. "Instead of leaving her to find it out for herself. I was with her yesterday when she read that paper, Mrs. Ridgeway. I saw her face. It ought to haunt you."

She had tried to turn him out, threatening to ring the police. Fisher invited her to do so; he also reminded her that they might like to ask a few questions when they knew of Black's connection with her family.

"What I really came for," Fisher said, "was to get two answers to two simple questions. Give me those, Mrs. Ridgeway, and I won't bother you.

"First, did your husband ever discuss escaping if Germany lost the war?"

She had looked at him with bitterness, almost with contempt. "If you had ever known my husband you wouldn't ask that," she said. "No one would have dared to mention the word defeat. Or escape. Also we detested each other; he wouldn't have discussed anything with me."

"Okay." Fisher lit a cigarette. "So you got the official notification of his death. You never doubted it?"

"Never. And I don't now."

"What did he do with the Poellenberg Salt?" She turned to him, her astonishment distorting her face.

"He had it, didn't he?"

"Yes. It vanished. I don't know where he put it; I wouldn't have asked."

"And you would swear to that, Mrs. Ridgeway?"

There was a movement behind Fisher.

"Swear to what? What the hell's going on?" It was the brigadier. The exchange between them was short; there was no doubt in Fisher's mind that the old man would bring the police to the house and have him forcibly ejected. He had no legal right to force himself upon them or to demand any answers, and he had bluffed the woman. He didn't try to bluff her husband. He was blazing with anger. As if to make it worse his wife suddenly dissolved into tears, and Fisher thought he was going to lose his head and throw a punch at him. "Get out of here, you bloody snooper—you try and come here again and bother my wife, and I'll take a horsewhip to you!" Fisher had left; his last sight was of the man cradling the woman in his arms, glaring in the direction of the door.

There was nothing he wouldn't do to protect her; Fisher filed that observation away. Paula hadn't exaggerated when she said they were devoted to each other. It must have been pretty solitary living alongside them. When he arrived at Paula's flat that evening, he brought a bottle of Riesling. He thought she looked rather pale; her hair was brushed back, and the blue eyes were very vivid in the artificial lights.

"Hello," Fisher said. He had an odd feeling in his chest when she smiled at him. "I'm sorry I'm a bit late. The traffic up was terrible."

"You're not late," Paula said. "Come in." He gave her the wine.

"Something pretty good from your country," he said gently. She looked at him.

"Good things have come out of it, haven't they," she said quietly. "I've been trying to think of as many of them as I can today. Beethoven, Mozart, Rhine wines, Goethe, Mann—I couldn't think of any scientist except Von Braun. Come and sit down, Eric. I'll get you a drink."

"Whisky please," he said. He watched her walking to the drinks laid out on a side table. She moved without any trace of self-consciousness, no hip swinging to call attention to a very good figure. And from the front she looked like a woman instead of a flat-chested boy. Fisher approved of that, too. He brought his mind back to a less personal appraisal.

"I went down to Essex," he said. He gave her a cigarette; she sat beside him on the sofa, and he was pleased about that. "I got nothing but an identification of Black as Schwarz. And one important admission, but I'll come to that in a minute."

"How was my mother?" The voice was cold. "She's still never contacted me. Oddly enough, I'm not even hurt any-more."

"I'm glad to hear it," Fisher said. "She was extremely upset. Cried her eyes out, as the saying goes."

"I can't imagine her crying," Paula said. "I don't think I've ever seen it. Go on."

"Your stepfather came bounding in, looking like a furious St. Bernard, threatening to call the police and give me a good horsewhipping! It must have had its funny side, but I felt he meant every word. I left them in each other's arms. Incidentally, she said one thing. She said she and your real father hated the sight of each other."

"I see. That may account for the way she avoided me," Paula said. "It must be a nuisance being saddled with a child by someone you hated. I always suspected it. What was the other thing she told you?"

"In a minute," Fisher said. "I promised to tell you who my employer is, didn't I? I got the permission this morning, before I phoned you. It's the Princess Von Hessel. You know who I mean—the armament family."

"I know the name," Paula said. "How very extraordinary this is. And they want you to find my father?"

"That's the idea. You see he took something from them during the war and they want it back." He had put personal considerations aside; he was a professional and he was watching her. She faced him without guile.

"I know what it is," she said. "That was why Black came to see me. He told me about it and I didn't believe him. I thought he was crazy. It's the Poellenberg Salt, isn't it?"

"Yes," Fisher said. "Yes, it is. And your father did have it. Your mother said so. Paula, what did Black tell you? This could solve the whole thing!"

She extended her hand, turning the cigarette between her fingers.

"He said my father had hidden it. He said he had hidden it to give to me." She raised her eyes to Fisher. "I suppose that makes a difference."

He kept his surprise under control. "It could, only you don't have any legal right to it," he said. "It was stolen."

"Black said it was a gift. He emphasized that. He said he had promised my father to find me and give me the clue to where it was."

"Are you going to tell me that clue?"

"I don't want the Salt," she said. "I looked it up—it's belonged to that family for hundreds of years. I'd like to give it back to them. But it's only a clue. Black said my father didn't trust him with the whole secret. He was certain that my father was alive. The message he gave me doesn't make any sense at all."

"For Christ's sake," Fisher said, "what was it?"

" 'Paris, Twenty-fifth June, 1944. Tante Ambrosine and her nephew Jacquot.' That was all. Jacquot is a man's name. It sounds like gibberish to me."

"Your father was no fool," Fisher said grimly. "He knew what he was doing. That message must make sense. Paris, Twenty-fifth June, 1944. Tante Ambrosine and her nephew Jacquot. I'll just have to find out what it means."

"We'll both have to find out," Paula said quietly. "By the way, what would happen if my father was found alive now?"

"He'd be extradited to West Germany and put on trial. He was a big man in the Nazi Party. He's wanted for war crimes."

"But if you find the Poellenberg Salt, that will be enough for you, won't it? You won't have to look for him?"

"No," Fisher said, "I won't. My clients want the Salt, that's all."

"They can have it," Paula said. "And that's a promise. Because I believe Black; I believe my father owned it legally and it's mine. But I'll give it back on one condition."

"That I lay off looking for your father?"

"No. That you help me to find him, if he's still alive."

Fisher hesitated. "You really mean this? You know what you're doing?"

"Not really," Paula said. "I'm still confused. I'm still looking for something and I haven't found it."

"Does it have to be a father?" Fisher asked her.

"I don't know that either. He must be an old man now; I've been thinking about it all day, thinking of what he was and what kind of man he must have been. An S.S. general. I've grown up with the idea of the bogey men in the black uniforms. But I want to see him for myself. That's as far as I can go at the moment. I've helped you, and I trust you to help me. It's not your job to expose him, but it's mine to help him if he's still alive and needs it. I want to search with you, Eric. And even if the Salt is legally mine, I'll hand it back. Is that a bargain?"

"All right." She turned and held her hand out to him. He thought she was crazy and he wanted to say so. He also wanted to kiss her, which was nothing to do with Nazi generals or hidden masterpieces. He had expected almost any development but this one. He had undertaken to find the Poellenberg Salt, and she wanted to find the general. So for good or evil they were in it together. He took her hand and shook it. He went on holding it for a few moments until she drew it away.

"All right," he said again. "It's a bargain. Next stop is Paris."

"Well," Dunston said, "so you're off to Paris? Lucky you."

"I'll be busy," Fisher said. "Don't tell me you've still got the musical-hall-Englishman's idea of Paris—all tits and Folies Bergère! I've got a lousy assignment, and you're welcome to take it over any time you like!"

"No, thanks." Dunston laughed. They were sitting in a public house down the street from their office; Fisher had ordered beer, and Dunston had a double whisky on the counter in front of him. In Fisher's opinion he drank too much. He was a tall, thick-set man, with bushy black hair and eyebrows, a genial ugliness redeemed by splendid white teeth. He laughed very easily, showing them off. He had a pretty little wife and three children; he was a lot cleverer than his cheery personality indicated. On his own admission, he was no gentleman, and he professed a passion for making money. "No trips to Europe for me at the moment," he said. "I'm up to my balls in work right here. How do you think it's going?"

"Don't know," Fisher said. "My guess is the general is alive and hiding out somewhere. Everything points to it. My second guess is that when he does show up, if he does, he'll make for his daughter. From what I've heard so far, he was crazy about her as a kid. And he's apparently made contact now through Schwarz. So he's still interested in her. And he wants her to find this Salt. From the point of view of our clients, that does worry me. She seems to think she's got a legal claim to it, from what Schwarz said to her. So there could be quite a fight over the bloody thing. Of course she's saying now she'll give it back to them."

"That's all very well till she sees it," Dunston said. "I've heard those generous gestures taken back before. You've told Princess Von Hessel about this?"

"I sent her a long report. Personally, I think Mrs. Stanley might keep her word. She's a funny sort of girl, not the usual grabber at all."

"Oh?" Dunston's bushy eyebrows lifted and the spectacular teeth appeared. "First time I've heard you giving a bird a good character reference. Taking her to Paris with you, aren't you? I suppose that'll go down on the expense account. . . ."

"I'm not taking her; she's coming." Fisher answered rather more sharply than he intended. Dunston's grin irritated him.

"Have fun."

"Get stuffed. Have another whisky?"

"So long as you're paying. When do you leave for Gay Paree?"

"Tomorrow morning. We're staying at the Odile; that

shouldn't break the expense account. I'll be in touch with you to let you know how things are going. I wish I knew what the hell it means. Tante Ambrosine and her nephew Jacquot."

"Try the telephone directory," Dunston suggested. "It could be a restaurant. Suppose some poor bloody foreigner was told to find the Great American Disaster, what do you think he'd make of that? Tante Ambrosine and her nephew—could be anything. You've checked around about them?"

"I got straight through to Joe Daly at Reuters in Paris," Fisher said. "It meant nothing to him either. It's got nothing to do with any contemporary pop Paris 'scene' or he'd have known it. Anyway, we'll see what happens when we get there. My first move will be to check on whoever thought they saw Bronsart."

"I'm off to Manchester this afternoon." Dunston stretched a little. He was very powerfully built.

"No wonder you're so narky about Paris." Now it was Fisher's turn to laugh. "You won't get into much mischief there."

"No, but I might make some money for us. Nice little five-hundred-guinea fee for a background check. Rich daddy with silly bitch daughter who wants to marry the little pouf who does her hair. If I can get some real dirt on him for daddy to show darling daughter, I might even get a bonus. I'm off now. Good luck with Aunty Ambrosine."

"Thanks." Fisher nodded to him. At the door Dunston turned and waved again. They got on very well together; as men they were completely different in type; they proceeded in different ways on an investigation. Fisher used intuition and took risks; Dunston was methodical, unswerving, and possessed a remarkable instinct for anything crooked. Their friendship was not deep, but they spent odd evenings together and never seriously disagreed. Fisher enjoyed his company. He could be extremely vulgar and very funny. He paid the bill and left to go back to his office. Outside, Dunston hailed a taxi. Inside, he leaned back and lit a menthol cigarette. His choice of the brand was an idiosyncrasy which Fisher sometimes used against him. He couldn't give up smoking, but he had a morbid horror of lung cancer. Fisher was going off to Paris with Mrs. Stanley. Well, well, Dunston said to himself. He'd picked himself up a piece of crumpet on the way; trust him. He never passed up a chance to get a slice. Fisher didn't think much of women; Dunston knew that. He always chose the same type. They were all loose and hard, and good-looking. There had never been a snowball's chance in hell of Fisher falling for any of them. If he bothered with a woman, it was to lay her and for nothing else. He was curious about this Mrs. Stanley. She was divorced from Jimmy Stanley, and everyone who read the newspapers knew what a high-powered little playboy he was—always firing on all six cylinders. So she was probably the same type as Fisher's usual, but a better-class edition. And she claimed a legal title to the Poellenberg Salt. Dunston had looked it up, and the photograph of it had been enough. People murdered for a thing like that. She wouldn't give it back. If it was hers, by any unsuspected twist, she'd hang on and fight for it till the blood ran. And that was probably why he was going, not to Manchester, as he had told Fisher, but to Germany, at the urgent and secret request of the Princess Von Hessel.

"Get in, Mr. Dunston. We are going for a drive."

The rear door was held open for him by the chauffeur; he had a glimpse of a woman sitting in the seat, her face pale and grim. He got in and sat beside her.

"I am Princess Von Hessel," she said. She spoke in German to the chauffeur, and then pressed a knob on the arm of the seat. The glass partition slid up and closed them off from the front of the car.

"It's very kind of you to meet me," Dunston said. He wasn't

quite sure how to address her. The size of the car, the uniformed chauffeur and the patrician arrogance of the woman beside him had shaken his self-confidence. He wouldn't have been ill at ease if he were dealing with the newly rich. But a face like Princess Von Hessel's was the result of centuries of aristocratic breeding and power.

"I didn't come to meet you," she said. "I came to have our interview. That's why we are going for a drive. You know my original letter was addressed to you?"

"Fisher showed it to me," Dunston said. "I was in Portugal, on holiday. I followed your instructions; I didn't tell him I was coming over here. I presume that you're not satisfied with him, is that it?"

"He was not the man I wanted," she said. "But since I've got him, he can continue his inquiries. He's made a lot of progress in a very short time."

"Then may I ask," Dunston said, "why you sent for me?"

The princess glanced at him; there was something in the eyes which made him wary; he had a faultless instinct for the unexpected, and he knew, by blind intuition, that the interview was not going to be what it seemed.

"You spent quite a time in Germany five years ago, didn't you, Mr. Dunston? When you were with Interpol."

"Yes. I know the country very well."

"And your last assignment was breaking up a gold smuggling ring, I believe?"

Now Dunston's skin was crawling. "That's right. You've made quite an investigation of the investigators."

"Naturally. I always prefer to know what I am dealing with. And what I discovered convinced me that you were just the man I needed. It was unfortunate that Mr. Fisher came instead of you. It appears he is of honest character." She turned toward him and smiled; it was an expression of amused contempt. "You have gone red, Mr. Dunston. Please don't be insulted. Taking offense is a luxury which I don't believe you can afford."

"I don't know what you're trying to say." Dunston began angrily. "But if you're suggesting, Princess Von Hessel, that there's anything wrong—"

"How much money did you take from the smuggling ring to slow up that investigation?"

The question caught him in mid-speech. He stopped and floundered. She went on, still smiling and implacable. "You left Interpol under a suspicion of accepting a bribe. Nothing could be proved against you, but you had no future after that episode. The sum mentioned was a miserable ten thousand pounds. Perhaps not so miserable to you in those days, but surely a contemptible amount by present standards. I wouldn't insult you by offering anything so paltry."

Dunston took out a packet of cigarettes. He was bright red and he was sweating.

"Put those away please. I object to smoking; it's a disgusting habit!"

For a moment Dunston hesitated. His composure had been shattered by her direct attack. He felt naked, sitting in the car with the old woman staring him out, the intangible force of her authority browbeating his will. Slowly he closed the packet and put it back in his pocket.

"All right," he said quietly. "You've got some proposition for me. It must be pretty shady or you wouldn't have brought up that old rumor. And it was just a rumor. There wasn't any truth in it; but the damage was done. I cut my losses and left."

"Mr. Dunston," the princess said, "if you convince me of your moral probity, I won't be able to put any proposition to you. Luckily, I know that you began your detective business with a sum of capital which wasn't there before. So I am sure you took the bribe and that you are a man who has a price. Shall I go on, or are you going to persist in this little fiction about yourself?"

"There's never any harm," he said, "in listening."

"Good. You know the facts about our loss of the Poellenberg Salt; you know as much as Fisher knows, is that correct?"

"He keeps me briefed," Dunston answered. "You want it back and you believe that General Bronsart is alive and can lead you to it."

"Exactly. I am determined to recover it." For a moment she glanced out of the window, frowning. "Determined. Nothing will stop me. But there are complications. Mr. Fisher is not aware of them."

"Too honest?" Dunston asked her. He was recovering himself now.

"Much too honest. My younger son tried to persuade him to go behind my back and drop the case and he refused."

"Why should your son do that? Doesn't he want the Salt back?"

"He's not prepared to take the risk," she said. "I am. I am prepared to risk anything and to do anything. That's why I've sent for you."

"What are the complications?"

"The general has a legal right to it," she said quietly. "It was moral theft, but he took it legally. For reasons which don't concern you, we can never have a public fight about its ownership."

"He's not in a position to fight," Dunston said. "He's a wanted criminal. He can never come into the open."

"No." Princess Von Hessel turned right around and faced him. "No, but his daughter can. I wanted somebody to find the general and the Salt, and then remove him."

"I see," Dunston said; he nodded slowly at her. "I'm getting it now. But you hadn't reckoned on the daughter."

"Exactly."

"When you say 'remove' "—Dunston sounded casual—"what do you mean by that?"

"Just what you think I mean," she said coldly. "Dispose of —kill, if you prefer plain language. I want the general dead."

"And the daughter? She could claim the Salt and get away with it. That's the real trouble, isn't it?"

"Yes," she said. "Once she came into it everything changed. Mr. Dunston, I will pay two hundred and fifty thousand pounds into a numbered bank account in Switzerland. Fifty thousand on account, as a retainer, and the rest later. But I want the Poellenberg Salt, and I don't want anyone alive to claim it."

"Christ," Dunston said softly. He pursed up his lips and whistled, but no sound came. "You're asking for a murder. You're asking me to kill that girl."

"I'm asking you to kill them both," she said. "And I'm paying you a quarter of a million pounds. Think of the money, Mr. Dunston. Think how rich you'll be. You don't have to give your answer now. Just think about it."

"You're taking a hell of a risk, trusting me with this. What's to stop me from going to the police and telling them the whole story?"

"Nothing but your common sense," she retorted. "Nobody would believe you; you have no witnesses, no proof. On the other hand you have the chance to be a very rich man. I believe you'll make the right choice."

"I believe I might," Dunston said. "But only if you double it. And that's my answer. Half a million, and I'll take care of them both. You'll have the Salt and there won't be any Mrs. Stanley around to make counterclaim."

"If I agree to double the money, you'll do it?"

"We can shake hands on it now," Dunston said.

"Very well. Half a million."

"By the way," he said. "Just what did the general have on you to make you give it to him?"

Again her slow, contemptuous smile appeared.

"If you knew that, Mr. Dunston, your life wouldn't be any safer than Mrs. Stanley's is at the moment. Now we will take you back to the airport."

4

Paris in July was full of tourists; the heat was not as intense as it would be in August, when the Parisiennes fled their city and left it to the foreigners, but there seemed a preponderance of English and American faces among the crowds sauntering along the elegant boulevards and parading up and down the Champs Elysées.

Paula noticed the numbers of Germans wandering around and going into the expensive shops. She felt no sense of identity with them; they were strangers, speaking the harsh language which she had never learned. Fisher had booked them into a comfortable middle-group hotel near the Madelon; their rooms were not adjoining, but they were on the same floor. They had dinner together in the hotel restaurant the first evening, and Fisher came to the door of her bedroom with her. He pulled her close and kissed her. She put her arms around his neck, but she didn't repeat that earlier invitation. She went inside and closed the door, leaving him in the corridor.

The next morning Fisher went to the offices of the Sûreté; he suggested that Paula amuse herself for an hour or so and that they meet for lunch.

"What are you going to the police for? How can they help us—"

"They can tell me the name and address of the woman who thought she identified your father. Let's get her out of the way before we start trying to find out who Tante Ambrosine and Jacquot are. That's going to be the real problem. You go and buy yourself a hat and meet me at the Tour d'Argent at one o'clock. I'll buy you lunch and tell you what happened. And don't get picked up, will you?"

"Why not—it might be fun." She had smiled at him, her eyes with a gentle warmth in their depth. He hadn't seen her look at him like that before.

"Because I wouldn't like it," Fisher said. He laid a hand on her shoulder. "From now on, Mrs. Stanley, you're with me."

He saw a superintendent after half an hour of arguing and refusing to accept the blocking tactics of a junior officer, who was determined not to help what he described acidly as *flic amateur anglais*. The senior police officer was a fat man of middle age, chewing on the stem of a very blackened pipe. He greeted Fisher without enthusiasm. Fisher showed his card, explained that he was working for private clients in Germany, and asked for the name and address of the woman who thought she saw the former S.S. General Bronsart in the street.

"Why don't you look up the newspaper files instead of troubling us?"

"Because it says a Madame Brevet and gives no further information," Fisher answered. "How many hundred people of that name are there in Paris, monsieur?"

"About five, maybe more. You could have placed an advertisement in the newspapers. We have other things to do, you know."

"So the officer outside explained," Fisher replied. "Less politely than you. I appreciate that this is a nuisance for you, but it only takes a moment to consult your files. And if you would be kind enough to tell me your conclusions in the business—"

The superintendent shrugged. He looked as if he were bored by life, as much as by people like Fisher who made demands upon his time. "I will get the file. I can't offer you a cigarette; I only smoke this." He waved the revolting pipe.

"Thanks, I have my own." Fisher took out a packet. He knew the French and liked them; he had worked in Paris for nearly two years and grown to love the city and understand the peculiarities of its citizens. They were usually described as the most insular, hard-headed people in the world, who would see you dead before they did you a favor. Taken in the right way, with allowances made for mood and suspicion, they were obliging, hospitable, and kind. The superintendent proved this by settling down to a long discussion of the Bronsart case and showing Fisher everything in the Sûreté file on him. Having complained of the waste of his time, he spent over an hour with Fisher, smoking and going over his memories of the war.

"We followed the lead at once," he said. "Nothing would please us more than to find that bastard still alive and able to face justice. He was here in Paris for six months. I could show you the graves of men and women who were executed at Fresnes by his personal order. Humble citizens who had done nothing but be caught on the streets by his murder squads, looking for hostages.

"But the woman didn't make any sense, Monsieur Fisher. She babbled on, insisting she had seen him, but it was nothing. Just a face in a crowd. Just her imagination. He's dead, I'm sure of it. But there is the address if you want to prove it for yourself."

Fisher got up and the two shook hands. "I agree with you," he said. "But I have to earn my fee."

"Make it a fat one," the policeman advised him. "They are all the same. Boche. Make them pay."

Fisher saw Paula walking along the street as he arrived in a cab outside the restaurant. The sun was shining and he felt happy. It was a strange sensation, quite unlike his normal mood. It was powerfully connected with the presence of the girl who was coming up to him, waving, one hand holding a wide-brimmed felt hat on her head. Fisher was not a coward; he would have faced anything physical, and he had proved himself at other times. But the implication of Paula Stanley, and the way his heart kept jumping every time he saw her, required a different kind of courage, and he didn't have it yet. He took her arm and guided her to the table which had been booked that morning. The waiters recognized him, and there was an animated exchange in French, while Paula sat down and watched him. His hair was on end, where he had brushed his hand over it; it was a habit she had noticed when he was concentrating. He was not a good-looking man, and nothing could be done to make him suave and establishment. He had the kind of body that resented anything but the most casual clothes, and a face that was wary in expectation of trouble. But with her he was gentle; she felt his sexuality whenever they made contact. When he kissed, he showed it, and when he handled her on trivial excuses like getting in and out of taxis or going into a lift.

He took a grip of her, and she could feel the proprietary attitude which was so clearly male. "From now on you're with me." James would never have said or thought such a thing. He had never been responsible for her in five years. Fisher had taken control of everything from the moment they left England. And it would need all her resolution to resist a final appropriation of herself.

"What happened?" He grinned at her over a glass of Cinzano.

"I got the name and address of the woman. But it's a dead end; they looked into it and found nothing. I'm half inclined to suggest we hire a car and drive through the Bois this afternoon and give the whole thing a miss for today. What do you say to that?"

"I'd rather see the woman," Paula said. "I want to get it over with, one way or another. And you won't find the Salt for the Hessels by driving through the woods with me."

"A day never made any difference. Besides I'm not all that enthusiastic for my employers. I'm inclined to agree with the superintendent this morning. They're real Boche. Sorry, I shouldn't have said that. I didn't mean it."

"Oh, yes, you did," Paula said. "But I don't mind. I'm sure they're awful. I remember reading an article in *Time*, I think it was, all about their money and how they'd come back after the war. Can you tell me about them? Don't look like that; I know you didn't mean anything by calling them Boche. I'm not that silly."

"I'm glad," he said. He reached out and took her hand. He was relieved to feel her fingers grip in return. "I'm a clumsy bastard. You know I wouldn't say anything to upset you? All right, the Von Hessels. The mother is the interesting one; she's just like a bird, something like a cross between an eagle and a peregrine falcon. About as feminine and inviting, I should say. Tough, arrogant, clever—runs the whole show. She didn't exactly treat me like dirt, but she showed that's what she thought of me. There are two sons; the old man died during the war. The eldest must be in his fifties; he was very odd. There was something about him I couldn't figure out at all. I had half an hour's interview with her, and he never said a word. He just stood there like a dummy."

"Probably frightened to speak with a mother like that," Paula said. "They sound ghastly."

"They are," he said. "But the younger son was less so. Quite pleasant, in fact; very good-looking if you like the blond superman type. Now he spoke up and seemed quite sure of himself. She must have really taken the guts out of the elder son. It was a very funny setup. The house was a nightmare; I thought I was in church when I first went inside. Stained-glass windows, potted palms. And everything the size of a cathedral. You could write a good play about a setup like that, only nobody would believe it. They'd say it was too far-fetched."

"Here come the *crevettes*. I hope you're hungry."

"I am." Paula smiled at him. "Your description is marvelous, but I forgot you were a journalist. And you speak perfect French."

"I'm a talented man," he said. "Why don't you take off that hat, I can't see your face."

"Oh, don't you like it? I took your advice and bought it this morning. I think it's very smart!"

"I think so, too, but I like looking at you. You're a very pretty sight, don't you know that?"

"If you say so."

"I do. Put it on the seat beside me and get on with your *crevettes*—they're delicious. You sure you wouldn't rather go driving with me this afternoon?"

"I'm sure," Paula said. "Let's go and see the woman—please."

"All right, we'll go. But tonight we will have dinner somewhere special. And we'll make a pact; we won't talk about your father or the Poellenberg Salt."

"What will we talk about then?"

"Ourselves," Fisher said. "I shall tell you the story of my life, and I want to hear all about that nice husband of yours. Incidentally, he must have been a shit."

"He wasn't too bad," she said. "I'm not very easy to live with either."

"So far"—Fisher wiped his mouth with a napkin—"I haven't found you difficult."

He had hired a car that morning and they drove. There was a fleet of boats traveling down the Seine, carrying merchandise and tourists. A huge coal barge floated past them, a solitary dog standing sentinel in the bows. The streets they drove through became shabbier and dirtier; refuse and prowling cats cluttered the narrow pavements; washing hung festooned out of the windows. It took forty-five minutes of crawling through the traffic in the narrow roads to reach the place where Madame Brevet lived.

It was a crumbling apartment building, the walls scrofulous with peeling plaster, the front door hanging ajar. They went into the dark hall and were assailed by a smell of cooking and cats' urine. Up one flight of wooden stairs, they knocked at another door.

It was a young woman who opened it and stood blocking their way; she carried a fat little two-year-old baby on her arm.

"Madame Brevet?" Fisher said.

"I'm Madame Brevet." She was about twenty-five.

"I think," he said politely, "that we want your mother-in-law. Could we speak with her for a minute? It will be worth her while to see us, madame."

"What do you want?" The woman hadn't moved. She had a tired, sullen face with small dark eyes that stared at them suspiciously. Her look at Paula was distinctly hostile.

"Information," Fisher said. He held out a fifty-franc note. "Would you ask Madame Brevet to see us?"

The daughter-in-law took the money; she gave the baby a comforting jiggle as it began to whimper, fingers stuffed in its mouth. "You can see her," she said. "But you won't get much sense out of her. She drives me crazy, monsieur. She had the police around here a while ago. Come in." She stepped back, and they went into a room which was crowded with furniture and dominated by a large, scrubbed, wooden table in the center. The smell of cooking was overpowering, so was the heat, for the windows were shut and a big kitchen stove was alight in the corner. An old woman, white-haired and dressed in frowzy black, was sitting in an armchair near the stove.

"There's some people to see you. What's your name, monsieur?"

Fisher came forward to the armchair; a lined white face looked up at him. "I am Monsieur Fisher and this lady is Madame Stanley. We are from England, Madame, and we wanted to ask you a few questions. Would you be kind enough to answer for us?"

The eyes were hooded in loose skin; they had a filmy look associated with age. "What questions do you want to ask? I'll do my best, but my memory is not as it was. She tells me I forget everything." The old woman jerked her head toward the younger woman.

"And you do" was the retort. "You drive me crazy the way you forget."

"Madame Brevet," Fisher began. "Not long ago you were walking down the Rue D'Auvergne and you thought you saw a man. A German officer who used to be in Paris during the war. Do you remember?"

For a moment there was absolute blankness. Paula moved a step nearer; it was useless, just as the police had said. The old woman was senile; she couldn't be relied upon for anything. The white head turned from Fisher to her and back again.

"What German officer?" she said.

"The one you said you saw!" Her daughter-in-law couldn't contain herself. "Jesus, you had the newspapers and the *flics* running all over us with that story! What do you mean, what German officer—stupid old cow!"

"General Bronsart," Fisher said. "You thought you saw him in the Avenue d'Auvergne. Can you tell us about it?"

"Ah, my God," the old woman cried out. Suddenly her eyes were bright, her face alive with excitement. "That devil—I saw him, monsieur! I saw him as clear as I see you, walking down the same side of the street; it was him and I knew him, even though it must be twenty years. . . ."

"Thirty is more like it," the younger woman said acidly. "Get something right, can't you? Old cow," she repeated.

"And you're certain it was him?" Paula stepped forward; she felt stifled with heat and anxiety. Her father's life hung by the thread of this old woman's credibility."

"Of course it was; I recognized him—I knew him!"

"When did you last see the general," Fisher asked her.

"Eh? I told you, a little while ago, I forget exactly when but a little while. . . ."

"When you saw him again," Fisher prompted, "had he changed very much? Wasn't he much older? How was he dressed, madame?"

She raised her head and looked at him. The expression was blurred.

"In black, of course. They all wore black uniforms."

"I told you," her daughter-in-law said. "That's all the police got out of it. But do you know she went to the station around here and reported seeing this man! Can you imagine it? The crazy old cow." She shook her head and humped the baby from one shoulder to the other.

"I don't think this is any good," Fisher said to Paula. He took her by the arm. "I'm sorry, but I think it was just a fantasy, reliving the past. We'd better go."

"Yes," Paula said. The atmosphere in the little room was at a furnace heat. It had been failure, and only now, faced with total disappointment, did she realize how much she had relied upon this interview.

The heat was suffocating. She took a deep breath and pulled off her hat.

There was a high, fierce little scream. The old woman was out of her chair and on her feet. One gnarled hand was in the air, balled into a fist.

"The eyes!" she shrieked. "That's how I knew him! He was

an old man and his hair was white, but I knew those eyes! And you have them—you have the same eyes as that swine who murdered my son!"

"Yes," Paula said quietly, "I am afraid I have. I am General Bronsart's daughter."

With two quick steps the old Madame Brevet had reached her. With a forward jerk of her head, she spat in Paula's face.

"Heinrich, where do you think this will end? If you interfere in this you can only do harm. Harm to mother and to all of us!"

"I should like to do mother harm," Prince Henry said. "It's time somebody injured her for a change. You will be here to hold her hand; why shouldn't I go to Paris? Are you suggesting that you'll miss me?"

His brother made a gesture of impatience. "You'll get into trouble," he said. "You force me to say these things. You'll get drunk, and it will be in the newspapers. Why can't you stay here—or go up to the Schloss, if you're bored."

"A drunkard is never bored," Heinrich Von Hessel said. "Or lonely. He swallows consolation for all his ills. I hate the Schloss. I spent three months shut up there with a male nurse who used to punch me black and blue when nobody was looking.

"But then nobody would have cared—so long as the family name wasn't damaged. And what a great name it is, eh? Making millions out of armaments, employing slave labor, financing the Nazis." He laughed out loud. "I'm going to Paris, and I shall stand with a placard around my neck saying who I am, and I shall piss in the street!" His brother went out and the door banged. The prince went over to the window; his mother's car had just driven up in the courtyard. In a few moments she and Philip would have a family conclave and discuss what best to do about him.

Their trouble was, he thought, that provided he stayed

within some bounds of sobriety, there wasn't much they could do. His last severe bout was only two months away; the accident with the car had happened before that. He had recovered and was soaking at a steady rate. He staggered, so to speak, but didn't fall. And unless he fell, there was no restriction his family could place upon him. He had a private fortune, inherited under a family trust which his father had been unable to break, and he couldn't be certified insane and put away without the scandal coming out.

That had always been his safeguard and it still was. He could move about with freedom and thereby torment his mother with suspense and fear. And he had told his brother Philip that he meant to go to Paris, partly for the pleasure of alarming him and partly from a sense of irresponsible curiosity. He had a juvenile habit of listening in to telephone conversations and looking in other people's drawers. He spied on his mother with a sharp degree of drunken cunning, as he had spied on her all his life, partly for self-protection and partly from malice because he knew himself to be excluded. He had discovered that Fisher was in Paris and that he had the general's daughter with him. And during the night, when he woke up to have a drink, the idea came to him of going there and making himself known. It would convulse his mother and cause his upright brother many anxious hours. They couldn't stop him. He could take his valet with him, who had acted as a private nurse for twenty years, and book in at the Ritz Hotel. He need never leave his suite unless he felt inclined. Or he could amuse himself by meddling, by indulging one of his infrequent bouts of self-assertion, like ordering a Ferrari motor car and driving it himself while drunk.

He had no recollection of killing the child. He remembered nothing till he woke up in his own bed and saw his mother standing near him, looking much older suddenly. They had bribed and cajoled and connived him out of a charge of manslaughter and kept the newspaper coverage to the minimum. He had accepted what was done, at the same time resenting it because it placed him under obligation, and gratitude was not within his capability. He hadn't been on a trip for months; when Philip suggested he was bored, he had denied it, but he realized that it must be true. He was tired of his surroundings, inhibited by his family's presence—required to be on parade, as on the occasion when the detective came and he had stood behind the sofa, trying not to sway about; and then locked in his bedroom because they were afraid he might stumble downstairs; at other times banished out of sight with the discreet connivance of his valet. He liked his valet; there was an understanding between them. Prince Heinrich paid his salary and gave him extra money when he felt in a good mood. The valet took orders from the princess in a crisis, but from day to day he set out to please the prince. He had made up his mind. He was drunk as usual but by no means incapable. He was going to Paris. He rang for his valet, gave him the news, and instructed him to pack.

Downstairs his mother and his brother Philip were in conference as he had imagined. "I won't allow it," the princess said. "God knows what he'll do when he gets there; imagine the Ritz if he has one of those drunken rages and begins to smash things!"

"He won't do that." Philip tried to comfort her. "The clinic cured him of those impulses. He simply drinks now, mother. I tried to persuade him not to go, but you know how obstinate he becomes if you argue with him."

"You're too soft," the princess said angrily. "You always plead and make excuses for him! I'm going to have him put away—I've borne enough from him! I'll get him certified and committed. Then we can have peace!"

"You can't do that," her son said quietly. "Henry's not mad; you can't do that to him. I won't agree to it. And you know it would leak out. We've covered him all his life, and you said yourself he hasn't long. You mustn't think of that solution. It's impossible."

The fierce glare turned on him like a light beam. She looked old and cruel with anger. "Nothing is impossible to us," she said. "As we have proved once already. It came to the Von Hessels and the might of Adolf Hitler's Gestapo and we survived. Never say to me that something can't be done."

"At a price, mother. But the days for paying it are over, too. We have power and we have money. We no longer have the right to abuse either of them. The old world permitted it, the new one won't, whatever you think. We hid the killing of that child because we set the parents up for life and moved them five hundred miles away to Frankfurt. But we can't put Henry in a lunatic asylum and hope to get away with it. He has trustees, and he's nominally head of the family. You don't want the scandal over the Salt to destroy us; this would be almost as bad."

"You have the new conscience, don't you, my son?" She sneered at him, standing at her full height, with the force of her patrician contempt for ordinary moral standards beating against him. "You talk like a bourgeois. You forget who we are."

"I could never do that," Philip reminded her. "I have lived and breathed the importance of this family from the moment I was born. I've watched you ruling our empire, mother, and I've accepted all my obligations. But the times have changed, and even we can't put them back to what we were. We're powerful, yes, but we're no longer the feudal barons of before the war. We can't dispose exactly as we like, even of our own blood. Society won't tolerate us if we try, and I'm very anxious not to put it to the test."

"That's not your reason for protecting that drunken maniac." The princess turned on him. "It's weakness!" She was so angry with him for this determined thwarting of her will that she was capable of saying anything to punish him. She loved him, as she had loved his father, but she loved her power of domination more than anything else. He was a Von Hessel, but he was of weaker stuff, with a silly conscience and a set of tepid morals that filled her with disgust. The temptation to tell him so, came for a moment, and she conquered it. Only a fool pulls down the house because a door squeaks.

"He's a danger and he's bad," she said coldly. "I've always known he would bring some dreadful tragedy upon us. Let him go to Paris, then. Let him meddle, let him blunder drunkenly into this hornet's nest, with Fisher and that woman. It is your responsibility if anything goes wrong." She turned her back on him and walked out of the room. Prince Philip watched her as she left him. His mother's anger lasted for days; she would move around the house and ignore him until he came and abjectly apologized. She was a woman who, when she once established contact, never let go. He felt her influence even when they were separated, the force of her affection, the pull of her willpower.

And he admired her for the super-human strength of character that had kept the Von Hessel factories in the face of government attempts to seize them, that had fought the accusations of Nazi sympathy and gathered the loyalty of thousands of workers to herself. She was like iron; the rock upon which he had leaned since his infancy, because the old prince died when he was still a little boy.

She hated his brother Heinrich, as only a woman of that determined cast can hate a weakling of whom she fails to rid herself. It would have surprised her to know that the feeling was returned; she thought the sodden, drink-distorted personality of her son was incapable of a coherent emotion or of a sensibility that could be wounded. And if she had admitted it, Philip knew she wouldn't have cared. He had disappointed her; he embodied everything she most despised. Lack of self-control, whether it was lying in a coma with his own vomit on the floor beside the bed or flying into violent tantrums when he broke the furniture or drove a car at lethal speed on the wrong side of the road. He had a keeper, a valet who was trained to clean up after him and nurse him, armed with a hypodermic when he fell into DT's. He lived with them, and yet he had an entity and freedom, which his mother had been powerless to take away from him. He seldom balked her, but when he did, as on this occasion when he had declared his plan to go to Paris, its effect upon her was alarming. Her solutions were the sweeping variety that suggest themselves to those with too much power. Put him away. Shut him up forever. But the terms of an old trust formed by her son's great-grandfather made this impossible to do without the maximum publicity. Philip wondered whether his brother understood the factors that had saved him, or whether he would capitalize still further to embarrass his family if he did realize. In any case it didn't matter. What did matter was this intention to go to Paris and involve himself in Fisher's activities. He would attract attention, because their name was like honey to a swarm of bees where the world press was concerned. Henry would be followed and photographed, and the old rumors of his illness resurrected, to be followed by veiled suggestions of what their exact cause might have been. Nervous breakdowns. Tuberculosis. That had covered a six-month stay in a Swiss clinic after a violent outburst which luckily took place in the Schloss Wurzen, far enough from the public eye to be disguised. Unmarried. The world's most eligible bachelor. The wealthiest recluse, who seldom left his hotel suite.

Philip had seen the press cutting his mother kept of the reports over the years during the early days of the war when Heinrich had got loose in Europe, for the second time. The efforts of his valet had brought him home without a major breakdown or the disclosure of his real malady. Alcoholic degeneracy. He had said Heinrich wasn't mad. Clinically this could be argued. Heinrich was the result of centuries of over-breeding, an unhappy genetic accident which he, Philip, had escaped. He maintained that knowledge of his own good fortune made him guilty in relation to his brother. He insisted to his mother that it could have been his burden instead of Heinrich's to carry through life the sins and intermarriages of his ancestors. He sighed and pushed the blond hair back from his forehead. It too was a genetic gesture, from the father who had died in a blazing Stuka over the English Channel. If Heinrich was determined to go, then he had better follow him. That might placate his mother and give them some safeguard against the future. Because the future could turn very dark if the detective's latest report was right.

In his opinion, and he had been very emphatic on the telephone, the newspaper report of a month ago had been correct. The general was still alive.

"Darling, why don't you sit down and relax? I've brought the newspapers; it's a lovely afternoon." The brigadier looked up anxiously at his wife. She wore slacks and gardening gloves; her face was lined and tired. Overhead, the sun was burning in an empty sky; the scent of roses was strong in the still air, birds perched in the beautiful old medlar tree beside their garden chairs and sang.

It was a dreamlike English summer afternoon, too hot to work, a time for peace and silence, for reading the Sunday papers and waking afterward from a light doze to drink tea and eat homemade cake. This had been their idyll for many years; their lives had passed in uninterrupted calm and mutual compatibility. They gardened, they read, they talked and held hands like lovers, which in spite of their ages, they still were. Their life together had been good. It was an almost Biblical phrase which the brigadier enjoyed using to describe something entirely satisfactory in the sight of God and man. He held out his hand to her, and she obeyed him, sitting at his side. She leaned back and closed her eyes. In repose her face was beautiful; it had a purity of feature that delighted him as much as the day he first saw it, in a freezing attic in her own home, that enormous stucco house in Munich which his commanding officer had commandeered. She had been a young woman then, frightened and hostile, facing an enemy intruder who had come up the back stairs and been a witness to her humiliation and despair. She had been burning pieces of broken furniture in the grate to keep herself and Paula warm. The child was in bed and coughing miserably. Gerald Ridgeway would never forget that first meeting with his wife. He had fallen in love immediately and for the first time in his life. There was a nice, conventional English girl at home whom he expected to marry one day; she disappeared from possibility as soon as he saw the German woman's sculptured face and flinched at the tragedy in her eyes. He had loved her from the first moment of their encounter, and his feeling was not diminished in its intensity. She didn't sleep well; she was restless and sad. The serenity which was their greatest achievement had disappeared.

"Darling," he said, "do stop worrying. It's all over now."

"I don't believe it," Magda Ridgeway said. "I lie awake, thinking it will all come out, that the world will know, and wherever we go, people will point us out. How do you think our friends would feel if they knew who I was—who my husband had been?"

"It's a long time ago," he said. "Nobody cares now."

"Our generation cares," she said. "They fought in that war; they were part of it all. The stain will never be washed away for them. It can never be washed away for me."

"You mustn't say that." He turned to her quickly. "You had nothing to do with what happened!"

"I was married to him for ten years." His wife spoke slowly as if it were an effort. "I entertained those creatures in my home; I lived with the spoils he took from families who were shipped away and murdered. I was part of it all, Gerald. I lived with death; I lay in its arms, and I bore it a child. That was the most horrible part—that obsession with the child." She shivered. "Without pity, without one human feeling for anyone or anything, and yet when it came to the baby he was besotted! Do you know, he used to spend hours in the nursery, playing with her? Sitting by the cot, watching every movement, holding her hand in his fingers. When I went upstairs, I'd hear him talking away to her, crooning and humming like a woman. If she cried, he would rush to the nursery and shout at the nurse—I was nauseated by it. I tell you, I found it so horrible that I couldn't go near her myself. And he knew this. He was very angry with me because he said I didn't love her. But I couldn't; she was his. Whenever she looked at me, they were his eyes. I felt as if I'd given birth to a monster; that was why he loved her, because she was the image of him. Poor Paula—I just couldn't help it. And in my heart I've never really got over that early feeling. It makes me very guilty."

"You've been a wonderful mother," her husband retorted. "Don't talk nonsense. I'm afraid she's just been spoiled, that's all. And losing James has made a difference. She's got soured. It's nothing to do with you, my sweetheart. And you can stop thinking about Bronsart and the past. He's dead, and so is that man Black. There's nothing to connect you."

"I remember Black so well," she said. "Albrecht Schwarz, a little man, very dapper in his uniform. He adored the general; he followed him like a shadow. I remember him standing in the room when they first brought the Poellenberg Salt to the house, and my husband laughing. 'How do you like your table center?' That's what he said to me. I knew where it came from; I'll never forget the shame. My father and the Von Hessel's grandfather were friends. I ran out of the room, and do you know what he did? He brought Paula down out of her cot and showed it to her! 'It's for her,' he said to me afterward. 'She touched it and she laughed. She liked it! So she shall have it—my gift to her!' Not long after that it was taken away, and I never saw it again. I never asked what he had done with it; I didn't want to know. He was like a madman; things were going so badly for us in the war. He was worse than I had ever known him. He talked of going to fight in Russia with his S.S. division and wiping every Russian off the earth. I used to pray he'd go and never come back. And that prayer was granted. Do you know, that's when I believed in God?"

"I know," the brigadier said. "You told me. And he is dead, and nobody can bring him back, whatever Paula does."

"And the Salt? What did Black tell her—why has she gone to Paris?"

"I don't know," he admitted, "but I am sure it will all come to nothing. You have no real reason to worry."

His wife looked at him. He too looked tired, and fresh lines had appeared around the eyes and mouth. She brought his hand up to her lips and kissed it.

"This has put years on to you," she said sadly. "I have only one fear. One terrible fear and I can't get rid of it. What if that devil *is* alive?"

"He isn't," Gerald Ridgeway said. "But if the impossible turned up and he had escaped—we'll face it, as we've faced everything, my darling. Together. And don't you worry. Whatever comes out of all this, I will protect you."

"By God," Fisher said, "look at this—Heinrich Von Hessel is here! It's in the paper; he's staying at the Ritz!"

He passed the newspaper to Paula; they were having break-fast in the dining room of their hotel. It was a morning ritual which had never appealed to Fisher. Sitting up and eating at an early hour had bored him, and he eschewed the habit as a waste of time. Now he looked forward to going down and waiting for Paula to come in; after the first few mornings he went to her room and they came down together. He could see by the hotel management's indulgent attitude that they were thought to be lovers. He only wished the grinning waiters had been right.

There was a bizarre horror about what had happened that clung to them both when they left the old woman. Paula kept rubbing her cheek, though the spittle had long disappeared. She shivered in spite of Fisher's arm around her. It was an unnerving experience, sudden and physically disgusting. Hate had come up and spat in her face. Fisher blamed himself for having taken her there. But if he hadn't, he would have gone away like the men from the Sûreté, believing the old woman to be suffering from senile delusions.

Senile she was, and mentally confused. But for that brief moment the fog of age had cleared from her mind. There was no doubt about the reaction when she saw Paula, or that angry scream. "He was an old man with white hair—but I knew him by the eyes—" The man was still alive. He was old and his hair was white, but he had the same distinctive eyes, and she had known him. She had remembered, with the terrible clarity of her maternal grief, the face of the man who had sentenced her son to death.

Shrieking and fighting to get at Paula, the old woman had brought back the terror and nightmare of the last phase of the war. Through her, Paula had been shown her father walking among a crowd of cowed and frightened men, dragged off the Paris streets as hostages, coldly selecting victims with a movement of his swagger stick. In this way he had sentenced Madame Brevet's son to death, watched by the distracted, weeping mother, who had gone to the prison in search of her son. There was no ban on relatives going to look for missing sons and husbands. It spread the agony when there were helpless witnesses to the daily executions. Through her words the figure of the general rose like a devil in the squalid little room, dressed in his sinister black, pitiless and inhuman, sending the shrinking boy to the firing squad. She had looked into his face; she yelled and cursed him. And she had seen that face again in a crowded street twenty-five years later and remembered it. If Fisher and her daughter-in-law hadn't held her, she would have attacked Paula with her nails. On the drive back Paula said nothing. Alone in the hotel, Fisher put his arms around her.

"That was terrible for you," he said. "I wish to Christ I hadn't taken you."

"It was so real," Paula said. "She made it so real; I could see it happening."

"I'm going to get you a drink," Fisher said. "You're shaking. Go and sit down."

"I suppose," Paula said slowly, "that I suspected it. When I heard he was S.S. and on the wanted list, I knew he'd done this kind of thing. But it didn't sink into me. I knew it, but I couldn't believe it. Do you understand that?"

"I think so. Here, drink this. Come and sit with me."

"She made me see it," Paula said. Fisher had his arm around her. She didn't seem aware of it. She went on talking, looking ahead, holding the glass of brandy in both hands. "The more she screamed and struggled to get at me, the more I could see her in the prison yard, begging and pleading with them not to take her son. And my father standing there, pointing with his stick. . . ."

"All right," Fisher said. "Now that you know it, now that you've accepted it, do you still want to find him? Are you quite sure?"

"Yes." Paula turned to him for the first time. "Yes, I have to find him. Nothing can alter that. He's my father; he's part of me. Whatever he's like, whatever he did, I have to see him face to face. I have to hear his side."

"But then what," Fisher asked her. "Isn't it better to keep the illusion? How will you feel if he turns out to be the kind of man that old woman talked about today—a soulless bastard or half cracked like you said Schwarz was—you've got to think what may be at the end of this."

"If he's sick," Paula said, "I shall take care of him. That would be the easiest of all. If he needs me, I'm his daughter. He's been in hiding for all these years; he must have paid for what he did."

"And you could forgive him?"

"I want to," she said. "I want to find him. I know you think I'm crazy, but when I was a child, I used to watch my mother and her husband going off together and think if only my father could walk through the door or up the garden and come and take me away with him. I created him, Eric, because I had nothing else. Now I know he's real, and everything in me is crying out to find him. To see him and touch him. To make the dream into a reality."

"And you're prepared to find that it's a nightmare?" Fisher asked her.

"I don't think it will be," she said. "I don't think anything he's done will matter to me. I don't think I'll care."

"I see," Fisher said. He got up and poured himself a drink. "I love you, Paula." He spoke quietly, watching her. "I know I'm not much of a substitute, but couldn't you make do with me instead?"

Paula shook her head. He looked unhappy and strained. It occurred to her suddenly that she had hurt him.

"No, darling. It's not the same thing. I'd never be happy with you if I walked away from him now. Our turn will come when this is over."

"It may never be over," Fisher said suddenly. "He may take you away from me forever."

"I don't believe that," she said. "But till I see him, I can't promise. You will go on helping me, won't you?"

"That was our bargain," Fisher said. "And I'll do it, if that's what you want. But don't expect me to be happy about it. Don't expect me to see you run into your father's arms and give three bloody cheers."

"I won't," she said. "But just remember this. I love you, too." She had gone up to him and kissed him, and nothing more was said. When he came to bring her down to breakfast in the morning, he was smiling and appeared relaxed, but he looked tired, as if he hadn't slept well. On the way to the lift she took his arm. Reading the *Monde* a little later over the breakfast table, Fisher had seen the news of Prince Heinrich's arrival.

"Now," he said, "why the hell has he come here? I cabled the mother about you and coming to Paris. I suppose he wants to check up. There's one thing I won't have, and that's the client breathing down my neck." He folded up the paper and threw it down. "I shall go and pay the gentleman a call and make that clear."

Twenty minutes after he applied at the reception desk, Fisher was shown up to the prince's suite. The hotel had been secretive and uncooperative when he asked to have a message sent up. The prince was not to be disturbed. Fisher suggested aggressively that this dictum did not apply to him and they had better put it to the test. Reluctantly the receptionist spoke to the deputy manager, who referred it higher still. Finally Fisher was taken up to the first floor by a page boy.

At the door of suite F/G the boy left him. He knocked, and a minute later a man in the dark coat and trousers of a personal valet opened it and, speaking in very bad French, invited him inside. Fisher spoke briskly in German and was answered with relief by the man. His Highness was expecting him—if he would wait in the sitting room for a few moments.

It was a charming little room, the walls lined with beautiful eighteenth-century boiserie; its color scheme and pictures were in the same period. It was delicate, restful, and quite unlike the usual uniformity of decorated suites even in a hotel of the Ritz renowned quality. Fisher heard the door open behind him and turned around. Heinrich Von Hessel was in a silk dressing gown, with dark trousers underneath. He wore a white silk muffler around his throat, and reminded Fisher of a character in a Noel Coward drawing room comedy. He advanced stiffly into the room—his legs seemed difficult to bend—and held out his hand. Fisher took it.

"Good morning," the prince said. It was the first time he had spoken; it was a deep voice, with a gutteral English accent.

"Good morning, sir. I saw your arrival in the paper this morning, and I thought I should have a word with you. Did you have a good flight?"

"Excellent," the prince said. "Very smooth." He lowered himself into one of the dainty little French armchairs. Fisher had noticed a tremor in his hand when he shook it. He moved with the uncertainty of someone who was either very old or very delicate. His physique was above average if anything. He was a tall, powerfully built man, bigger in proportion than Fisher. He didn't look in the least like a man suffering from any recognizable infirmity. But there was a deliberation about the way he spoke and handled himself that struck Fisher as abnormal. As abnormal as the stance taken behind his mother's sofa on that first afternoon.

"I find flying agreeable," he said. "Very relaxing." He seemed to be looking for something, his eyes glanced quickly around the room and came back to Fisher with an expression of abstraction in them. Fisher produced his cigarettes.

"May I offer you one?" He was more conventional in his approach to the man than he had been to the mother. There was no attempt to overwhelm or impress; he looked what he was, an immensely rich, pampered man, with nice manners and no desire to impose himself upon anyone. He looked through Fisher rather than at him.

"I would like a cigarette, thank you. Do you speak German, Mr. Fisher? Ach, Josef—" At that moment the valet came into the room. He carried a large glass in a silver holder on a salver. There was a look in the prince's face that made Fisher pause before he answered. It was satisfied, secretive.

He took the glass with both hands. On an impulse Fisher lied. "No," he said.

"Ah." The prince nodded. He looked around and spoke to his valet in their own language. "Bring me another brandy in fifteen minutes. And don't keep me waiting again." He spoke to Fisher. "This is my little indulgence. Cold tea. Would you like some coffee?"

"No, thank you." For a second Fisher almost asked for the same as his host, then he decided that jokes were not in order, even private ones. He watched the prince take a deep swallow. He cradled the glass in both hands as if he were afraid he might drop it, or it might be snatched away from him. Cold tea.

Christ, Fisher thought, brandy at ten thirty in the morning. And another one in fifteen minutes. So that was what it was all about—that was the wooden walk and the glazed aristocratic stare. The man was stiff drunk.

"I enjoy airplanes," he remarked. "Flying is very pleasant." Fisher didn't answer; he was so surprised he forgot to light his cigarette. Now the details began to make sense. He watched the man opposite him and saw the big body sinking downward in the seat, the hands with their alcoholic tremor gripping the glass of brandy like an animal's claws. For no reason that he could explain, Fisher suddenly felt sorry for him. The eyes were wretched.

"How is the princess?" Fisher asked. He couldn't think of anything else to say. The idea of talking seriously to someone in that state was out of the question.

"My mother is well," the prince said. He took another swallow. "She is a very active woman for her age. She dislikes flying. I like it. I find it relaxing."

Fisher recognized the single-mindedness of the alcoholic. He was likely to repeat the remark about flying every few minutes. "And Prince Philip?"

"He is on his way over here. He decided to come because

I came. They are afraid I will interfere with you, Mr. Fisher. They want the Poellenberg Salt very badly."

"Your brother doesn't," Fisher said. "He came out to the airport when I visited you and tried to persuade me not to take the case too seriously. Don't you want it found either?"

"Not very much." The prince put down his precious glass and, with some difficulty, negotiated a cigarette out of a box. Fisher got up and lit it for him. The stench of brandy was unmistakable; he must have been pumped full to ignite so quickly on one drink. He glanced down and looked at his watch. The time for another refill must be near.

"Why don't you want it back, sir?" Fisher asked him.

"Why should I?" He gestured with the cigarette. "We have enough. My mother has one of the finest Raphaels in the world in her bedroom. Why do we need any more? We have enough treasures to worry about. But she is determined, Mr. Fisher. My mother always gets what she wants, you know. Sometimes she does what Philip asks but never what I ask. Did you know I was head of our family?"

"Yes," Fisher said. He should have made an excuse and left, but he couldn't. The prince was not just drunk; he was the product of a permanent alcoholic condition. That was the meaning behind the "recluse, subject to ill health." He was pickled to the brain cells and must have been for years. Anything he said would be irresponsible. No wonder his brother was following him. To keep visitors away. And yet if he hadn't overheard that exchange between the master and the servant, if he hadn't seen himself, the valet come in with another glass and the same pantomime repeated, he might not have guessed. Which proved how deep-seated the prince's sickness really was. The genuine alcoholic is permanently drunk. It's only on occasions that they fall about and give themselves away. And that was where the valet and the family influence would raise a shield to hide him from the world. Poor bastard, Fisher thought suddenly. Poor sick, lonely bastard, killing himself by inches. I bet that bloody mother would be glad to see him dead.

"I am the head of the family," Prince Heinrich repeated. "But they don't listen to me. How will my mother feel if Bronsart tells the truth? How will she like that?"

"He can't tell anything if he's dead." Fisher was going slowly. The sad, pouched eyes looked at him, and there was a glint of something humorous in them. But it was gallows humor, and Fisher sensed this.

"He isn't dead, is he? I heard them talking. You don't think so, Mr. Fisher. Men like him don't die, they live forever. To plague and torment. She'll be sorry. He was the only one who beat my mother, do you know that? Most unusual. She always gets her way. But not with him." He fingered his empty glass. "I never liked him, Mr. Fisher, even before it happened. He got the better of her. Would you be good enough to give me a light—I can't find my lighter."

Fisher held his lighter flame to the trembling cigarette end. The hand was steadier now, but the heavy head was bobbing on the neck.

"What truth could he tell if he is alive? What happened between him and your family, sir?"

"I can't tell you that," the prince said. "No, that cannot be told. Besides, I have forgotten the details. In the end one forgets everything. But if you find him and you try to get the Salt back, it will all come out. My mother knows that. Has she asked you to kill him yet?"

Fisher went back to his seat. He took a cigarette and lit it himself. "No," he said, "she hasn't. And it won't do her any good if she does."

"She will ask you." The watch was being consulted again. He seemed as calm as if they were again discussing his flight in from Munich. "She will have to ask you, and you will say yes. Nobody says no to her for long." He smiled at Fisher; as a young man he must have been handsome in a ponderous way. "Josef, you are two minutes late. Ach, Mr. Fisher, perhaps you would like a drink? I only take tea."

"No, thank you." Fisher got up. One detail was nagging at him. He refused to take that last suggestion seriously. The man was crazy with drink. He would have said anything. How in hell had they let him appear at all that day? Fisher would never have noticed.

"If you and your brother didn't want the Salt to be found, why didn't your mother see me alone?"

"Because I am the head of the family. People are always saying they don't see me. She wanted you to know that there was nothing wrong. Once a newspaper said I was dead. I went to the opera with her that night. I hate opera. Philip was there because she relies on him. You see?"

"I see," Fisher said. He didn't see at all. With the erratic insight of his kind, the prince seemed to sense this.

"She's going to need you if the general is still alive," he said. "So you had to see me, Mr. Fisher. She won't be pleased that I've talked to you."

"I don't have to tell her," Fisher said. He held out his hand, and the prince released his glass of brandy and shook his hand.

"I'd be obliged," he said. "Good morning, Mr. Fisher. Thank you for calling on me."

As Fisher left the suite, with the valet bowing him to the door, he heard the voice raised from the romantic little sitting room. "Josef! Josef!"

"Tante Ambrosine and nephew Jacquot," Fisher said. "Jacquot, Paris, Twenty-fifth June, 1944. That's all we have to go on. That and the fact that I'm certain your father is still alive and in this city. The point is, my darling, where do we start looking for what?"

They were holding hands in the car, parked under the trees in an avenue of the Bois de Boulogne. He had given her lunch and then taken her for the drive out of Paris to the peace and beauty of the famous woods where the kings of France had hunted game and the fashionable used to parade in their smart carriages until the outbreak of the First World War. Now it was a place for trippers, for coach parties eating sweets and throwing ice cream wrappers in the grass, with the echo of the centuries returning as a group of riders trotted by.

Fisher had told her about Prince Heinrich. Paula had surprised him by her attitude. "So he's a drunk," she said. "That's not such a terrible secret; surely they don't have to go to all this trouble covering his tracks if that's all it is. There must be something more." Fisher didn't answer for some moments. The simplicity of what she said was obvious. There must be something more. And of course there was. There was the secret which concerned the Poellenberg Salt and General Bronsart of the S.S. for example. "Has she asked you to kill him yet?" He hadn't told Paula about that remark. He refused to take it seriously, and yet it had begun to worry him. Why hadn't the princess called in Interpol—with her influence she could have instigated a full inquiry into the report of Bronsart's reappearance and got further faster through official channels than she could hope to do using a detective agency, however competent. Why make a secret of the Salt, why not publicize and advertise, offer a huge reward for information. This was the normal course to take in her position, but she hadn't taken it. She needed secrecy; there was always a shame attached to the wish for a private investigation. Whatever the circumstances which gave Bronsart his treasure, they didn't reflect credit upon the Von Hessels, and the prince had let that much out during their conversation. And so little credit did the family derive from the affair that both the sons were ready to forgo the priceless heirloom, which was lost, rather than court discovery. It was intriguing and a little sinister.

But until he could begin to trace the Salt through the general's message to his daughter, Fisher hadn't a hope of solving anything.

"Jacquot," he repeated. "Who the hell is Jacquot?"

"What about the date," Paula said. "That means something, too. June, 1944. What happened in Paris in June, 1944?"

"A hell of a lot," Fisher answered. "D Day, for instance. There must be thousands of incidents which could be relevant, but which one and where to start?"

"Why not start with my father?" Paula suggested. "If he hid the Poellenberg Salt, it must have been then. Otherwise the message makes no sense at all. And I'm certain Black didn't know any more. My father told him just enough, but he didn't trust even him with the whole secret. Why don't we start with that date?"

"You ought to join the firm," Fisher said. He slipped his arm around her and kissed her. "Get out and let's walk," he said. "I've had an idea."

They made their way through the wood on a bridle path; the sun dappled the ground at their feet and glimmered through the leaves overhead. It was cool and still. "What's the idea?" Paula asked him. Their arms were linked, and he held her close against him as they walked.

"I'm going to try to knock out two birds at the same time," he said. "I'm bothered to hell by those Von Hessels. The more I think of it, the less I like to feel I'm working in the dark. The princess didn't tell me half the truth, and what I got out of that poor drunken sod this morning didn't reassure me either.

"He's the black sheep, and, as you say, it must be more than drink. So I'm going to do a little investigating of the Von Hessels for myself. I'm going to call an associate in Bonn and see what they can dig up. Especially in 1944, because I'm assuming that you're right and your father hid the Salt that year. I'm also assuming that that's when he got hold of it. So let's find out what the Von Hessels were doing at the time. Especially Prince Heinrich; he must have been serving in the army about then."

"What about the other part—Tante Ambrosine and Jacquot?"

"I had quite a chat with that chap from the Sûreté the other day." Fisher lit the usual two cigarettes and handed one to her. "I'll take a chance and go to see him. He remembered your father pretty clearly. I've a feeling he was in Paris around that time, too. It's just a chance he might have heard those names. Or he could think of someone I could contact who might know. It's all loose ends, but it's the best I can do at the moment. Why the frown—what are you thinking?"

"You don't suppose my father has been living here in France for all these years?"

"Not a chance," Fisher said. "Far too well-known; remember the old woman only saw him once and she remembered him. He was a famous man in his day; he couldn't have lain low anywhere in Occupied Europe. Most of them got to South or Central America through that underground organization of theirs. Code name—Odessa—did you know that? They had it all organized with the usual efficiency, when it became obvious the war was going to be lost. My guess is your father holed up in Switzerland or Spain, ditto our friend Black, and that's why he's been able to come here and Black could get to England. He'd been living in Switzerland under a phony passport for a long time."

"So why has my father come back to Paris?"

"Because he knew Black was going to deliver his message," Fisher said quietly. "So your father comes to Paris. To wait for you. Isn't that obvious? Didn't you realize that was what it meant?"

"No." Paula had stopped on the pathway. She pulled free of Fisher and stood alone. "No, I didn't think of that. You mean he's looking for me? We're looking for each other?"

"That's what I think." He said it quietly. She made no

move to take his arm again; she just stood there with the sunshine catching her brown hair, alone in the middle of the wood. Fisher didn't like the reaction. He caught hold of her and held her.

"He'll be somewhere near the Salt, that's my guess. So if we find one, we're almost certain to find the other. Or perhaps not—perhaps he just wants to make sure you get it."

"That's a terrible risk to take," she said slowly. "Tell me something truthfully. Do you think he killed Black?"

"I don't know." Fisher didn't lie to her. There was no intimacy between them now. She had completely withdrawn.

"He might have. Destroying the link when it had served its purpose. But I'm not sure. I can't honestly answer you."

"He must be mad if he did. I don't believe it."

"Not necessarily mad. Death didn't mean much to people like him. It was often the logical solution to a problem. Personally, I don't think there's a connection. Don't worry about it. I'm sure it wasn't your father."

"If he is looking for me," Paula said, "he won't come near me if I'm with you, will he—he wouldn't dare."

"Well, I *am* with you," Fisher said; he was beginning to feel angry. "So that's too bloody bad, isn't it?"

"It gives me the most extraordinary feeling to think he might be trying to get to me." She didn't seem to notice his irritation. "It's getting cool, let's walk back to the car."

"All right," Fisher said. "We'll take a drive through the Bois and then go back. I might invite the man at the Sûreté to have a drink with me. Then we'll have dinner out somewhere. How about Maxim's? Would you like that?" He wanted the distant look to leave her face and for the blue eyes to mirror some consciousness of him, instead of looking at and through him as if he were a shadow.

The silence that developed between them lasted all the way back to the hotel. Fisher didn't come into her room with her; Paula said she was tired and hot and wanted a long bath. He could meet his Sûreté contact and have drinks with him; she would be ready at eight or a little after, if he liked to come up for her. Fisher put both hands on her shoulders.

"What's the matter with you?"

"Nothing," Paula said simply. "I was just thinking of something else, that's all."

"Do me a favor in the next couple of hours," Fisher said. He jabbed her playfully on the chin, but his smile was strained. "Think about me. I'll come back around eight." He kissed her and went along to his room to telephone.

The first call was to Bonn. They had an arrangement with an agency there; they kept a small staff of half a dozen skilled operators, three of whom were former members of the West German police force. The single woman had worked for three years with the German Intelligence Service. He wanted information on the Von Hessels. The request was received with reservations; it was not easy to get anything except what was common knowledge or else unfounded scandal about the Von Hessels. They were well protected. All right, Fisher had said sharply, let's have the unfounded scandal as well as the society column crap. And where was Prince Heinrich during 1943 and 1944—there must be a record of his war service; that would make nice reading for the beleaguered German population, knowing the big industrial giants were out there fighting in the dust for the survival of the fatherland.

He ordered himself a drink before he looked up the number of the Sûreté office and called the detective inspector. The response was hesitant; it was almost four o'clock, and the inspector had promised to be home early. Fisher offered to come down to the office but suggested that a drink on the way home might be more pleasant. Finally there was a grudging acceptance. They arranged to meet at a small bistro around the corner from the Sûreté office.

It was a brightly painted modern place, with a record

player in one corner and plastic-topped tables. Fisher looked
around with distaste, regretting the garlic smells, checkered
cloths, and comfortable fustiness of the usual French bistro.
To his horror, the machine was belting out a noisy pop music
selection. The inspector was already seated in a corner, his
eyes closed, his pipe in his hands, with a thin plume of foul
smoke issuing out of it as if it were a volcano.

Fisher went over, sat down, and inquired what his guest
would like to drink.

"A Pression, thank you." The inspector's name was Foulet,
and he shook hands with Fisher across the table. They ex-
changed remarks on the weather; Fisher said he had spent
the afternoon in the Bois, and Foulet nodded, remarking that
it was a beautiful spot. There had been a hideous sexual
murder committed there only six weeks ago, and the criminal
was still at liberty. Woods attracted madmen, he observed.
Some psychiatrist had suggested that it was a return to primeval conditions, in which the retarded mentality felt at home.
Personally, he believed the assailant chose it because it was a
place favored by young girls out walking or riding alone. The
victim had been on a horse, dragged off it and horribly mutilated. Fisher decided that he had better interrupt before he
was given the anatomical details as well. The police, the law,
and the medical profession were all akin in one vice; they
found their own activities the only source of conversation. He
headed Foulet off homicide by offering him another Pression,
which he accepted.

"I went to see Madame Brevet," he said.

"Oh?" The inspector's pipe came out of his mouth for a
moment.

"She was gaga, just as you said. A waste of time. But thanks
for the help you gave me."

"It was nothing. We've had a dozen reports about Bronsart
since that one. They were all the same—cranks."

"Were you in Paris when he was here?" Fisher asked. He

had intended bringing the conversation around to the general without letting the police know that the old woman had not been mistaken. He had also decided to tell the inspector part of the truth.

"I was," the Frenchman said. He took the pipe out again and drank some of his beer. "He was here in 1942 on a tour of inspection; I was a youngster then. I'd come back from the army after 1940, been demobilized, and gone into the police. I thought it was the safest place to be, and also that I might get a chance to work against the Boche. The Wehrmacht were in control of Paris at that time; those other swine were longing to get a foot in and bring the Gestapo with them, but the army held them off. There was great jealousy between the two branches, you know that. It wasn't that those Prussians were humane—they shot as many hostages as the Gestapo when the trouble really started—but they looked on the S.S. as upstarts, not bred to be officers and gentlemen. *Merde* —how I hated them! But the worst of them was nothing compared to that bastard. When he came back, he was not just picking faults with the army people. He had power, Monsieur Fisher, and he used it."

"And when did he come back?"

"In May, 1944. He spent three months here in Paris. The Gestapo and the S.S. were established in force. Why are you so interested in this man?"

"I told you I was privately employed to try to find him." Fisher ordered a third beer and a Campari for himself. "If he's dead, that's only part of it. He stole a valuable work of art from my client during the war, and they are trying to get it back. The Nazis hid hoards of treasures all over Europe; this man Bronsart left some kind of clue with a relative, which my clients got hold of—I'm trying to figure out what it meant."

"And this is a very valuable art treasure?"

"Pretty well priceless," Fisher said. "Tell me, Inspector

Foulet, does the name Tante Ambrosine and her nephew Jacquot mean anything to you?"

He shook his head. "No, nothing. Tante Ambrosine, Jacquot. It could mean anything; everybody lived by pseudonyms in those days. I'm afraid I can't help you. Is that all of your clue?"

"Paris, June 25, 1944. That's all there is."

"Hmm. Well, he was here at that time. I can vouch for that. From May till the end of July. I know because all the districts were alerted for security. He was one of the most hated men in France; by the end of June every Resistance leader had promised to kill him. But they couldn't get near. He moved with an army of S.S. I saw him once or twice at Fresnes. He used to go down there to watch the execution of hostages. I've seen women weeping, going on their knees, begging him for the life of a husband, a son—"

Fisher was beginning to wish he would stop. He kept seeing the look on Paula's face in that shaded wood, the distant light in her eyes, as if she were seeing something or someone from far away.

"He had no pity," he said.

"I was told that."

"No pity," Foulet repeated. "Some of them were sadists; they got real pleasure from the things that were done. And there were Frenchmen among them, don't let us forget that. The Vichy militia were worse than the Gestapo. But Bronsart was above that. He was just inhuman. Tante Ambrosine, Jacquot." Again he shook his head. "I can't help you, Monsieur Fisher. It means nothing to me."

"Thank you anyway," Fisher said. "At least you've established one thing; Bronsart was here in June that year. That's something."

He decided to walk back to the hotel; it was a warm evening, and Paris was preparing for the night and its activities. The streets were filled with slow-moving crowds. Fisher found himself staring at faces as he passed. Somewhere in the teeming human mass, in some part of that city, the man he wanted was alive and waiting. Waiting for what? For his daughter to solve the riddle passed to her after a lapse of nearly thirty years. To see her recover the Poellenberg Salt as a silent watcher in the shadows, then to disappear forever. Fisher didn't think so. His instincts rejected this romantic supposition. Men like Bronsart didn't efface themselves from selfless motives. This man was old by now; Madame Brevet, shrieking her hate and grievance at his only child, had talked of him as old with white hair. But the burning blue eyes were not dimmed by time, nor was the tenacity and toughness which had kept him alive and safe when his fellow criminals had paid for their crimes. The general was in the same city as Paula, and if they couldn't understand the meaning of that message and find the Poellenberg Salt, then they would never find the general. Which, in the interests of his own happiness, might be the best of all solutions.

5

The receptionist at the Ritz Hotel saw a shadow fall across his counter, and he put down his pen and looked up. A tall man, white-haired and distinguished, wearing tinted glasses against the hot glare outside, stood in front of him.

The receptionist had a sharply tuned sense of a guest's social and financial status; he could almost scent wealth and titles, even in the most unobtrusive.

The man was well dressed in a lightweight gray suit, a plain silk shirt, and a dark tie; he held himself like a soldier, and before he spoke, the receptionist reckoned that he was a German. It was something about the cut of the hair and the set of the shoulders.

"Good afternoon. I wish to book a suite." He spoke in French.

The man behind the desk shook his head.

"I regret, monsieur, there aren't any suites available. We are fully booked. I can offer you—one moment please." He opened his register and looked quickly through. "I can offer you a double room and the usual private bathroom. But not until the day after tomorrow."

"I wanted the Louis XV suite on the third floor," the tall

man said. "I am not interested in a room. How long is the suite booked for; I am not in an immediate hurry."

"I can't say," the receptionist answered. "The present occupant hasn't given any date for leaving."

"And who is the present occupant?"

"I'm sorry, monsieur, I can't say that."

"Is the Prince Heinrich Von Hessel in the hotel?"

"Yes." The receptionist was very guarded now. "He is staying here."

"And you cannot tell me if he is in the Louis XV suite."

"I'm sorry," he said again, "I am not allowed to give anyone information about him. All I can tell you is that the suite is occupied, and I have no idea when it will be vacant. If monsieur is not in a hurry, I have a very nice suite on the second floor which I can offer in ten days' time."

"I'm afraid that will not do. The Prince Von Hessel is an old friend of mine. Would you be good enough to connect me to his room."

"Certainly, monsieur. If you will go into the cubicle over there, number six, I will put the call through the switchboard."

The general walked across the foyer and into the little sound-proofed cubicle. Coolly, he lit a cigarette and drew in the smoke. Without meaning to, the pompous little Frenchman had given him the information. If Von Hessel had been staying in another room, he would have denied his presence in the suite the general specifically mentioned. He now knew where he was. The idea of the telephone call had come to him in the last few seconds while he spoke to the receptionist. He had come into the hotel without any plan in mind except to check up on the prince and set a certain anxiety at rest. He had read the account of Von Hessel's arrival in Paris, and the idea of him staying there at that particular time had begun to suggest more than coincidence. He knew all about Heinrich. He smiled a little to himself as he waited in the cubicle.

He had known him many years ago; the screen of rich recluse
didn't protect him from the general. In fact, he could remember the time when he had seen him last, swaying drunkenly
with his mother beside him, ashen-faced and trembling,
rounding like a tigress on her son because he was demeaning
himself by crying. The general had enjoyed that scene, not
because he relished the misery of the unhappy alcoholic but
because it occasioned the humiliation of the most arrogant
woman he had ever known, so proud and disdainful of the
outside world and everybody in it. He knew that she toler-
ated him and his kind because she dared not do anything else,
but that she hated and despised them. The general had endured her freezing condescension and her repeated snubbing
of his wife, whose birth was irreproachable, and he had been
revenged at last.

He knew Heinrich better perhaps than anyone outside his
mother and his brother; he wondered whether the prince
were mentally capable at this stage of even remembering. But
the roots of fear went deep; he would remember if the general mentioned certain things. The telephone rang beside
him; he picked up the receiver and spoke into it in German.

"Prince Von Hessel?"

He recognized the throaty voice immediately. It hadn't
changed during the twenty-five years since he'd last heard it.

"Yes. This is Heinrich Von Hessel. Who is that?"

"Ah," said the general, "now listen very carefully to me."
A few moments later he put the telephone down, lit another
cigarette, and walked down the lounge to one of the armchairs. He chose one which had a view of the lift and sat
down in it, one leg crossed over the other, perfectly relaxed.

Fisher had been out since lunch time, going through the
old press cuttings of *France Soir*, whose editor had been a
friend of his in the days of journalism.

It was a long and tedious task on a hot day; the files

smelled dusty, and the bright strip lighting in the filing room had given him a headache. There was enough material about the general to occupy him for more than two hours, reading and making notes. His first visit to Paris had been in 1942; there was a picture and a short piece about him visiting the then-military-governor of the city—General Von Stuplagle. It was a poor photograph, taken from a distance. By 1944 the scant references to him flying here or there for brief visits to different parts of France had become a steady flow of propaganda handouts, which the French newspapers were obliged to print. There were items about him attending the opera, spending the weekend with some of the notorious collaborators, and finally taking charge of the situation in June, 1944, when there was an outbreak of sabotage and the murder of German troops increased in proportion to the success of the Allied invasion forces.

This was what Fisher wanted to find out—the exact duration of the general's stay in Paris, and whether there was an item which could account for his choice of the twenty-fifth of that month. But there he had met failure. There was nothing. He handed back the files and returned to the hotel. As he crossed the foyer, he glanced at the notice board and saw something white in his room slot.

There were in fact two messages, both telephone calls. One was from Prince Heinrich Von Hessel, who had called twice in fifteen minutes. The other was from Inspector Foulet. The prince had phoned in more than an hour ago. Foulet's was more recent.

There was little to be gained from another conversation with Prince Heinrich. If he had made up his mind to telephone, he would do so again and again until the pattern broke. Fisher had known a number of drunks, and they all followed the same type of routine. It was like a record, and obsessive repetition was a part of it. But the call from Inspector Foulet might be very important. He had learned long ago not to get excited in his profession. He looked at his watch; it was nearly five. Foulet might be in his office still. But the switchboard at the Sûreté said that the superintendent had left the building, and advised him to try again tomorrow.

Fisher swore. He dialed the Ritz.

The valet, Josef, answered. Fisher asked for the prince. Josef sounded worried; his English was very bad indeed as he tried to explain.

The prince was not in the hotel. He, Josef, had gone out for a moment on a private errand, leaving the prince settled comfortably in his sitting room with a television program (and a bottle of brandy, Fisher said to himself), and when the valet returned, the prince had gone out. He was very anxious, but as he had no idea where the prince had gone, there was nothing he could do but wait.

Fisher said that the prince had tried to telephone him twice; had Josef any idea what he wanted? No, the answer came quickly, no, he didn't know anything except that the prince had a telephone call which seemed to disturb him, and he began trying to contact Fisher after that. Fisher decided it was some alcoholic foible and told the valet not to worry. He would telephone again in an hour and see if the prince had returned. He went upstairs to find Paula and forgot about him.

Heinrich Von Hessel came down in the lift and walked carefully across the hotel vestibule. He had found his hat and walking stick. The hall porter sprang forward to open the doors and asked whether His Highness wished a taxi. The prince hesitated; the bright sunlight in the street hurt his eyes, people were hurrying past him, the effect was confused, and he had an impulse to turn back and resume the shelter of the hotel. He wasn't used to the outside world without Josef there to cushion the impact for him. But the hotel

wasn't shelter. That was why he had left it. Josef had gone
out; when he discovered that, he had panicked at the thought
of being alone in his suite after that call. His first reflex was
to try to get Fisher. But there was no reply, and he had sat
by the telephone, muddled and becoming increasingly afraid,
while the hotel operator tried to reach him.

Josef had given him a lot to drink because he sensed that
his master was upset about something, and the prince had not
intimated his intention to go out because the impulse was a
direct consequence of finding himself alone. Now the porter
was beside him, asking about a taxi. The prince had no idea
where he wanted to go.

He shook his head and said, "No, thank you," and began
walking slowly away toward the Place de la Concorde. He
was a very distinguished-looking man, and people turned to
stare after him. He walked stiffly and with the deliberation of
the unsober, holding his walking stick in the right hand, not
knowing where he was going to or why he should feel safer
in the street. Normally Josef answered the telephone. He had
been sitting beside it, having a drink and watching the racing
program on the television in a pleasant haze, without much
detail to disturb him, when the phone rang, and he auto-
matically picked it up. It hadn't been a long call, and he had
only spoken twice. The first time he announced himself in
answer to a question, and the second time he had asked who
his caller was. But no reply was given. The message was brief.
If you want to go on living, get out of the Ritz. Today. That
was all. No more and no less than an ultimatum, and then
silence. The prince had replaced the receiver and spent some
moments looking at it in surprise. He hadn't been frightened
until a little later when he thought about it. That was when he
tried to enlist Fisher. Fisher was a detective; he would know
how to deal with threats. From past experience the prince
was conditioned never, under any circumstances, to go near
the police. He had a hearty dislike of them after the accident

in which the child so foolishly ran in front of his car. The fact that the car was mounting the pavement at the time had escaped his attention. He distrusted the police; they were only interested in nailing some scandal on his family. He never considered calling them. And because Josef was a servant, he didn't confide in him either. He merely demanded more to drink and felt comforted by the fact that Josef was in the suite and could afford protection. But after the second abortive attempt to find Fisher, he grew restless and called for the valet. That was when he found himself alone, and for the first time he was overcome by an irrational panic. The charming little suite seemed unpleasantly quiet. His bedroom, the bathroom, the sitting room, all assumed a sinister aspect, as if something were about to happen. He had been told to leave the Ritz immediately or something *would* happen. So he had seized a hat and his stick and left. Now his fear had subsided. The sunshine was bright, but not too warm as it was late in the afternoon; he found it agreeable to walk. He had always liked Paris; he had better memories of France than of places like Switzerland and Denmark, where he had spent a long time in a particularly unpleasant clinic before the war. He had hated the Danes ever since; the Swiss he regarded as jailers, but amenable to rank and money, so life was not made too uncomfortable for him under their care. Paris was his favorite city; he felt quite calm and in a nostalgic humor. A walk would do him good; he would show his displeasure very clearly to Josef when he went back to the hotel. It had only been a telephone call, and he shouldn't have taken it seriously. No harm could have come to him. He had forgotten what had frightened him. *The voice.* He was walking up toward the Champs Elysées when he suddenly stopped. A man bumped into him from behind. The prince removed his hat and apologized. The man swore at him and hurried on. There was a café immediately opposite, and he crossed the wide street without even considering whether he should go in or not. He sat down, placed his cane and hat upon a chair and signaled the waiter.

He needed a drink. It was a simple need, but it had to be satisfied. Then the panic would go away and he wouldn't feel anything. He drank two cognacs straight down and then lit a cigarette. It was a pleasant place from which to watch the crowds walk by. Two more drinks followed, and he had forgotten why he needed them. He had forgotten about the telephone call. It was growing dark, and lights were glittering along the beautiful central avenue, as the shops and cafés prepared for the evening trade. There was a dusty smell, with the fumes of gasoline mixed with the human scents and the odors of cooking, which were coming through to him from the kitchen. He thought that he might eat something, but there was no hurry. He smoked again, and the waiter, who by this time was hovering near his table, came at once and brought another drink. Heinrich had spent two months in Paris just before the war; he had made the trip with his paternal grandmother, a stately old lady who took a floor of the Ritz to accommodate herself and her staff of maids, hairdresser, and nurse.

She had been kind to Heinrich, whose illness she didn't understand. He had liked her; love was too strong a word to describe any of his emotions. He had never loved. Not really loved . . . he existed, and he drank to make that condition easier. He had gone to Paris with the old princess and found a special kind of happiness. A very special kind. He thought of it then, with the sights and smells of the city crowding memories back upon him. They were disjointed and distorted, but they had reality at their core. He fingered his glass of brandy and smiled into the distance. The waiters were watching him and whispering. He was very drunk indeed; he lifted the glass as if his right arm were a crane negotiating a huge load. His cigarette burned unnoticed in the ashtray, and there was a glaze over his eyes as he looked rigidly ahead of him.

The waiters were taking bets on when he would keel over. It grew dark; the cars racing up the Champs Elysées were a stream of flashing lights; the prince sat on, stiff as a waxwork, swallowing drinks. He raised his hand and clicked his fingers when he wanted more. Somewhere in the recess of his brain a signal warned him feebly that it was time he went home.

They got him to his feet; he took some minutes finding his wallet and trying to extract a note. A man at the next table, who had been drinking coffee and reading the newspaper, got up, paid his own bill, and came around. He looked sympathetic.

"I'll get him to a taxi," he said. "I'll see him home. Poor devil—I had a brother like this once." He picked up the hat and the cane and took Prince Heinrich by the arm. "All right," he said, "take my arm and lean on me."

They didn't find a taxi. The prince struggled to extricate himself. He felt he was able to walk alone, and he resented being guided. He got his arm free, but immediately he staggered, thrown off balance. It was held again and he let himself be supported. They were walking near the Seine, making a slow progress up toward the elegant outline of the Pont Neuf. They didn't speak. Couples passed them, strolling with their arms around each other. The prince had no idea of the time; stars glittered overhead, reflected in the black water of the Seine. The reflections danced and twinkled in the tide. A boat glided past them, its port and starboard lights preceding it like eyes in the water. They had stopped, and the man had taken his support away.

"Now," the general said, "why are you here?" The prince looked at him, dazed and unable to focus. "I wish to go home. My hotel—back to my hotel."

"You shall go when you've answered me. Why have you come to Paris—why have they let you come back here?"

The prince grinned suddenly. He had no idea of what he was doing near the river answering questions. He didn't recognize the man who asked them, who had suddenly taken his supporting arm away just when the prince most needed it. His mind registered nothing but the last thing he had heard. He thought of his mother.

"She couldn't stop me," he said. "They don't want me interfering. But I am the head of the family. I have a right to know."

"That is correct," the general said. "I hope you make yourself a nuisance."

"I don't want the Salt back," the prince mumbled. "I told my mother to leave it alone. But you know her. She always gets her way." He swayed and clutched clumsily at the parapet.

"Oh, yes," the general said softly. "I know her. But she doesn't always get her way. What do you mean about the Salt? It's gone; it's lost to you."

"She thinks she may find it." Prince Heinrich gave a bark of laughter. "She thinks that Bronsart is alive. I hope he is, I hope he is—do you know something? He's the only man who ever frightened her? Do you know that?"

"Yes." The general nodded. "I know that. When are you going home?"

"I'm not," the prince said. "I like Paris. It has happy memories for me. Very happy memories. I'm staying where I am. I may stay here forever. Why should I go home? I want to go now. My legs are tired."

"You are a tired man, I can see that," the general said.

"It is kind of you to take me back to my hotel." Prince Heinrich raised his head and peered at him.

"It is a pleasure. Shall we go now?"

"Yes. Yes, let us go now." They were walking below the parapet on the dark bank of the river.

"And you are quite sure you mean to stay in Paris? Wouldn't you be safer somewhere else than in the Ritz?"

"No, no. We have a detective. He is looking for the Salt. He will take good care of me. I thought I telephoned him . . . I want to go now. Why don't we go?"

"We are going," the general said, "but separate ways." There was nobody in sight; the river was empty of traffic. He stepped back a pace and struck the prince full on the jaw. Before the heavy body buckled and fell down, he had caught it and was supporting the weight. The general heaved and pushed, and suddenly he stepped away. There was a splash and drops of water spattered the pavement and spotted the front of his jacket. He brushed them away and went to the side. There was nothing but a turbulence in the water and a circle of bursting air bubbles. Even if he hadn't stunned him, the prince was too drunk to swim. The general looked down and saw his walking stick, lying where the prince had dropped it. He left it there and walked away, crossing to the other side of the road. As he waited for a taxi to come by, he lit a cigarette. Now when he next inquired, the suite at the Ritz would not be occupied.

The next telephone call that came for Fisher was from Prince Philip Von Hessel with the news that his brother had walked out of his hotel and disappeared.

By the next morning the newspapers carried the story, and on their front pages there was a photograph of the prince's silver mounted cane lying on the pavement by the riverside.

"It's so horrible," Paula said. "It's the second death."

"I know," Fisher said. He held her hand; she looked very pale and unhappy. He hated to see it. All he wanted was for her to smile and come into his arms.

"I know it is. It's getting rather creepy. Listen, darling, I've been thinking. I know you won't like the idea, but all the same I think it's not a bad one. I want you to go home to London."

"No!" Paula turned to him immediately. "I knew you were going to say that! Why should I go home? We made a bargain and you promised."

"I did," he agreed. "I promised to help you find your father. But I'm not sure now it's a very good idea. Be a good girl and give it up. Let me get on with it and find the bloody Salt, if I can. And if I can't, then it's too bad, and the Von Hessels can have their deposit back, as far as I'm concerned. I just don't want you mixed up in this. I don't like the way it's shaping up at all."

"I'm not going back to London," Paula said. "I'm not giving it up now. You said you loved me; I told you what this means to me. If you go back on me now, I'll never forgive you."

"You know bloody well I can't risk that," he said. "As for loving you, hasn't it struck you that this is just a bit one-sided? I know how you feel about your father, but I'm not sure how you feel about me."

"You ought to be," she said. "I've told you. I love you, too. It's only that I have to do this first!"

"I wonder," Fisher said slowly. "I wonder if you're not fooling yourself. Maybe there's no room for anyone else in your life but this phantom you've created. There is a name for it, you know."

"I know." Paula got up. "And as I told you before, I don't care. I've got to have the chance to judge for myself. Otherwise I'll live for the rest of my life with the things that old woman told me! Can't you understand at all?"

"No," Fisher said, "honestly, I can't. All I know is that I'm not enough for you, and I find that very hard to take. It's a funny thing; you're the first woman I've ever cared a damn about. Are you going to marry me, or has that got to be put on the waiting list, too?"

"Oh, don't let's quarrel." She came and put her arms around him. "Please don't say things like this to me. I know it's difficult for you, but try to be patient. How can I say I'll marry you at this moment—my life is in chaos. I've only been divorced a few weeks, and now I'm going to find my father after thinking he was dead since I was a tiny child. You're not being reasonable."

"No, I suppose I'm not," he said. He put his arm around her and kissed her gently on the mouth. "I'm so bloody scared of losing you, that's my trouble."

"You needn't be," Paula said. "I need you, too. And I'm probably going to need you even more before it's finished. All my life I've been pushed out to fend for myself, and women hate that. I did it, but I hated it. With you I know it'll be different. You're a real man, darling, that's why I love you. And you're probably the first one I've ever met."

"And the last, if I have any say in it," Fisher said. "You wouldn't like to prove what you've just said?"

"How?"

"By letting me make love to you."

"Will it convince you?"

"I don't know," he said. He pressed her around the waist. "But I think it would certainly help." She didn't answer; she stood against him, feeling the tension in his body, letting him open her mouth and explore while his hands stroked her back and picked at the fastening of her dress. It was a different kind of love making from her husband James'. It was more forceful, yet controlled. Fisher knew what he was doing; he took the initiative at once and never let it go. He brought her to the bedroom and went on kissing her; he didn't say anything, none of the superlatives she had heard about how great she was and what a swinging trip they were going to make together. He didn't talk at all. He used his body to arouse her, to confuse and compel her, and he gave the act of love a significance which Paula had never known could exist. He loved and he was serious about it. For the first time she felt dignified by sex instead of used. When it was over, he looked down at her.

"I love you," he said. "And nobody and nothing is going to take you away from me. Never forget that."

"I won't," Paula whispered. "And after this, there isn't anything that could." For the rest of that night Fisher believed her. But by the morning when he woke and left her sleeping, he had already begun to doubt.

At eleven o'clock he arrived at the Sûreté office and asked for Superintendent Foulet. The superintendent was very busy; he looked harassed and not very pleased to see Fisher; then his expression changed. He asked him to sit down.

"You must excuse me," he said. "I have very little time. This Von Hessel case is driving me mad. Why should someone as rich as that want to jump into the Seine? Poor little girls and penniless students, but not that Boche, with his millions!"

"I knew him," Fisher said. "And I may be able to provide an explanation. Analyze the contents of his stomach and you'll find enough alcohol to drown anyone. He didn't jump in, superintendent, he fell in!"

"You are sure of this?"

"Dead sure. Princess Von Hessel is the client I am working for." He saw the older man's jaw slip.

"The Von Hessels? They want to find the war criminal? Is that why the prince was here?"

"Partly," Fisher answered. "And partly to meddle. I don't think he knew what he was doing half the time. Poor bastard, what a lousy way to die!"

"Not at all." The Frenchman's dark eyes were hostile. "There's nothing to pity about him or any of them. The Von Hessels are just a gang of millionaire criminals, guilty of everything the Nazis did. Slave labor, collaborating to the limit, growing fat on German victims. Don't waste your sympathy on any Von Hessel. They are all the same. All bad."

"If you say so," Fisher said. "I just take their money and do my job. And speaking of that, you were kind enough to telephone me."

"Ah, yes, so I did. It was about your question—Tante Ambrosine and Jacquot."

Fisher was on the edge of the chair. "Yes? You've found them?"

"Oh, no." The superintendent shook his head and frowned. "I don't work miracles. The names are a mystery to me; but I have a friend you might go and see. He worked in the Resistance during the war, and he operated in Paris when Bronsart was here. He might be able to think of something. I wrote down the name and address—one moment while I find it."

He passed a sheet off a memo pad to Fisher. "You will get on well, I think," Foulet said. "He's an old friend of mine, a most remarkable man. He used to be a hard-line Communist, and he ran the most successful Maquis réseau in the central Paris area. He's mellowed now; politics have sickened him, as it has most of us. But he could be helpful to you if anyone could. Would you excuse me now? That telephone has never stopped ringing all morning, and I have a lot of paperwork."

Fisher thanked him. He stopped in the street outside and reread the name and address. Albert Montand, and the number of a house in sixteenth arrondissement. For an ex-Communist, it was an exceedingly smart place to live. He put the paper in his wallet and drove to the Ritz Hotel to see Prince Philip. The princess was flying in later that day, and it was planned to take Prince Heinrich's body back to Germany for burial. He wondered on his way there whether the family might not be too concerned with the scandal to want to look for anything, even Cellini's masterpiece.

And that was the first thing the prince said to him after Fisher had expressed his sympathy.

"I want this stopped," Philip Von Hessel said. "I want you to accept a check from me, Mr. Fisher, which will cover all your expenses and leave a substantial sum in compensation for the time we have wasted. I tried to persuade my mother to drop this investigation, but I failed; now I know she will be glad to forget the whole affair."

"Do you have her instructions to do this?" Fisher asked. "Written instructions, I mean."

"No," the prince said. "She is too upset about my brother to be worried at the moment. But you can take my word for it."

"Unfortunately, I can't," Fisher said. "I thought I'd made this plain to you before. I'm working for your mother, and if she wants it dropped, I'll be happy to oblige. For personal reasons, Prince Von Hessel, I'm anything but anxious to find either General Bronsart or the Poellenberg Salt. But I have my responsibility to my client. Please don't try to offer me money again because I shall walk right out of here if you do. I'm not amenable to bribes."

For a moment the prince looked at him; suddenly he made a gesture.

"Mr. Fisher, please sit down and listen to me. Forget that you are working for my mother. I want to talk to you as one man to another. Mine is an old and honorable family; during the war we lost our good name and we did things of which I am personally deeply ashamed. What would have happened to us if we had refused to go with the Nazis can be argued several ways. I'm not prepared to judge my parents because I wasn't old enough to know the issues, and it's easy to criticize in retrospect. But I want to make up for the past. I want to reestablish my family as a force for good in the destiny of my country. This is my life's work, if you like to put it in rather dramatic terms. And the Poellenberg Salt can destroy everything I mean to do. Now that my brother Heinrich is dead I am in a position to do it. My mother still has the power, but she is old, and I can persuade her to hand it over to me. I can build something constructive and even noble out of our resources. Call off the investigation. I'm asking you as a personal favor to me. Not for money, if that offends you, but for much greater, more important reasons. Leave this thing alone."

For a moment Fisher was tempted. It sounded very sentimental and noble—real tears to the eyes stuff. It would have
been easier if he could have dismissed the prince's appeal as
a piece of emotional blackmail, but he was genuine. He
meant what he said, with the passionate idealism which was
yet another contradictory facet of his race. But Fisher also
had his ethics, and they were not to be discarded for the sal-
vation of the Von Hessel soul.

He stood up. "I'm sorry," he said. "I told you, dropping the
case would suit me just as much as it would you. But I can't
do it. Not unless I get instructions from your mother. If she
asks my opinion, I'll advise her to forget about it. But that's
all I can do."

"Thank you," Prince Philip said. He didn't look as if he
were grateful; he rang the bell by the fireplace. A servant in
livery appeared.

"Show Mr. Fisher out," he said.

"I'm sorry about your son," Dunston said.

"Thank you." The princess' voice was brisk. She showed no
inclination to discuss the matter.

"Why have you telephoned me?"

"I received a letter from Switzerland," Dunston said.
"You've made the first payment. Thanks very much. I thought
I'd let you know I'm getting ready to take action on that business we talked about. I'll have to go and spy out the land a
bit, meet the person concerned, you understand."

"So long as it's successfully concluded I don't care what
your methods are," the princess said. "But your partner is very
confident; I hope you prove to be as efficient in your conduct
of our business."

"Oh, don't worry," Dunston said, "when it comes to a fee
like that, you'll get the very best I have to offer."

"What do you intend to do now?"

"I'm going over there. I want to be on the spot."

"Good. I don't think we should be in touch again. When you've completed your part, the bill will be settled in full. Good-bye, Mr. Dunston."

"Good-bye." He hung up and for a moment sat looking at the telephone. There had been times in the past two weeks when he had woken in the night, his wife soundly asleep beside him, and wondered whether he could do what he had promised, even for the huge fortune involved. Dunston didn't suffer from scruples or from a sensitive imagination. No ghosts would haunt his conscience, no guilty qualm allay his enjoyment of a leisured, wealthy life. He would never look back. But in the still hours of the early morning he considered the problem and pondered the means. He had killed once before in the exercise of his police duties, and the experience had left him quite unmoved. He had a low opinion of human beings and an even lower sense of their ultimate value in the scheme of life. He had an affinity with the dishonest, owing, he supposed, to his long association with crime and criminals. It was known that in some cases some of the dirt of law breaking tended to rub off on those engaged in its suppression. The bent policeman was a familiar phenomenon; Dunston's acceptance of the bribe from a front man for the smuggling ring was the logical progression of his attitude toward his work. It hadn't been too difficult. Ten thousand pounds was a lot of money. And what he was asked to do was simple. He had delayed operations and once quietly suppressed evidence. In retrospect his action had been foolish. He had jeopardized his career for insufficient gain, and after he left Interpol with the question mark above his character, he made up his mind never to take an uneven chance again. He had run his agency with scrupulous honesty, assisted by the rigid attitude of Fisher to anything which wasn't according to the rules.

But what he was going to do now was in a very different league from taking money and obstructing an investigation.

This was murder. He said the word aloud to himself during his night-time meditations. He had to kill a woman in such a way that no blame could ever attach itself to him. Or to anyone. Which meant her death must be an accident. He liked the sound of the word. It conjured up scenes of cars leaping over cliffs, of trains thundering toward a hurtling body, of windows high above the ground. However he got rid of Paula Stanley, it mustn't look like murder. Because he was a professional and he knew that once an investigation started, no matter how carefully the killer plotted his course, the chances of discovery were higher than those of getting clear away with it. One difficulty presented itself, and that also worried him. Fisher's involvement with the girl. He had to find out just how close they were; he had to go to Paris and begin by watching the victim and noting her routine. This was the first step toward the ultimate goal of isolating her for death. It wasn't going to be easy; he knew the odds and he hadn't tried to minimize the risks. But balanced against all was a sum of money so enormous that he couldn't believe he'd had the gall to ask for it. The first payment was a fortune in itself and that was safe in Switzerland in an account of which he had the number. The final sum would take him and his family anywhere in the world, away from the agency and the necessity ever to think about money again. He could buy a villa in Portugal, where they had spent such a good holiday. A motor yacht. Any kind of car he fancied. There would be some fancy jewelry for his wife, who was a good girl and solid as a rock with the children, and any amount of women to be had on the side. It would be a golden world for them all. He picked up his office telephone and began making the arrangements to go to Paris.

Fisher arrived at the Montand address and found an elegant private house, with a charming eighteenth-century façade. A uniformed maid opened the front door and showed him to a first-floor drawing room. Fisher had been trying hard to reconcile Foulet's description of the man as a hard-line Communist with the exclusive area and expensive house; the sight of a Modigliani hanging on the wall as he walked through the door removed any preconceived notion of what he could expect. It was a long room, discreetly lit by ceiling spotlights which were directed on the pictures, and the pictures, even to Fisher's disinterested eye, were very good indeed. It was a modern room, subdued and comfortable, with a hint of an art gallery about it; there were several large pieces of avant-garde sculpture.

"Monsieur Fisher," the maid said. A woman got up from a long white leather armchair and came toward him, holding out her hand.

"Good evening," she said. "I am Madame Jenarski. Albert won't be a moment. Please sit down. What can I offer you to drink?"

She was a woman somewhere in her fifties, dark-haired, with black eyes that glittered like coals, a handsome face which had once been beautiful but was disfigured by lines across the brow that cut deep into the skin. She was superbly dressed, and she wore a gold and ruby pin in the shape of a tiger on one shoulder. Rich—very rich indeed. The scent she used cost ten pounds an ounce.

She smiled at him; there was a gleam of gold in her mouth. She was not a Frenchwoman; Fisher made a guess and came up with Greek.

He sat down and accepted a glass of whisky. She offered him a cigarette out of a small gold box. He made a remark about the weather. She sat opposite him and smiled.

"Why do you want to see Albert, Monsieur Fisher? His friend Jean Foulet said you would be coming. I hope it's nothing that will worry him."

"I hope so, too, madame," Fisher said. "But I'm making an investigation, and I hope he can help me."

"Something to do with the war? Not with the camp, I hope. I can't let you talk to him about that. It upsets him too much."

"No." Fisher shook his head. He admired her directness at the same time as he resented her tone.

"I'm not concerned with any camp. I presume you mean he was a prisoner."

"He was in Dachau for eight months," she said. "When you see him, you will understand what was done to him there. People have tried to interview him, wanting to write his life story—you know the sort of thing. It would be too much for him to be asked questions about that time. It took me five years to get him as well as he is, Monsieur Fisher."

"You look after him, I understand." Fisher decided to clarify the position. "Is he an invalid?"

"No," she answered. "He can walk now, thank God. I took him to the best specialists in Europe to see what could be done. The Germans crippled him, you see. He suffered terribly. When I found him after the war, he was in a hospital for incurables, dying of loneliness and despair. It was so fortunate for me that I heard where he was."

"And for him, too," Fisher said. The black eyes burned at him.

"No, for me. He saved my life during the war. I loved him when he was the great Resistance hero with every Boche in Paris looking for him, and I love him better now than I did then. Caring for him has been my privilege, monsieur."

"Thank you for telling me about it. I won't worry him, I promise you."

"I'm sure you won't." The smile appeared, and she was charming again. "He will be glad to see you. He likes visitors."

When the door opened, they both got up; the man who came through it was on two sticks, one leg grotesquely twisted up. He was almost bald, with a seamed and wrinkled skin that made him look very old. He wore a patch over his right eye. Fisher came forward and introduced himself.

Madame Jenarski had come to Montand's side and slipped an arm around him. "Come and sit down, Albert. I have been entertaining Monsieur Fisher for you. I will get you a drink."

Fisher didn't begin a conversation. He let the old man settle in a chair and accept the drink first. Then it was he who spoke.

"What can I do to help you?" he asked. "Jean Foulet told me a little about you. You're a private detective, aren't you?"

"Yes," Fisher said. "I can't go into any details of my job, as I'm sure you'll understand, but very briefly I'm interested in the career of a General Bronsart, who was S.S. commander in Paris around June, 1944."

Montand had pale gray eyes; at least the one remaining looked that color—it was sunk deep in his head. Fisher thought suddenly how difficult it was to judge emotion in a man without the guide of two good eyes.

"I knew of him," Montand said. "What interests you about him, monsieur?"

"He stole an art treasure," Fisher said. He felt that, without some amplification on his part, the old man and the Greek woman would refuse to tell him anything. "Its original owners are anxious to get it back. There are one or two pretty flimsy clues, and one of them is a man's name. Inspector Foulet thought it might mean something to you."

"He told me," Montand said. "Tante Ambrosine and her nephew Jacquot. Isn't that it? You want to know its significance."

"Yes," Fisher said. "Yes, I do. It's very important. Who are Tante Ambrosine and Jacquot?"

It was all so simple, without effort on his part. He asked the question and suddenly, unexpectedly, there was an answer.

"Tante Ambrosine was the code name for my réseau during the war," Montand said. "And Jacquot was the code name of a member of it. But there is nothing he can do to help you, Monsieur Fisher. He is dead. He was shot by personal order of General Bronsart that June."

The room was silent; none of them moved. Then Fisher said quietly, "Goddamn it. I was afraid of something like that. How well did you know him, sir? Why should Bronsart use his name in connection with hidden loot—"

"Why did the general have him shot? He was a humble man, very young and unimportant. He was arrested and questioned. Then they executed him the next day. His mother told me how it happened. Now you tell me there is a connection with some hidden treasure. . . ." The single eye switched from Fisher to Madame Jenarski.

"What do you think, Madeleine?"

"I think it is all very fascinating." She smiled at him, tenderness softening her face. "Hidden treasure—fascinating," she repeated.

"Poor little Jacquot; I can't see what he could have had to do with such a thing. I remember him well." She turned to Fisher. "You see he worked for Albert, as I did. Although I'm not French, I was in Paris when they invaded Greece, my country. So I met Albert and became one of his couriers. He didn't think very much of me in those days—he didn't approve of the rich. Did you, my darling?"

Montand shook his head; the scalp glistened under the spotlight above him. "No. I did not. But I tried to redeem you, didn't I? I was a fervent Communist, you see, Monsieur Fisher, and I hoped to save Madeleine's soul in spite of her money. I still do, even though I am fortunate enough to live on it." He laughed and she joined him.

"And there's nothing else you can tell me about Jacquot?"

"Nothing." They both seemed to shake their heads in unison.

"He was a courier for me," Montand said. "A quiet, simple

young man, loyal and a good patriot. He was captured by a piece of bad luck; he was picked up in the street in a Gestapo swoop for hostages. They took the poor devils to Fresnes Prison to hold them for a few days before they shot them. Jacquot was brought out the following morning, picked out at a parade by the general, and executed minutes later. I got all the information I could from others in Fresnes. They said Jacquot was away during the night but came back without a mark on him. And when they questioned you, monsieur, believe me, they left marks." He put up a hand and touched his eyepatch. Madame Jenarski got up suddenly. She looked at Fisher.

"Thank you for coming to see us," she said. "I'm sorry we haven't been able to help more. I will see you out."

Fisher shook Montand's hand. Close to, he could see some horrible scar tissue at the edge of the eyepatch. Down in the front hall, the Greek woman turned to him and held out her hand.

"I saw a report in the newspapers some month or so back," she said. "Bronsart was reported seen. It was a curious coincidence. It was poor Jacquot's mother who thought she saw him."

"Thank you for your sympathy." The princess was sitting, her back as straight as a steel rod, dressed from head to toe in black, her pale eyes clear and undimmed by any sign of recent weeping. Fisher had come the morning after her arrival to make his report. He had offered his sympathy as a formality, and she accepted it curtly, as if she despised him for wasting both their time. Looking into the hard face, the features accentuated by the black dress and a chiffon scarf of the same color, Fisher remembered the blurred features of her dead son, with the lurking wretchedness in the eyes, and felt sorry for him all over again. "It is a disgusting business," she said suddenly. "I was besieged with photographers when I arrived. Reporters have been hiding in the hotel. I warned the management that if one intruder got near me, I should move immediately to the Crillon!"

She had taken up quarters in the Ritz on the floor below her son Philip. "To drown in the Seine," she said. "It's unbelievable. It's such a vulgar thing to happen to us, Mr. Fisher. If my son had died in any other way I could have faced it with more equanimity!"

Fisher could well imagine it. She made so little pretense of being sorry that it was grotesque. He felt his dislike of her increasing in ratio to his pity for the unhappy alcoholic whose passing was so little lamented. "I went to see Prince Heinrich," he said. The steely glance shot at him.

"Why did you do that?"

"I wanted to make a report." Fisher couldn't resist it. "I must tell you, Princess, that I thought he had been drinking." The remark was prompted by sheer lower-middle-class malice; that was how Fisher analyzed the motive to himself. He wanted to see the arrogant bitch wilt a little. Her mouth actually curled—with contempt for whom—Fisher couldn't be sure it wasn't for his effort to score off her.

"My son did drink from time to time," she said coolly. "But he held it like a gentleman. And that is all that matters. What progress have you made?"

"Not very much since I last checked with you," he said. "I've traced one man who seemed to be a vital part of it, but he's dead. I'm afraid this could bring us to a dead stop."

"Why should it? You are sure the general is alive—I agree with you—his daughter has been contacted; all that remains is to solve the riddle he set for her."

"The dead man was part of that riddle," Fisher said. "I'd hoped he was alive and could supply us with some answers. But he's dead, and it was done by the general's personal order." As soon as he said it, the irrationality was obvious. He wondered how he could have missed seeing it before, when he spoke to Roulier. But as soon as he left them he had joined Paula and that drove everything else out of his mind. It didn't take the princess long to see what had eluded him.

"Bronsart must have known he gave a dead man as part of his clue, so his being dead is not important. What must matter is something else about him. Really, Mr. Fisher, what am I paying for?"

"That," he said slowly, "is what I've been wanting to ask you. Which is the most important to you, Princess Von Hessel—finding the Poellenberg Salt or getting our hands on the general?"

"The Salt," she said; the answer was a little too quick. "That's what I engaged you to find. If you find the man who stole it from us, well and good! I don't understand your question."

"Both your sons have tried to dissuade me from going on with it," Fisher said. "Your eldest son talked of a scandal. I want to know what's behind this, what you haven't told me. I don't like working in the dark."

"My eldest son drank," she said sharply. "Sometimes his imagination wandered away from the facts. I've no idea what he was talking about."

"Your second son said the same." Fisher wasn't going to back down now. "There's nothing unreliable about him."

"Philip came and talked this nonsense to you? I don't believe it!"

"Twice," he said. "He came to the airport to see me off after my first interview; and the day before yesterday in this very hotel, he as good as ordered me to throw my hand in."

"I see." The eyes were narrow, watchful. "And what did you reply, Mr. Fisher?"

"I said I was employed by you and didn't take instructions from him or anyone else. If you said to drop it, I would, but not otherwise."

"I appreciate your loyalty." It was a sneer, and Fisher reddened. "You did the right thing; disregard everything my son Philip says to you. I'll deal with his objections."

"I'd rather you dealt first with mine." That stopped her; she moved abruptly in her chair.

"I don't have to deal with anything with you," she said. "You're being paid. That's all you need expect from me."

"I want the truth," Fisher said. "You can stuff the money unless you tell me what the general had over you that you gave him the Poellenberg Salt."

She took it well—he had to grant her that; she didn't lose color or betray herself by a single flicker of those implacable eyes. She glared at Fisher. "What do you want—more money? Is that what this quest for truth is all about? Don't try to fool with me; I know what your profession is—once removed from the criminal classes!"

Fisher didn't answer. He got up and walked to the door. Her voice rose above its normal pitch.

"Mr. Fisher! How dare you walk out!" He turned at the door.

"That poor devil was married, wasn't he?" He spoke quite calmly. "What was the matter with her—why did you have to hide it?"

"Come back, please." She offered the invitation in a normal way, but now there were two red patches on her face, and both hands, festooned with diamond rings, were clutching the chair arms like rafts in a tossing sea.

"Please," she repeated, "sit down and let us both be reasonable. We won't gain anything by losing our tempers."

Fisher didn't move. "I'm not losing mine," he said. "And you haven't answered my question."

"Why should I answer it?" She rounded on him bitterly. "Who are you to pry into my family and try to confront me!"

"You've just told me, once removed from the criminal classes. What are you afraid of—blackmail? You needn't be. But I want the truth or I won't go on with the case. There happens to be an innocent person involved apart from you."

"I see." The princess stood up; she seemed taller than Fisher remembered. "Very well. Come away from the door and I will tell you what you want to know. How did you find out about my son's marriage?"

"There was a report in a Swiss newspaper in 1943. The prince was said to have got married secretly in Paris during a trip over here. I had my office check it out, and they discovered a similar report in a local French paper. He was married in a small village about twenty-eight kilometers from Paris, wasn't he?"

"Yes." She spat the word out. "But how did you find out—there are no records."

"I know that," Fisher said. "My operator spoke to the mayor of the village, and he remembered the prince simply because there was such a fuss about it afterward, and his records were removed and returned with the entry taken out. So he couldn't tell us anything about the marriage except that it took place, because he officiated."

She made a gesture with her hand. "You must be very stupid if you can't guess," she said. "She was a Jewess. Heinrich was completely irresponsible. My fool of a mother-in-law took a fancy to him and insisted on having him travel with her. And that is when he married this girl, while he was staying in Paris with his grandmother."

She moved across the room and took a handkerchief out of her handbag. "You can imagine what that would have meant to us, in the middle of the war. It was hushed up; we separated them and brought him home, but we failed to keep the secret. Bronsart discovered it, and you can understand now why he was able to take the Poellenberg Salt."

"In return for his silence?"

"Precisely. And you can appreciate why I am determined to get it back!"

"What happened to your daughter-in-law?" She seemed to wince at the title. "I have no idea. She was just an adventuress who had her schemes frustrated. She disappeared after we took Heinrich home."

"It can't have been very easy being Jewish at that time."

"It was before the German persecution of the Jews in France," the princess said. "That came later. I expect she had escaped by then. Most of them did. It doesn't concern me now."

"I see," Fisher said. "Thank you for telling me."

"If this becomes generally known," she said quietly, "I shall make it a personal issue between you and me, Mr. Fisher. And believe me, neither you nor your detective agency would win."

"I can believe it," he said. "Don't worry, nobody will know your son fell in love with a Jewish girl and you dragged him home to Germany and left her to fend for herself."

"If we hadn't," the princess said, "if that had come to Hitler's notice, my son would have been sent to a concentration camp. And we could have lost our factories. We did what had to be done because of the circumstances at the time. You may disapprove, but you have no right. You were not there, and you can't judge. I had to protect my son."

"I can see that," Fisher said. "I'll keep you in close touch with everything that happens. And I'd be obliged if you'd get your son Prince Philip off my back. I don't want any more calls from him telling me to lay off."

"You will go on working for me?" she demanded. "You will get the Salt back?"

"I said I would," Fisher answered. "And even though I'm only a common Englishman and pretty near being a crook on your reckoning, I always keep my word. Good morning to you."

When the door closed, she stood looking at it for a moment. Then she went to the telephone and asked for her son Philip's suite. Her right foot tapped an impatient rhythm while she waited.

"Philip? I've just seen Fisher."

"What did he say?" The voice sounded anxious through the receiver.

"He wanted to know the truth," the princess said. "You fool, you only aroused his curiosity by trying to go behind my back! This isn't your affair, and I forbid you to interfere!"

"I'm sorry," her son said. "I thought it was for the best, mother. What did you tell him?"

"He had found out about the marriage. I confirmed it. That was all."

"And he was satisfied with that?"

"Yes. Please God, he won't look any further."

6

"She's dead," the young woman said. The same child was balanced on her hip, greedily sucking its fingers; she stared at Fisher with hostility, holding the door half shut in case he tried to come up.

"I'm sorry. When did it happen?"

"The day after you came here," the woman said. "The excitement was too much for her; she went on raving after you left—I blessed you and your lady friend, I can tell you! Then she just went to pieces; the next afternoon she had a heart attack and that was the end of it. Thank God!" She rolled her eyes upwards. "I ought to thank you—I thought she'd live forever, the old cow—"

"Then perhaps you could help me?" Fisher was desperate to keep the door open; one hand was in his coat pocket holding a wad of notes. The woman looked at him, suspicion closing her face against him.

"Help with what? Not that old wartime stuff again?"

"Your brother-in-law Jacquot, the one who was shot by the Germans," he said, "I want to know about him."

"There's nothing I can tell you." She shrugged, dislodging the baby's fist from its mouth. "Christ, monsieur, how old do you think I am! My husband was six years old when it happened. I wasn't even born. The old cow told you all there was to know. He got himself caught like a fool, meddling with what wasn't his business, I daresay, and the Germans did for him. Always talking about him, she was, raving on and on. She drove me crazy; thank God, she's gone. Old cow."

Fisher brought his hand out of his pocket without anything in it. He gave the young Madame Brevet a look of disgust.

"I expect your mother-in-law's glad, too," he said. "Living with you can't have been much fun for her." He turned and walked away; she was shouting abuse after him. At the end of the shabby street he said out loud to himself, "Hell's teeth, now what?"

The only source of personal information about Jacquot was gone; he had been full of hope when he left the hotel to see her again that morning.

He was ready to spend hours with the old lady if necessary, until he could dredge up something about her son which might make sense of the general's inclusion of his name. Now hope was gone. The door which appeared to be opening had slammed shut; added to which his partner Dunston had phoned early that morning to say that he had to make a trip to France on another case and intended stopping over in Paris. Fisher liked Dunston, but he didn't want him intruding at that moment, booming on about the Von Hessels, putting his foot in it about Paula. Most of all, he didn't want Dunston meeting her, eyeing her up and down and making his barroom jokes to Fisher afterward. He was a clever man and a good drinking companion, but he had the finesse in personal relationships of an elephant in a china factory. Now Fisher had another reason for resenting Dunston's visit. He had come to a complete dead end. He had pinned his hopes on the old lady; the senile have a happy facility for the past, whereas the present confuses them, as Fisher knew. He had memories of an old aunt in a dreary home near Brighton, who could talk with amazing clarity about the First World War but didn't

know which day of the week it was, and had difficulty with
her own name. He thought of the vixen-faced daughter-in-
law and swore. Jacquot was as clear in his mother's mind as if
he had met his brutal death on the day before. She could have
answered questions; Fisher was certain of that. But he had
come too late. With her death there was nobody left to ask
about Jacquot. He searched through his pockets for the cigarettes; there was only one left in his packet, and when he
tried to light it, he found a split in the paper. He swore again
and threw it away. He saw a tobacconist on the other side of
the road, and he crossed over.

Three children were playing a game with colored chalks
on the pavement; they were hopping from foot to foot among
the chalked-out squares, calling to one another and laughing.
Fisher sidestepped them and went inside the shop.

It was dark and the air was stale; there was a woman inside, counting out money, and a man waited behind the
counter. He wore a soiled shirt, collarless and open at the
neck, showing thick black hairs like creeper at the base of
his throat; his mustache was bushy and stained yellow at the
ends. He looked up at Fisher as his customer handed her
coins across the counter and pushed past him to the door.

"Monsieur?"

"Forty Gauloise." Fisher found his money; the man scooped
up the coins with a horny workman's hand; instead of turning
away he peered at Fisher for a moment.

"Excuse me," he said, "but you are a friend of Madame
Brevet?" He spoke hurriedly, as if he had been waiting to get
it out since Fisher came into the shop. The question took
Fisher unawares.

"Which Madame Brevet?"

The man jabbed with his thumb out of the window.

"Not that bitch. The old lady; I heard the other one shouting after you. I saw you standing at the front door. She
wouldn't let you in, eh?"

"No," Fisher said. "I came to see her mother-in-law. She told me she was dead. I was sorry to hear about it."

"Don't be sorry." The shopkeeper leaned over the counter; garlic and sour wine sighed over Fisher. "It was a mercy that she died. For ten years she lived in that house with that vixen—nag, nag, nag at her all the time. Always calling her dirty names, never a kind word. It broke our hearts, monsieur, to see the poor woman go to pieces as she did. Just for the want of a little kindness in her old age. And what a woman she used to be!"

"Oh?" Fisher had been about to turn and go. He wasn't in the mood for a back-street gossip. "You knew her well?"

"She lived in this street all her life," the old man said. "We went through the war together, her family and mine. One never forgets something like that!"

"No." Fisher came and leaned against the counter; he took out the Gauloise and offered one. "No, I'm sure you don't. Then you must have known her son, too."

"I'm glad to meet you," Dunston said. He held out his hand and Paula shook it. Fisher had been so unwilling to introduce him that it had been funny. He hadn't been pleased to see Dunston either; he didn't listen to Dunston's alleged reason for being in the city, which was a fictitious client with a business problem. He had tried very hard to avoid Dunston's request to meet Paula and entertain them both for dinner, but Dunston refused to be put off. He was genial and thick-skinned, and finally he won. They met in the lounge of their hotel, and immediately he gave his partner credit for good taste. The girl was certainly attractive. He appraised her very quickly without making it too obvious. Good figure, nice legs, pretty face, with marvelous eyes. He shook hands with her and smiled, showing his bright white teeth. Pity it had to be her. But still. He took them both to the bar of the Tour De France for a drink and settled back to get as much background information as he could. He thought Fisher looked hung-up over something; probably she hadn't gone to bed with him yet. He kept watching her. Dunston didn't like it. He had never seen Fisher behave like this with anyone before. He was deeply hooked by this one. Which might prove to be a bloody nuisance. He hadn't reckoned on having to fool Fisher with whatever method he decided to employ, but now this factor couldn't be ignored. The bloody fool was mad about her. And she, so cool and gentle, with her upper-class manners and her elegant clothes—how did she feel toward him? Dunston made small talk about the city and the weather for the first half hour, and watched them very closely. He couldn't decide about her. He couldn't be sure how she felt about Fisher or how closely she was involved. And this could be important. If he were going to set something up for her, she had to be alone, and he had to be sure that she would walk into his situation without suddenly referring to anyone else. He decided to play along and see what happened.

"Now tell me"—he leaned forward toward her—"how do you feel about finding this treasure, Mrs. Stanley?"

"Not very enthusiastic," Paula said. "I've said all along to Eric that if we do find it and I do have a legal claim, I don't intend to keep it. The original owners can have it back."

"That's very noble of you," he said. "Mind you, you might change your mind when you actually see it! I don't think I'd give it up in a hurry!" He laughed and looked across at Fisher.

"And what do you do all day while our boy here is out playing Sherlock Holmes?"

"She comes with me," Fisher interjected. He wouldn't have put it past Dunston to try to make a date. He found the steady grin and the eyes flickering up and down Paula so offensive that he could hardly keep his temper. He had never imagined he could dislike Dunston. Now he could have taken him by the collar and told him to keep his dirty looks to himself.

"Does she? Everywhere?"

"No, of course not," Paula said. "I do quite a lot of sight-seeing and, I'm afraid, I shop. Paris is a terrible place for spending money."

"And that reminds me," Dunston said. "I must look around for something nice for Betty. That's my wife—maybe you'd come along with me one day and help me choose a dress—I've got her size."

"I'd be delighted," Paula said.

"How long do you expect to be here?" Fisher asked. He didn't want Paula going shopping with Dunston; he didn't want her going anywhere with anyone. He caught himself up with surprise. His latent jealousy had surfaced until he was sullen and suspicious when they were apart.

The fact that they were lovers had not improved the relationship for Fisher; it had transformed his uncertainty about her into an obsession. The more he made love to her and she responded, the more he wanted to relinquish the search for her father, and the deeper his resentment when she showed no sign of doing so. He should have filled the vacuum in her life; he couldn't accept that there was any need for what was just the fantasy of a neglected child, if she was really in love with him and not merely happy on the physical level. He looked across at her, talking to Dunston whom he had expected her to find objectionable, and was irritated that she was smiling and seemed to be at ease with him. Why the hell should he ask her to go shopping for a present for his dreary wife?

"How long are you staying?" He repeated the question.

"I don't know," Dunston said. "Depends on how the sleuthing goes. I shall not hurry back though; it's very pleasant here. You'll be staying to the end of the business, Mrs. Stanley?"

"Yes," Paula said. She avoided Fisher's look. "I'm staying."

"In for the kill," Dunston said and laughed. He turned

slightly toward Fisher. "Since it's all in the family, how near are you to finding it?"

"I'm going to England," Fisher said. He reached across and took Paula's hand; he didn't care what Dunston thought. "I need to see Paula's mother just once more. And then we start digging."

"Literally?"

"Figuratively, I think," Fisher answered Dunston. He felt Paula's fingers stiff and unresponsive in his grasp. He hadn't mentioned the trip to England before; he found it difficult to discuss the progress of the search with her now. Every forward move was a move toward the general, and however hard he strove as a lover, Fisher had no surety that in a confrontation, the woman he loved would choose him and not her father. In his darker moods, he would have bet on the general every time.

"You mean you've solved the little riddle about Aunty Ambrosine?"

"It was a code name for a Resistance group," Fisher explained. This much he had told Paula. "Jacquot was another code name for a courier in the group. I managed to get enough information about him to make sense of most of it. The last bit, your mother may be able to fill in." He addressed Paula and squeezed her hand, asking for forgiveness. She gave it, and for the moment Fisher relaxed. Dunston ordered them another drink. The subject changed to Dunston's business in Paris, and Paula withdrew from the discussion. She sat holding Fisher's hand, looking at both of them and wondering what they had ever had in common. The moody, possessive, tender man beside her was a different breed of human being. The other was cheerful and self-confident; she applied that elusive word "breezy" to him, and it was an apt description. Nothing would bother Dunston, whereas the more she knew Fisher the more complicated she discovered him to be. Sexual surrender hadn't satisfied him; he conducted what could only be termed a war when they went to bed, a campaign of calculated seduction which was designed to dominate her completely. And the tragic truth, which she could never let him see, was that his success in one field insured its failure in another. Paula would not be sensually dominated; her body and emotions were interdependent; she was not yet ready to surrender both to Fisher, even though she loved him. And she did love him; she insisted upon that. She needed to love him in order to deny his constant assertion that she didn't. When he left her at night, she often cried. It could have been a happy, fulfilling relationship, so different from the shallow, unsatisfactory one she had experienced in her marriage, but his possessiveness was ruining it for both of them. She should have warned him of the consequences, but she couldn't. He was too strong for her and, at the same time, too vulnerable. She felt unhappy and confused. Fisher was not enough to fill the wasted years; he couldn't answer the question which had to be answered if she was ever to know peace or independence of spirit. What manner of man was her father, the general? Was he the inhuman brute of old Madame Brevet's wild denunciation or the warm, tender father of a little girl, doting and sentimental.

Fisher couldn't forgive this hunger to know. He saw it as a personal slight, a proof that she was still free of him and able to choose something else. And she was free; with her hand imprisoned in his, Paula felt a desperate need of that liberty of choice, of the freedom to see her whole life in true perspective once, before she submitted it to the dictates of someone else. She had been alone too long, and independence had been thrust upon her. Now a man had come into her life who wanted her to give herself completely, to surrender herself in body and mind to his passionate care. She couldn't do it. She gently withdrew her hand on the pretext of lighting herself a cigarette. He was asking too much of her too quickly. Dunston was speaking to her again.

"Are you going back to England to see your mother, too, Mrs. Stanley?"

"No," Paula said. "I'm not. I'm staying here."

"And when are you going?" he asked Fisher.

"Tuesday," Fisher said. "I'll be away only one night."

"Oh, well." Dunston's smile beamed at both of them. "In that case, Mrs. Stanley you could come and help me with my shopping. That would be great. All right by you, Eric?"

"Why not." Fisher was surly. "If Paula wants to—"

"And don't you worry," Dunston said happily. "I'll take good care of her while you're away. Now let's go and eat some dinner. I'm starving."

Paula was sitting in the lounge of the hotel; she had taken a chair facing the entrance, and as soon as the tall, fair man walked through the door and stood for a moment, looking around, she knew that this must be Philip Von Hessel. She had the opportunity to study him while he paused, looking around the room. He was one of the best-looking men she had ever seen; he stood very upright, with an arrogant grace that was without self-consciousness. So did a man look, with a hundred million and an ancient title to buttress his personality. Added to which were the advantages of youth and that Wagnerian face. He caught Paula's glance and moved toward her. She got up and came to meet him, holding out her hand. "Prince Von Hessel?"

"Yes. Mrs. Stanley—"

He took her hand and kissed it, bowing a little. The telephone call had been such a surprise that when he asked her to meet him for a few minutes, in Fisher's absence, Paula hadn't been able to think of an excuse. He had sounded older on the telephone, very precise and rather grave, like many foreigners who spoke good English but were out of practice.

The reality was very different. He took a seat beside her, offered her a cigarette, and asked if he might order her a drink. He smiled, and Paula felt an impact of charm. It struck her suddenly that except for her mother, this was the first of her countrymen that she had ever met.

But she had forgotten Schwarz, with the bright eyes that burned at her, sitting hunched up in her office. He had been German, too, like the handsome young man sitting at her side.

"I hope you'll forgive me for intruding myself on you," the prince said. "I had hoped to talk to Mr. Fisher, but I have also been anxious to meet you. When the hotel said you were in, it seemed too good an opportunity to miss."

Paula noticed that he wore a black tie. "I'm very glad to meet you," she said. "May I say how sorry I am about what happened to your brother."

"Thank you." Philip Von Hessel looked down. "My mother is here; we are taking my brother's body home as soon as the formalities are completed. Have you been to Germany, Mrs. Stanley?"

Paula changed the subject gladly. "No, never. I shall go one day, but my mother left at the end of the war and she's never been back."

"A number of people have cut themselves off because of the past," he said. "Even people like your mother, who were only innocent bystanders. I think it is a pity. Do you mind my saying this?"

"Not at all," Paula answered. "I was brought up to be ashamed of what I was, without ever being told the reason. Now at least I know it."

"You are not responsible for the past either," he said gently. "No more am I, Mrs. Stanley. Your father committed crimes; well, so did my family. We are just becoming acceptable to the civilized world, both ourselves and our nation. Because, of course, they need us. So don't feel too guilty. We are not so black and the rest of the world white, I assure you."

Paula looked at him. "My father stole a family treasure

from you," she said. "But you're not bitter—you can talk about him so calmly. I think it's very admirable of you. And I'm glad to meet you, Prince Von Hessel, because I have something to say to you."

"Please," he said. The expression in his eyes was gentle. "You don't have to say anything to me."

"But I want to." Paula turned toward him. "It's possible that I have a legal claim to the Poellenberg Salt. I don't know if this is true, but if by any chance it is, I want you to know that, as far as I'm concerned, the Salt belongs to your family. I shall hand it over to you immediately."

"That is a very generous thing to say," he said. "I appreciate it deeply. But do you know how valuable it is?"

"I know," Paula said. "It couldn't be priced. But that's not my concern. I don't want it. It was taken from you; by whatever means within the law, it was morally illegal, I'm sure of that. And you must have it back. I just wanted to tell you this. There won't be any difficulties or wrangling about ownership. It's your property."

"Mrs. Stanley"—he spoke quietly, twisting the broad gold signet ring upon his little finger—"I repeat, that is the most generous thing I've ever heard. But can I ask you something?"

"Yes," Paula said, "ask me whatever you like."

"If you don't want the Poellenberg Salt," he said, "will you use your influence with Mr. Fisher to call off the search? It's terribly important to me. I don't want it found, Mrs. Stanley. I don't ever want to see it again. I can't make any impression on him or my mother. I shall continue to try with her if you could possibly talk to him."

"Why don't you want it?" Paula asked. "It's one of the treasures of the world. Why wouldn't you have it back?"

"I can't tell you that," he said seriously. "So please don't ask me. I know I have no right to say this because I'm only a stranger to you, but you must believe me when I tell you that it is a bloodstained thing, and it's better left wherever your father hid it. Please—would you do this for me?"

He had nice eyes; as he talked, he had leaned across and laid his hand on her arm. Suddenly it moved down and closed emotionally upon hers. It gave her a shock to feel its warmth. Slowly she shook her head.

"I can't do that," she said. "It's just not possible. I'm not with Eric Fisher to find the Poellenberg Salt; I'm here looking for my father. If I find it, I believe I'll find him. I can't help you, Prince Philip. I only wish I could."

"I see," he said. He took his hand away. "I'm sorry I became emotional. I didn't know this or I wouldn't have asked you."

"I don't expect anyone to understand," Paula said. "Anyway, nobody does. I never knew him. I told you, I was brought up to be ashamed of being his child, ashamed of being German. My name was changed, my nationality, everything. And then I was told about him. He began to take shape for me. Nobody ever loved me, Prince Philip; forgive me, if I'm being emotional now, but it's true. My mother didn't and my husband didn't. I need my father. I need to see him and judge him for myself. He's a war criminal, and he's been on the run for nearly thirty years. And whatever he's done I must be the only person in the world who cares about him. Or would help him. That's why there's nothing I can do."

"I understand," the prince said quietly. "I too would feel the same; it is our German blood. We all have a strong sense of family. For your sake I hope you find him—without the Salt. The irony is, only one person wants it. My mother. It has become an obsession with her."

"Why did you say it was bloodstained?" Paula said. "What did you mean?"

"I can't explain that either," Philip Von Hessel said. "Mrs. Stanley, would you do me a favor?"

"If I can," Paula answered.

"Would you have dinner with me before I go back to Germany? I promise not to talk about the Salt."

"That's very nice of you." Paula stood up. She held out her hand and he kissed it, touching her fingers with his mouth. "I could tell you about your country," he said quietly. "We have much to be ashamed of but also much in which we can take pride. It would give me great pleasure. Say you will come."

"I will," Paula answered. "I shall be alone on Tuesday evening. Perhaps we can meet then."

"I have an engagement for Tuesday," Philip said. "But I shall cancel it. I will come here at eight. Good-bye, Mrs. Stanley. Or better still, *auf Wiedersehen!*"

The garden in Essex was famous for its roses. The formal rose garden was one of the sights of the district; the Ridgeways had been persuaded to open the gardens for charity, and on a blazing July afternoon a crowd of well over a hundred were walking through the trees and lawns, wandering alongside the wide herbaceous border which was the loving work of Paula's mother. The brigadier hovered on the perimeter, pausing to answer questions about the various plants and some of the rarities in the small-walled enclave which he tended himself. Gardening was a passion, taken up as a hobby in the years following his retirement and developed into an absorbing pastime in which his wife shared with as much enthusiasm.

He could see her walking among the roses, smiling and talking to the visitors; he felt a pang of pride and love as he watched her, cool in a pastel linen dress, her gray-blond hair shining in the sunlight, as beautiful and dignified in old age as she had been as a young woman.

There was nothing he would not do or had not done to preserve that air of serenity, to see her smile and pass through life untroubled by care. She had suffered too much to endure even a moment's disquiet or a qualm of pain. She had given him a love and a contentment which he had never imagined. The debt could be repaid only by a lifetime of watchful care and fierce protectiveness. It made him happy just to be alive and act as a buffer between her and life. He was answering a middle-aged couple's inquiries about a miniature species *Clematis* which rioted in shades of purple and white along the edge of an old red brick wall, when the elderly cook who had worked for them since they moved into the house came down the path toward him.

He was wanted on the telephone; he excused himself and went toward the house, walking slowly in the heat, wondering irritably which of their friends had been inconsiderate enough to call on a day when the garden was open to the public. The local Red Cross was the Ridgeways' favorite charity, and they benefited every year from this occasion.

The line crackled with the atmospherics peculiar to English rural telephone systems.

"Brigadier Ridgeway?"

"Yes. Who is it?"

"Eric Fisher—Dunston and Fisher Detective Agency. I came to see you and your wife about two weeks ago."

The brigadier held the receiver closer to his ear. "Who? I'm sorry, the line is bad." He hadn't wanted to hear the name; his denial was instinctive. The words were repeated. This time he couldn't pretend to himself; there was no escape. He swore, one hand over the mouthpiece.

"I've nothing to say to you." He raised his voice. "And you've chosen a very inconvenient time to telephone."

"I'm coming to England tomorrow. I want to come see you. It's very important. You know Paula's with me."

"I know," Ridgeway said. "What my stepdaughter does is her own affair. It's nothing to do with us."

"It's very much to do with you. I have to talk to you and her mother. Will you see me?"

"No." The brigadier was shouting down the telephone. "No, certainly not. I won't have you here bothering my wife!"

"There's a strong possibility that she's not legally married to you." He could hear Fisher clearly now; the crackling on the line had stopped, and the awful words might have been spoken in the room.

"I'm pretty sure that General Bronsart is alive. I think you'd better see me. I'll fly over tomorrow morning and drive straight down."

"Go to hell!" He rammed the telephone down and stood there looking at it as if it had a malevolent life of its own. Slowly he sank to a chair, an old man whose knees were trembling. His legs were the only part of him to show the sign of age; that and the weakness of his chest, which worried his wife every time he caught a cold. He put his hands over his face and his head dropped.

"Oh, my God," he said. "Oh, my God, my God." Outside in the bright sunshine the couple who had been waiting for him to come back gave up and decided to walk on.

Philip Von Hessel faced his mother; she was sitting up in bed, the breakfast tray across her knees. It was a brilliant morning, and the room was full of sunlight. Paris was emptying as the summer advanced; there were few native Parisiennes left in the hotels and bistros; the tourist crowds abounded, making the city an alien place. The Ritz was full of Americans, which annoyed the princess who found their accents and their presence in the hallowed places of the European aristocracy particularly irksome. She glanced at her handsome son, and her expression softened. Of all the human beings with whom she had made contact in her long life, she loved her younger son the best. No qualm of regret or sentiment for Heinrich had troubled her mind. She was a relic of an age when grief was regarded as an indulgence, the luxury of the inferior classes whose women shrouded their heads in their aprons and cried. Marriage with Prince Von Hessel had withered any sensibilities she might have had. She held out her hand to Philip; he bent over and kissed her.

"You're sure you don't want me with you?" he said.

"No, it's better you stay here. Fisher will be away in England for a day and a night. The funeral will take place privately; I shall give it out that you're ill. You must be here in case he comes back with something decisive. He seemed very confident on the telephone."

"There will be photographers at the airport," Philip said. "There are half a dozen hanging around the entrance already."

"The authorities have promised that we shall get away without being bothered by them," she said. "As soon as it is over, I shall fly back. In the meantime I leave it in your hands. I feel it will all turn out for the best for us. Promise me you won't worry. This will be the end of a long and troublesome period for our family. From now on it will be up to you to expunge the past and build up what I have preserved. I know you'll do it."

"I will," he promised. "You have my word."

She thought how much he resembled his father, that gallant airman who had come so briefly and decisively into her life. Power, wealth, world influence. She leaned against the pillows, a little tired with the onset of emotion, yet mellow in her triumph that in spite of everything she had succeeded, and through her son, the future would be safe. For a moment their hands clasped. "My son," she said gently, "I'm very proud of you."

7

It was midafternoon when Fisher's car drove up to the front door of the Ridgeways' house in Essex. He got out, and the Labradors came leaping up to investigate him, barking a welcome. Fisher didn't like dogs; he had been ravaged by a stray when he was a boy. He could honestly say that it was his only fear, that instinctive recoil from the leap and the bared teeth. He swore at them and they went backwards, puzzled and hurt. It was some moments before the door opened, and then it was the brigadier who stood facing him.

"I told you not to come," he said.

"I know," Fisher answered quietly. "But I have to see you. I'm not trying to be difficult or upset anyone. I told the truth on the phone. It's very important."

The older man turned away, leaving the door open for him to follow. Within the shadowy hall he turned.

"All right, come in then. My wife's waiting."

Paula's mother was in the drawing room; she looked white, and there were shadows under her eyes. At the first sight, Fisher saw a resemblance to Paula in the way she stood and the carriage of her head. He should have felt distaste for what he was going to do, but he didn't. They had had their life together, these two, standing with their arms linked, united against him as they had been against her daughter.

"My husband told me what you said," she began. "Why do you say my first husband is alive? What proof have you?"

"He was seen in Paris," Fisher said. "That newspaper report was right. I interviewed the woman. She remembered the general, and she had good reason to—he ordered her son's execution. She saw him in the street and then he disappeared." He saw Paula's mother clutch at the brigadier's arm.

"I'm certain he's alive," Fisher said. "And in the circumstances you'd be well advised to help me get this business over. If he's recognized again and the police pick him up, I imagine you'd find it rather embarrassing."

"We married in good faith," Ridgeway said stiffly. "My wife was told he was killed in action. No blame can be attached to her."

"It's no use, Gerald," Mrs. Ridgeway said suddenly. "He knows what we have to fear. Public knowledge of my past, isn't that right? The wife of a war criminal, a woman who was arrested when the Allied troops marched into Munich and held for weeks in prison. You didn't know that part, did you, Mr. Fisher? I was the wife of a man who consorted with Hitler. I was spat upon, abused, humiliated—accused of complicity in my husband's crimes, denounced for having slave labor in my house. If one thing could have been proved against me, I'd have been sent to prison for years! When they let me go home to my child, there was a screaming mob, howling and spitting at me outside the gates—I was almost broken; I thought of suicide. Then Gerald found me, burning the furniture in the grate to keep myself and Paula warm, without enough food to eat, and too ashamed to go out and beg for it like the rest of the German civilians. I hated my first husband; he was a cruel and heartless brute, and I thanked God when I heard he was dead! But I was the only one who could be punished for what he had done. I suffered,

Mr. Fisher; it's taken all these years of living with a man like my husband to make me forget it. If I have to live through that shame again, I shall die. So there's no point in your talking about 'embarrassment' and trying to frighten us. We know what we have to fear. Can't you see it? War criminal's wife discovered in Essex village. Brigadier committed bigamy during the war—my God, embarrassed! This means the ruin of the rest of our lives. We're respected and liked here; Gerald has had a distinguished career. We've lived happily and decently for nearly thirty years. If you want to ask me questions, I shall answer them. But understand that nothing you can do or say can frighten me now. No, darling"—she turned to her husband—"let me do this. We can't go on hiding. We will always have each other."

"One moment." The brigadier interrupted, speaking to Fisher. "One moment—before my wife says anything to you, I want to ask one question. If you find the general, what do you propose to do?"

"Nothing," Fisher said. "I'm looking for the Poellenberg Salt; I'm not interested in catching war criminals. As things have turned out, I'm as anxious to keep him under cover as you are. You know Paula's looking for him? She's got an obsession about him; she thinks she's going to find a helpless, hunted old man who needs someone to take care of him. I don't think she knows it herself, but she hasn't the slightest intention of seeing him once and then letting him go out of her life. And if they come together, I shall lose her. She'll go off with him. I don't want that to happen."

"We didn't know you were involved," the brigadier said.

"You didn't ask," Fisher said sharply. "You've left Paula to get on with the whole dirty mess, just thinking of your own position. If I may say so, Mrs. Ridgeway, you had no right to keep your daughter in the dark about her father. If you'd told her the truth, she wouldn't have this terrible hang-up. God knows what effect it'll have on her if they ever do meet.

That's why I want to find the Salt without Paula being there. If he's going to appear at all, that is where he'll choose, hoping to find her digging it out. I'm not going to let things happen that way. I want to marry her. I hope you get the picture now."

"I see." Mrs. Ridgeway turned to her husband. "Darling, this could be the best thing for all of us. How can I help you, Mr. Fisher?"

"I know he was in Paris," Fisher said, "in June, 1944. But I can't find out where he was living. It was naturally kept a secret because the Resistance were after him; he was high on their murder list. Do you know where his quarters were, Mrs. Ridgeway? Believe me, everything depends on my finding this out."

"Of course, I know," Paula's mother answered. She had her arm linked through her husband's; now she disengaged it and made a movement with her hand.

"I know exactly where he was. I spent a weekend with him. Why don't we all sit down?"

"Mrs. Stanley? Good morning to you. Joe Dunston here."

"Oh, hello," Paula answered sleepily. Fisher had left her in the early hours. She was tired and depressed after the night they had spent together. For the first time she had been unresponsive, miserable, and tense in spite of all his efforts to arouse her. He had failed, and the effect upon him was profound.

He had said very little, sitting up in the bed, apart from her, staring into the darkened room. "You're not in love with me anymore, are you?"

When Paula denied it, he didn't seem to hear.

"I know you're not." He had continued as if she hadn't spoken. "I know it's over with you. You didn't feel a damned thing with me, did you?"

"I'm tired," she protested, close to tears. "Darling, it's the first time it hasn't been wonderful for both of us. Don't make something out of nothing."

"Nothing," Fisher had said, throwing back the bedclothes, "is the operative word. I'll let you go to sleep now. I'll try to call you from England; I'm leaving early in the morning." And he had gone, letting in a brief shaft of light from the passage outside as he opened and then closed her door. Paula had lain awake for a long time. She had cried, and it was more for him than for herself. She was empty, unable to be rushed away on the tide of his urgent sexuality. By accident, by an abdication of nature, not by the deliberate cooling which he suspected. It hadn't worked. The thought came to her that it might never work again. When she finally fell asleep, it was an uneasy rest, disturbed by anxious dreams of journeys where she was prevented from arriving. As she took Dunston's call, she looked at her watch and saw that she had slept on until past ten o'clock. Fisher had caught the eight thirty plane.

"I didn't wake you up, did I?" The hearty voice broke into a laugh.

"Just as well you did," Paula said. "It's terribly late."

"You must have had a gay evening," Dunston said.

"Yes," Paula answered, "yes, I did."

"I know our boy's gone to England today and I wondered whether you might take that shopping expedition with me." There was a few seconds' pause, and then the tone was diffident. "I'd appreciate it very much if it wouldn't be a nuisance to you. My taste in clothes is terrible."

"Of course, it wouldn't be a nuisance." She pushed the hair back from her face and leaned against the pillow, which still bore Fisher's imprint.

"I'd be delighted. Where do you want to go?"

"No idea," he said. "Somewhere not too cheap, but not exactly Christian Dior. I'd like to leave that up to you."

"Well, let me think—how about Lafayette's—they have

some nice clothes, and they're not too desperately expensive."

"Anything you say." Dunston sounded delighted. "Where is it? I'd better go direct there, if you don't mind, because I've got an appointment in about twenty minutes. Say about eleven thirty, quarter to twelve?"

"That would be fine," Paula said. "I'll meet you downstairs in the main entrance. A quarter to twelve? It's in the Rue St. Honoré."

"Wonderful. And thanks a million. Bye-bye."

Paula got up and went into the bathroom. Under the electric light she looked pale, and the dark shadows associated with a night spent making love were deep under her eyes. The first man in her life hadn't cared enough about her; now she was caught up with one who cared too much. He wanted what she couldn't give him—the full possession of herself. James had complained of her shyness; for a time it seemed that Fisher had smashed through the reserves which kept her partially aloof. But now the barriers were going up again, and this, more than the failure of one night together, was what he had sensed and what had driven him to leave her in despair. Despair threatened Paula, too, the despair of her returning solitude, of the knowledge that she was moving away from Fisher, from loving and being loved, back into the world of lonely waiting. Waiting. That was the right description. She showered and dressed, getting ready for her appointment with Dunston. Waiting for something or for someone. And what made her glad to spend the time with Dunston was the fear that the someone was not Eric Fisher after all. For a moment, dressed and ready to go out, she dropped back on the bed. She hated herself for hurting him. He too was independent, previously invulnerable. He had told her she was the first woman he had ever loved, and she believed him. And unlike her, there had been no holding back, no reservations.

She owed him too much; she even owed herself the chance of being happy. She got up, checked her bag for the room key, and made a resolution to be especially affectionate and reassuring when he phoned.

Outside the hotel, seated at a café on the pavement opposite, Dunston watched over a newspaper and saw her come out into the sunshine, hail a taxi, and get in. He paid for his coffee, threw his newspaper away, and went around the side to the back entrance. He had got her room number from the switchboard when he phoned. There was nobody around when he opened the door and stepped inside a grubby passage; there was a smell of kitchens and rubbish, and a dark furred cat fled into a closet as he came upon it. Dunston moved carefully, trying doors. He found the entrance to the service stairs and began to climb them. At the first floor he came out into the main landing and went to the elevator. It was automatic, and after a short wait it arrived, with two passengers on the way up. Dunston got in, touched his hat to the elderly couple, and pressed the button marked 3. At the third floor he got out, while they continued higher up, and he went up the corridor toward the room which he knew was Paula's, 339. There was no one around; at that hour all the beds had been made. His only danger was the chambermaid coming in to tidy up that particular room. It was a chance he had to take; he went up to the door, and in less than a minute he had picked the lock.

It was untidy, the bed in confusion; he walked carefully to the window and pulled the blind. Then he switched on the light and began to look around. It was not a very luxurious room; the color scheme was pastel blue and the furniture was mahogany and vaguely modern in design. A large bowl of roses stood on the writing table. Dunston guessed they were from Fisher. He went over to look at them and open the table drawer. There was nothing inside but some sheets of hotel writing paper, a few envelopes, and a laundry list. He glanced at the bottles of cleansing lotion and the rank of lipsticks, ranged like soldiers. Powder, very expensive scent, in a five-ounce bottle. He wondered whether that were Fisher again. Then he went to the closet and looked through Paula's clothes. He searched everything without knowing yet what he was looking for; he picked up the silk nightdress she had worn, and suffered a brief qualm of lust.

Then he went into the bathroom. More bottles, tooth-brush, paste, combs, and a hairbrush. No pills of any kind. Obviously not a neurotic. There couldn't be any accidental overdose. The floor of the bathroom was still wet. On an impulse Dunston pulled back the shower curtain; drops of water spattered him. He looked up, and then suddenly he stood quite still. He hadn't gone to look for it; he hadn't even thought it could be found—the idea was so old-fashioned. But there it was. A long barred electric fire, high up on the wall above the bath. He reached over and pulled the cord. The element began to turn red. It was above eye level; he was tall and he had to tilt up to see it, burning away there on the wall, designed to warm the bather's naked body as he got out of the water. He pulled the cord again and the heat faded. Twice more he jerked at the cord, and each time he used less pressure. Sometimes they could be stiff. This one was loose. He began to whistle softly. He took the end of the cord and slipped the tiny knob under one of the plastic rings holding the shower curtain. Then he switched the curtain around the bath. Immediately the fire turned on. He un-hooked the cord. Then he slipped off his shoes and climbed on to the edge of the bath; this brought him level with the fire. He made a careful examination of it and then stepped down. He would need time, and no fear of being disturbed. His watch said it was already eleven forty-five. She would be waiting at Galleries Lafayette. He had to go before the cham-bermaid decided to come and make the bed. He went out of the bathroom, pulled up the windowshade, and slipped through the door. As he hurried down the passage to the lift, he saw the maid come through the service door, pushing her trolley for the dirty linen. Fifteen minutes later he arrived, breathless and full of excuses, to meet Paula at the store.

When Fisher telephoned the hotel that afternoon, there was no reply from Paula's room. He had lunched at a pub an hour's drive from the Ridgeways' house, and wondered why he didn't feel elated. The end of the search was only a flight away across the Channel, a matter of making the necessary arrangements and letting the Princess Von Hessel know that she would soon be in possession of the Salt.

Fisher had sat in the pub bar, eating sandwiches and drinking beer, wishing he were able to see or speak to Paula. He intended breaking his promise to her. He believed that her obsession with the general was the barrier which prevented her from committing herself to him completely. She was keeping apart in order to be free when the moment of choice came. He smoked and sat on, moody and unhappy, despising himself for cheating her and yet convinced that he had no alternative. She wanted love; he could satisfy that need—he had proved that his was more than just a sexual hunger. He wanted her as he had never imagined he could want anyone, and yet she aroused such a dread of losing her, that he no longer recognized his own personality. He had become jealous, obsessed. He would do anything to prevent Paula from escaping on some crazy, mixed-up pretext that her father's need of her came first. Fisher had seriously thought of turning the general into the police if he appeared; if he did come forward, it would be when the Salt was found. He had no other way of contacting his daughter, except by waiting till she came to where the Salt was hidden. And she just wasn't going to be there; Fisher left the pub and began to drive to London; she wasn't going to be anywhere near the Salt, and if her father materialized, then Fisher could either scare him off or turn him in. In his present frame of mind he would have preferred the latter course, but fear of

Paula's reaction made that impossible. If he was caught and tried, she would never forgive Fisher. If he never appeared, as far as she knew, then Fisher felt he had a chance of being accepted as a final substitute. As for her claim to the Salt, he was only too anxious to waive that, too, if indeed she really had one. Let the Von Hessels have it; let the whole bloody business come to its conclusion and let him get her back, safe with him where she belonged. They could get married and start looking for a home. Fisher, the professional nomad, who had never bothered to do more than rent a furnished flat, found himself yearning for a home, with possessions and a wife. And children. He had even thought that far ahead. He reached his agency's office and put through the call to their hotel. When she was out, he swore and banged down the receiver. The uncertainty of their parting remained until he could talk to her and repair the damage. And he had done damage, walking out like that. His male pride had been affronted, and his insecurity had overwhelmed his common sense. He had behaved like a fool. He booked in another call for an hour later and then telephoned through to Princess Von Hessel in Munich. Her response was short but full of suppressed excitement; he could hear the tone of her voice changing as he talked.

"When will it be?"

"Tomorrow, if you can fix it with the hotel."

"Leave that to me. I shall fly down tonight. You've done very well."

"Thanks," Fisher said. "I'm coming back to Paris tomorrow and I'll contact you." He hung up. It seemed almost unreal that the explanation was at once so simple and so clever. He was a clever man, the general, with an ironic twist of mind. No caves in isolated places, no chilly Swiss lakes, for his treasure. He had hidden it where nobody would ever think of looking and where it was easily accessible to anyone who knew. Very clever. And not to be discounted even at the end.

He would emerge; Fisher was sure of it. At some moment he would step forward out of the shadows, to claim his daughter and the loot he had secreted all those years ago. And Fisher was going to make sure that he got neither of them.

The second call came through after a short delay. It was no more successful than the first. Paula had not returned to her hotel.

Dunston gave her lunch after their shopping expedition. They bought a smart coat and dress for his wife; the first of many, he reminded himself privately, when his assignment was complete. He set out to be cheerful and amusing; he had a way with women, which had come in very useful over the years. He had joked his way into some inaccessible beds, rather to the surprise of the women who found themselves seduced. He would have given Fisher serious competition with Paula Stanley if he hadn't been otherwise committed. . . .

"Well," he said, taking her arm as they came out of the restaurant into the street, "now where to? Back to your hotel?"

"No," Paula answered. "I'm going to have my hair done; it looks awful."

"Not to me it doesn't," Dunston said. "You look good enough to eat, if I hadn't had a good lunch already. Speaking of lunch, what are you doing for dinner tonight?"

"I'm going out," Paula said. "But thanks anyway. I do hope your wife likes the dress."

"She'll be thrilled"—Dunston grinned—"so long as she never knows a beautiful girl helped me to choose it. Where's the hairdressers? I'll drop you off."

He got out of the taxi, shook hands with her, still showing his excellent white teeth in a friendly smile, and waited until she had gone inside and he saw her checking in at the desk for her appointment. He told the taxi to take him to an electrical suppliers. There he bought pliers with a cutting edge, a screwdriver with an adjustable head for large and small screws, a yard and a half of cable, and a roll of insulating tape. He hailed another cab and gave the address of Paula's hotel.

He went inside and up to the reception.

"Mrs. Stanley, please."

"One moment, I'll call her room."

Glancing around the hotel foyer, Dunston waited, the package with his purchases under one arm. She just might have used the hairdresser as an excuse to get rid of him. She might have gone in without booking an appointment and been told they were full up. He had to make absolutely sure she wasn't in her room.

The reception clerk looked at him and shook his head. "There's no reply, monsieur. Mrs. Stanley went out this morning, and I haven't seen her come back."

"Never mind," Dunston said. "I just took a chance."

"You wish to leave a message?"

"No thanks. I'll phone this evening." He walked out into the street and turned left. He passed a couple of women conversing earnestly; he opened the service entrance to the hotel and went inside. He reached Paula's room through the back stairs, avoiding the lift. At that hour in the afternoon none of the hotel staff were around in the corridors, and he didn't wish to be seen by any of the residents. He picked the lock on her door, as he had done earlier, and went inside, closing the door very carefully after him. He slipped the catch down; if anyone should come, or Paula herself return unexpectedly, he would have warning and be able to clear away any tools.

The room was clinically tidy; the bathroom was hung with clean towels, and there was a smell of abrasive cleaner. He saw a trace of white powder on the shelf above the lavatory. The shower curtain was pulled back. He undid his parcel, laid the cable, the insulating tape, and the screwdriver on the lavatory seat, took off his shoes, and climbed on the bath edge to inspect the electric fire above it. He got down, picked up the screwdriver, and began to work. Ten minutes later he lifted the fire carefully away from the wall. It came down some six inches and then hung, caught by the cable connecting it at the back. Dunston gingerly let it go; the cable was thick and strong, and the fire held. He hesitated a moment, making up his mind. Then he gave a slight shrug and pushed it back against the wall; he screwed in two main screws to secure it temporarily and then got down. Outside, he found the corridor empty and began walking the length both ways, looking for the fuse box. It wasn't there. He opened the service door and saw it on the wall. It was too high to reach. He swore unpleasantly. There must be some way of getting up to it. He found a door and opened it. It was a cupboard, and inside, among the feather dusters, brooms, tins of cleaning powder and polish, he found the stepladder. He opened the fuse box and looked at his watch. It was three forty-eight. Nobody was likely to have lights on or be using electricity on the floor at that hour. And by the size of the fuse box, he knew that each floor had its own separate electrical unit, so that failure on one floor didn't mean cutting off the entire electricity supply for the hotel.

Dunston pushed the main switch to off; quickly he replaced the stepladder in the cupboard, glanced around the door into the corridor to make sure nobody was walking down, and went back to the room at a run. Inside the bathroom he worked very quickly. He disconnected the fire from its cable and joined the extra length to the end; this he then reconnected to the fire. Gently he let it hang, and the result satisfied him. Fully extended on the new lead, the fire hung down into the well of the bath. It was directly in line with the shower head. He lifted it up and pushed the extra cable length into the hole in the wall; then he wedged the fire with one hand and fitted two screws loosely into their holes, giving each a couple of turns. The fire held; he caught the cord and pushed the knob through the ring of the shower curtain. He pulled the curtain, the cord jerked, and at the same moment the fire came loose and toppled down. Dunston caught it long before it had reached the end of the cable. He was standing in the bath, and if he hadn't been prepared it would have hit him. As it would hit anyone standing naked and wet who pulled back that shower curtain. The fire would turn on and fall at the same moment. With the extra length of cable it would be as lethal as a bullet. She would be instantly electrocuted. If she were sitting in the bath and touched the curtain, the effect of the fire hitting the water would be the same. And it would be an accident. The hotel would be held responsible for a faulty fitting, and he would collect his half a million in Switzerland. He replaced the fire again, put in all the screws, and turned the two biggest ones just enough to give a slight purchase. Holding the fire against the wall, he fixed the end of the cord into the curtain ring. He stood for a moment looking up. It was high on the wall, and the shower curtain itself obscured it. If she was going out to dinner as she said, she would come back and take a shower. And that, Dunston said coolly to himself, would be that. Fisher would be very cut up. But then breaking eggs was an intrinsic part of making omelettes. She was a nice girl, and he didn't wish her any harm. It was just her bad luck to be the price of being very rich. He put his tools and the paper they had been wrapped in, in his pocket, opened the door, and went back to the service passage and the fuse box. He switched on the electricity supply, left the steps in their original place in the cleaning cupboard, and ran down the stairs to the side entrance. It had been completed in just under an hour. He went back to his hotel in a taxi, ordered himself a bottle of brandy, and lay on his bed to wait. After the second drink, he fell asleep.

*   *   *

"I've been trying to get you all day. Where the hell have you been?"

Paula was undressing when the telephone rang. She had got in, hot and exhausted after an afternoon spent having her hair done and then taking a walk through the warm streets, enjoying the peculiarly Parisian atmosphere of the city in the early evening, when the cafés were filling up and the army of tourists paraded up and down, window shopping and staring around them. She should have gone back to the hotel, but there was something bleak and uninviting about the empty room. Paula avoided it, and in the meantime her telephone shrilled unanswered, until Fisher's call came through again and she was there.

"I went shopping with Joe Dunston," she explained.

"Not till this hour, for Christ's sake," he said. He sounded angry. "What were you doing?"

"We had lunch and then I went to have my hair done, and I've been wandering around. Why do you sound so upset, darling? I'm sorry I wasn't here, but I didn't know what time you'd be telephoning." She lay back on the bed, one arm above her head, listening to Fisher's sharp, accusing voice. The room was hot and still, the light just beginning to fade. She felt tears come to her eyes. This was not what she had planned; this wasn't the mending of the breach. It was opening still wider, and she couldn't stop it.

"I suppose he made a pass at you? He always does."

"Please don't be silly. He was very nice and we bought something for his wife. I don't know what's the matter with you. Tell me, did you see my mother?"

"Yes, I saw her. What are you doing now?"

"Lying on the bed talking to you. What did she say?"

"Nothing much." Fisher lied. "She wouldn't cooperate at all. I wish I were with you. I'd make up for last night. I'm crazy about you, you know that, don't you? I'm even jealous of that bloody fool Dunston."

"You needn't be," Paula said gently. "I wish you were here, too. When are you coming back?"

"Tomorrow. I'm not sure what time. Do you still love me?"

"Yes," she said, "yes, of course I do."

"All right then," Fisher said. "Take care of yourself. I'll see you tomorrow."

"Good-bye," she said. She put the telephone down and lay still. She should have told him about Philip Von Hessel, but she hadn't. And if he was jealous of someone as harmless as Joe Dunston— They had parted on a better note; he sounded mollified, happier. And her mother had told him nothing. Paula closed her eyes. She wouldn't help. It had been a wasted journey. The phone was ringing again. She glanced at her watch and sat up. She wanted to have a bath before she changed to meet Philip. But it was Philip on the line.

"Mrs. Stanley? I wonder if I could come around earlier. Have you spoken to Mr. Fisher?"

"Yes, just a few minutes ago."

"Then you must be excited. My mother told me; she is coming down late tonight."

Paula sat up. "What do you mean, excited? What's happened?"

"Didn't he tell you? He knows where the Salt is. We are going to get it tomorrow."

"No," she said. "No, he didn't tell me. What time do you want to come?"

"It's seven o'clock now. I would like to meet my mother's plane; it arrives at eleven. If I could come to your hotel in about twenty minutes, we could have dinner a little early. Would you mind?"

"No, of course not. I'll be ready by half past seven. Good-bye." She got up slowly. Fisher had lied to her. Whatever he had wanted from her mother, he had got it. He knew where the Salt was, and he had denied it. She went into the bathroom. The window was open, but it was stifling hot. She went to the bath and dropped in the plug, turning on both taps. They were going to find the Salt. Tomorrow, Prince Philip had said. Fisher had alerted the Von Hessels and said nothing to her. Suddenly she felt sick, sick with the sense of his deceit, whatever the motive. She had trusted him, loved him. In his way he had been no more true to her than James. Philip had told her; Fisher hadn't counted on that twist of circumstance when he said he loved her and lied to her at the same time. The prince would soon be calling for her. There wasn't time to have a bath. Paula shut off the taps and jerked out the plug. She washed at the basin and changed into a dark silk dress. She wore a long string of pearls which James had given her; her hair was burnished and chic; she made up lightly and used Fisher's expensive scent. A glance at her watch showed the time to be seven thirty. She went out and down in the lift to wait for Philip Von Hessel.

A great number of women had tried to capture Philip. From the time he was in his teens, girls had ogled and simpered in his direction, and their activities became more serious as he grew older and more eligible. There had been flirtations and love affairs; he had a mistress of three years standing who was already married and had long since abandoned any hope that he might marry her. But he had never fallen in love to the extent of asking any girl to be his wife. Like royalty, the Von Hessels either married cousins or into other families of similar eminence. It was unthinkable that Philip should look outside his own circle or have serious intentions toward a woman of lesser background. As a result, he remained an obdurate bachelor, waiting for the improbable to happen, and the appearance of someone suitable with whom he could be in love. Because, without love, he rejected all his mother's arguments that he should marry. She had called him a sentimentalist, in some surprise and not with approbation, but once again he had shown a strength of will in parity with her own. He never balked her, except on an issue which he connected with his conscience, and this again baffled and irritated his mother who denied the existence of a moral code which wasn't dictated by the expedience of the moment. He had no intention of doing more than meet Paula and try to enlist her help in getting Fisher to drop the search for the Salt. The invitation to come to dinner was spontaneous, and afterward he was a little surprised by his own action. He was not a man who acted on impulse, and this had been impulsive to a degree. She was not the most attractive or the most beautiful woman he had met. His mistress was a magnificent blonde, acclaimed in her wealthy circle as a dazzling example of German womanhood. Paula could not compare in respect of elegance, presence, or importance with the women who frequented his circle; they were exotic, pampered creatures divorced from the reality of ordinary life. He had felt when he talked to her that he was with a living woman—vulnerable, uncertain, dignified, and shy. When he arrived in the foyer of the hotel and she got up to meet him, he felt elated, as if something unusual were about to happen.

"It's very kind of you to make our dinner earlier," he said. He had taken her hand and kissed it. He looked down at her and smiled; he thought she looked pale and aloof, but after a brief moment she smiled back at him, and suddenly the atmosphere relaxed. The success of that evening was assured from the moment Philip took her arm and led her outside to the car. Again, he seldom indulged in physical contact. He had been brought up to abhor the casual pawing which was generally accepted as social mores—the kissing of comparative strangers, the instant use of Christian names, all the debased practices which had once dignified a relationship between two people. He never took a woman's arm and held it on a pretext. He settled into the back of the limousine and offered her a cigarette.

"Thank you," Paula said. "Tell me about the Salt. Where is it?"

"I don't know," Philip answered. "My mother only had time to tell me she was coming here and the search would be over tomorrow. She was hurrying to catch a plane. I can't understand why Mr. Fisher didn't tell you; I thought that's why you were here."

"I think I understand it." Paula looked at him. "The trouble is, I trusted him. Where are we going?"

"To the Grand Vefour," Philip answered. "It is quiet, but I think you will like it. I hope so."

"I'm sure I shall," she said. "Let's wait till we get there and then we can talk about it."

"We don't have to talk about it if it distresses you," he answered. "And I feel it does. You look upset. I want this to be a pleasant evening for us both. After all, you won't accept another invitation if you don't enjoy yourself."

"I don't suppose you get that many refusals," Paula said. "You're not married, are you?"

"No. I am a bachelor and the despair of my mother. She wants grandchildren, and I want to be happy. So it is stalemate. Here we are."

It was an elegant restaurant, with the subdued atmosphere of the very exclusive and expensive, a haven for the rich gourmet who wished to concentrate upon the food and the company without distractions. There was no music, only a three-star menu and soft, immediate service that anticipated everything. Paula took her place at the table, and he noticed that several men were watching her.

"May I pay you a compliment?"

"Please do."

"You are the most attractive woman in the room."

"Thank you. Why do you laugh?"

"Because you have a simplicity that I find delightful, Mrs.

Stanley. I say something flattering, and you don't simper at me or try to deny it, you just say thank you. Where do you get your blue eyes? I've never seen such a color."

"I get them from my father," Paula answered. "Are you going to pay me a compliment about that?"

"No," Philip said. "I am not concerned with him. But I know that you are. You are no nearer finding him?"

"No," Paula said, "and if I depend on Mr. Fisher, I shall never do so. He doesn't want me to find the general. That's why he didn't tell me he had solved the clue about the Salt. He wants me to go back to England and forget about it all."

"Why should he do that? Why is he involved in your life?"

"He's in love with me," she answered. He had ordered a fine dry sherry and she sipped it. For some reason which she couldn't explain to herself, she wanted to tell this man the truth. He had a habit of looking very intently at her when she was speaking; it focused all his attention upon her. She found it intimate rather than disconcerting. He had fine eyes, with a serious expression in them that invited confidence. But basically she wanted to shock him and retreat.

"And you," he asked her. "I can understand him, but surely you are not—"

"I've been living with him," Paula said slowly. "He wants to marry me."

"He has very good taste," Philip remarked quietly. "I am surprised that he appealed to you."

"I was surprised, too," she said. "But then he's very much a man, and this was something new to me. Very decisive—I felt so safe with him."

"And do you love him?"

"I don't know." She shook her head. He thought how narrow and white her neck was. "I'm so angry with him and so disappointed. He's tried to cheat me. He knows that finding my father is the one thing in the world I have to do, and still he's cheated me and lied. I can't get over it. He's coming back tomorrow, and I don't know how I'm going to face him. I wish I could move out of that hotel and not be there when he gets back."

"Why don't you," Philip said. "Why don't you leave tonight?"

"I'd never get another room; Paris is full of tourists this time of year. You wouldn't have to worry about it; you probably have a permanent suite at the Ritz."

"We have the suite my brother occupied," he said suddenly. "Why don't you move in there? That's an excellent idea! It's empty and no one will use it; my mother has her own suite and so do I. It's completely wasted."

"I couldn't do that," Paula said.

"Why not? For a day or two, until we have recovered the Salt. Then you will be going back to England. It would save you the embarrassment of seeing Fisher in the same hotel."

"It might be easier," she said. "I want to break with him. I've made up my mind."

"Then you don't love him," the prince said. "And I would suggest that you never did. You were alone and perhaps unhappy, and he seemed to be the answer. But he wasn't and no doubt you see that now."

"I don't see anything except that I can't go on, and I don't want a hideous emotional scene," Paula said. "I'm so angry with him and so sorry for him at the same time."

"You have a kind heart," Philip said. "I've never enjoyed hurting people either."

"Especially," Paula remarked, "when one has been hurt oneself. My husband was an expert at crushing other people's sensibilities. By the time he and I were divorced, I didn't have an illusion left about myself. Eric gave me a lot of confidence. But he's lost his own, that's what has happened. He's afraid I shall find my father and choose him, and that's why he's broken his word to me and gone behind my back. He never thought I'd know."

"And would you choose your father?"

"If he needed me," she said. "I don't know. Nobody could answer that. When you find the Salt, I want to be there."

"You should be," he said seriously. "It may prove to be your property."

"That's not the reason." Paula turned to him. "There may be some message from my father, something to lead me to him—I told you, I don't want the Salt!"

"I know you did," he answered. "And I promise you, as soon as I know what is going to happen, I will tell you. I promise you. And you will find that unlike Mr. Fisher, I don't break my word."

"You haven't the same motive." Paula said. "I've destroyed him. He'll be better off without me anyway."

"I don't think he'd agree with that," Philip said. "I feel sorry for him. If you will excuse me for a moment, I can telephone to the Ritz and tell them you'll be using the suite. It will be very much easier for you."

"I know it will," she answered. "I'll take advantage of your offer; I can move in tonight."

A few moments later he was back; he looked down at her and smiled.

"It is all arranged," he said. "You will be very comfortable. And nobody can trouble you there."

"You're very kind," Paula said. "I do appreciate it."

"It isn't necessary; I'm glad to help. Now let us enjoy our dinner and forget about unpleasant things. You have a charming smile, Mrs. Stanley; I want to see it from now on."

"You forget," she said, "it's the Austrians who are supposed to be gay. I'm straight middle German."

"So am I," he said. "Perhaps that's why we understand each other. I know our temperament; we are the only race in the world who have ever tried to live their legends."

"But only the sad, destructive ones—the Götterdämmer-ung," Paula said. "The awful thing is I love Wagner, too."

"I hate him," Philip said and laughed. "It is Mozart for me. You're fond of music?"

"Very fond. Orchestral more than opera, always excepting Wagner."

"Then you must come to Germany," Philip said gently. "There you will hear our music as it should be played. By Germans, for Germans." He reached over, and for a moment his hand rested upon hers. It was warm and the pressure lasted for some seconds. "You must remember the good things about our people," he said. "The world will remind you often enough of what is wrong with us, of what we did in the past. But my answer to them is that it *is* the past; our duty now is to the future. And it's your duty, too, Mrs. Stanley. You are a German, and you have a place among your own race. Understand that, and you won't need anyone like Eric Fisher."

"I was brought up to be ashamed of it," Paula said. "It was never mentioned; my father was never mentioned. My name and nationality were changed. And yet I've never felt English."

"Our blood is strong," Philip said. "It isn't easy to suppress. Why did your mother do this to you?"

"Because of her own shame," she answered. "Because she hated my father and everything he stood for. And I believe now that she hated me; in a quiet way of course, not admitting it for a moment, but she hated me just the same."

"Your life has not been happy," he said. "I'm sorry."

"What about yours? What is it like to have so much money and so much power?"

"It is a heavy responsibility which often becomes a frightful burden," Philip replied. "But there are compensations, and I don't mean obvious advantages like being able to buy whatever you want or go anywhere in the world. I mean the opportunities for doing things, for shaping events in the right way. I must sound very pompous to you, Mrs. Stanley—a dull man with a sense of mission—"

"Not at all," Paula said quietly. "I've never been more interested. Please go on."

"I too have been ashamed of what I am." He lit a cigarette. "My family name has been blackened by our association with the Nazis. And we did associate. My mother tried to resist them; she's proud and she doesn't understand the meaning of fear. But my father wanted to survive. The price was collaboration with Hitler. We collaborated. We used forced labor in our factories; we gave funds to the Party. We protected our interests by participating in their crimes, and as far as the rest of the world is concerned, we were equally guilty. You know this; you know what the name Von Hessel means to non-Germans. Now that my brother is dead, I am the head of the family and responsible for the future. I want to prove that the image has changed. I want to do good, with our money and our power. I want to redeem my family name. I want to serve my country."

"And you'll do it," Paula said. "I really believe you'll do it. Do you know what someone once said to me—at a party—they didn't know anything about me; if you find a good German, kill him before he goes bad."

"I know." Philip smiled briefly. "But you mustn't mind. We are a new generation, you and I. That is what matters. We're different from our parents; I love my mother and naturally she influences me, but I don't think the same way. I can't; I belong to a new world. And I am determined to help bring Germany into it. That is the only excuse for being as rich as we are, Mrs. Stanley, and having this kind of power. To use the money and the power for the right purposes. Otherwise as a family we are damned—and doomed. I am sure of that."

"I wish you luck," Paula said. "You're going to need it. But I think you may succeed. And in a way I envy you, having something to work for."

"You could work for it, too." He leaned toward her; she thought irrelevantly that he was the handsomest man she had ever seen, and the least personally conceited. "You should go back to Germany and see what is happening for yourself. I told you before—don't be an exile."

"And I said I might," Paula answered. "But who knows? Who knows where I'll be in three months' time."

"You could be with your father, is that what you mean?"

"I could—if it worked out that way. Or I may never see him, and just go back to England, to the same empty life. Anyway"—she shrugged and smiled at him, deprecating her own prophecy—"who knows? I may well go to Germany some day."

"And when you do," the prince said, "you will be my guest. I'll get the bill and take you back to the hotel. We can go to the Ritz together."

"You fool," Margaret Von Hessel snapped, "you incompetent, bungling, fool! She's in the Ritz! My son moved her into the suite last night—"

Dunston held the receiver a little distance from his ear. He was in the foyer of the hotel, phoning through to the princess. He had gone to make a report, albeit prematurely, because he was feeling very confident. He had tried to call Paula the previous evening at about seven thirty, judging that she wouldn't have left for any dinner date so early, and got no reply. He had hung up with a mental picture of her lying naked and dead in the bath. He hadn't telephoned again. There would be an inquest, that was normal procedure. He had no intention of being called as someone who lunched with her the day she died.

He kept quiet and assumed that all had gone as he intended. When he phoned through to the Von Hessel suite, he made the mistake of telling the princess that everything was being taken care of, according to her wishes. The furious retort took him completely by surprise; he held the receiver and gasped. Then he swore, obscenely and briefly, without caring whether she heard him or not.

"What the hell's your son doing with her!"

"Never mind that," the princess barked at him. "You leave my son to me and get on with your part of it. She's here, on the floor above—so much for whatever you thought was happening somewhere else. You damned bungler," she said again. "You've had plenty of time to arrange something. Now there's no time left—Fisher is arriving today, and he's found the Salt! If you want our agreement to be honored, you get on and do something at once! Within the next few hours! And don't think you can keep that first payment—the bank will block it on my instructions."

"You mean this," Dunston said. "It's coming to a head today?"

"Tomorrow at the latest. That's what Fisher said."

"One thing"—Dunston was thinking at full speed—"how much does your son know—about you and me?"

"Nothing," she said. "And he never must know. He wouldn't pay you; he'd hand you over to the police! For God's sake, keep away from him!"

"All right," Dunston said. "I'll have to get on with it and do it somehow. But don't be surprised if it's messy. And you can blame your son for taking her out of the hotel. If he hadn't, it would have all been over!"

"Never mind that," she snapped back at him. "Finish it now. Otherwise you won't get a penny!" She hung up. He stood there in the cubicle, looking at the telephone. He'd get nothing—not even the money paid in as a deposit. The old bitch had hemmed him in on every side. He'd tried the accident angle. But if he wanted that money, he couldn't afford to be nice. As he'd said, it would be messy. The floor above, the princess had said. He glanced up at the ceiling. Three floors.

High enough. Bloody messy. But in the time and the circumstances, there wasn't any other way.

"I'm sorry, sir," the receptionist said. "The Louis XV suite is occupied." He remembered the tall German gentleman with the white hair and the tinted glasses who had come in a few days earlier with the same query. He appeared to be fixed on that particular suite in the hotel, and the reception clerk was becoming irritated. He had told him already it wasn't available, and he appeared not to have heard because he asked the same question.

"You are certain?" the man persisted. "I thought it would be vacant now that Prince Heinrich Von Hessel died so unfortunately."

"It is still at the disposal of the family," the clerk said. "There is a lady staying in it now. She arrived last night."

"Oh," the general said, "how disappointing. I had counted on staying here."

"I have no suites available now; the one I offered you before has been booked. But there is a room on the third floor with private bathroom. That became vacant the day before yesterday because we had a cancellation."

"On the third floor?"

"Yes. One moment and I will look up the number and I can tell you the position; I believe it faces to the front."

The general waited; one hand buttoned his top button on his jacket and then unbuttoned it again. Otherwise he remained quite still and calm. A lady. Where exactly was the vacant room in relation to the Louis XV suite. They were both on the same floor.

"It is number 370, monsieur. And it looks out onto the Place."

"Thank you." The general nodded. He unbuttoned his coat for the last time. "I will take that. For a week."

"You will register, please? And your passport."

"Certainly. Here it is. My name is Weiss." The Swiss passport came out of his inside pocket, and he filled in the details
in the register. He gave his address in Spain and signed the
name under which he had lived for ten years.

And that was when he saw the name Paula Stanley written on the line above. He paused, underlining his signature,
and read the address in England which she had given. It was
the same, the place to which he had sent Schwarz. A very
faint color showed around his cheekbones and came in a
patch on his forehead. He was very pale skinned, the coloring of a pure blond. The flush of excitement faded quickly.
She had come. His hands were quite steady, his voice un-
changed.

"You have a friend of mine staying here, I see," he said.
"Mrs. Paula Stanley."

The reception clerk glanced down at the register. The
Swiss passport had changed his attitude; he had a profound
dislike of Germans. He actually smiled at the general. "Yes,
Monsieur Weiss. In fact, the lady is staying in your suite—
she came last night."

"What a coincidence," the general said. "I shall move out
of my present hotel and return in about an hour with my
luggage."

"You'll find it more comfortable here," the clerk said.

"I am sure I shall." The general nodded. "I always used to
stay here." He walked out toward the street, very straight-
backed, one hand in his pocket. It was a stance only too familiar to his subordinates in the days to which he had referred with secret irony, the days when he walked through
the foyer of the same hotel and everyone in sight made way
for him and his entourage. He was back as he had said, within
the hour, carrying a single lightweight suitcase and a heavy
canvas duffel bag, which surprised the porter by its weight.
He traveled up in the lift and followed the porter to his room

on the third floor. His bags were put inside, and he gave a handsome tip. He was saluted and left alone.

He looked around the room; it was beautifully furnished, combining taste and comfort to an extent which he had not enjoyed for many years. Even the smell reminded him of the past; it was a pleasant aroma, peculiar to the Ritz, with its fresh flower arrangements in every room and the scented furniture polish used by the cleaners. He remembered it all. The Louis XV suite was two doors down the passage. He lit a cigarette and went to the window; it was fastened, excluding the noise and dust of the busy street outside. The air-conditioning kept the room a pleasant cool temperature. There was a handsome private bathroom, tiled in primrose yellow. He opened the window on an impulse and glanced down; the sound of the traffic was a steady rumble. He fastened back the catch, preferring the noise of activity to the carpeted silence. Then he removed his jacket, folding it over the back of a chair, and lay on the bed. It was the wrong time to go to her; the mornings were busy in any hotel; rooms were being cleaned, guests arriving and leaving. They would need a slack period, preferably during the heat of the afternoon, or the hours between seven and nine when everyone was dining.

Now that the moment had come to him, he found to his surprise that he was less prepared for it than he had imagined. He had a speech ready; it had been rehearsed ever since that afternoon in Madrid when he opened the English newspaper and saw her photograph. He had read the cutting so many times and fingered it so much that it was frail and frayed. His daughter. The only link with his past life, his only claim to a future beyond his own shrinking span. He was an old man, with nothing to aim for now but a peaceful death in bed and the frustration of his enemies. A sad and feeble ending to a career which had reached such levels of power and found such depths of hunted failure. He had a sense of the grandiose; it had enabled him to add a singular glamor to his role, to speed in his big black Mercedes on a mission of death, like an infernal angel, blond and terrible, something beyond an ordinary man. He had fled the debacle and preserved his life, because the alternative of public trial and a sordid death by hanging repelled his sense of what befitted him. Destiny had denied him for nearly thirty years; he had lived the mean, petty bourgeois existence of a businessman expatriate in Madrid, and counted himself fortunate. But back in the surroundings of his past, the present day and its realities receded; distant as an echo the trumpets sounded in his brain, the haunted music of a *danse macabre* played out before a frightened world. He had lost; everything he had believed in had crumbled away and disappeared, leaving nothing but a memory and a huge genetic crime. Nothing was left to him now but obscurity; for his daughter it could still be different. For her there could be wealth and power in the possession of the Poellenberg Salt, and for him the final satisfaction of seeing his blood triumph through the one living creature he had ever loved. She would be immensely rich, sought after, famous—his thoughts ran on, rioting without discipline, breaking the bonds of common sense he had imposed upon himself. Emotion fought with him and won. The fatal German love of sentimental drama fastened upon the ideal of father and daughter; it swept him forward until he had forgotten the need for caution and concealment. He lay back with his eyes closed, waiting.

"What the hell's happened?" Fisher exploded. He had returned in the early afternoon and gone straight upstairs to Paula's room. The door was open and the room was crowded with people. He pushed his way through.

"Where's Mrs. Stanley? What's going on?"

Suddenly he found himself facing the manager; the man's face was pale and two sweat streaks glistened down each cheek.

"There's been an accident, monsieur!"

"What accident?" Fisher shouted at him. "Where's Mrs. Stanley?"

"One of the cleaners; she was found a few minutes ago. She was cleaning the bath and she was electrocuted—please, monsieur, you must excuse me."

"A cleaner—" Fisher's mind registered only one fact. Whatever the accident, it hadn't happened to Paula. "Look, where's Mrs. Stanley?"

"She left, monsieur." The manager turned back to him with impatience. "She checked out of the hotel last night. That's all I can tell you. Now, please—excuse me!"

Fisher could see two men coming out of the bathroom, carrying a limp body in a blue linen dress and a rumpled white apron; he caught a brief sight of a head lolling back and a blackened face from which two round eyeballs protruded. For a moment he felt sick. Electrocuted cleaning the bath. He turned away and went to the stairs, too anxious to wait for the lift. He went down them so fast he was short of breath when he reached the reception.

"Mrs. Stanley," he said. "She left last night. Did she say where she was going?"

"No, monsieur. She just checked out."

"But you've got a message for me?"

"I don't think so. One moment and I will make sure—no, nothing. There is nothing for you."

"I don't believe it," Fisher said. "She must have left a message. What did she say? Why did she leave?"

"I can't help you," the receptionist answered. "There was a gentleman with her. They came in, collected her luggage, she paid her bill, and she left. I'm sorry, but that's all I know."

"A gentleman," Fisher repeated. "She had a man with her?"

"Yes, monsieur."

"I see," he said. "Thanks. Oh, wait, did they go in a taxi? Would the porter know where they went?"

"You can ask him," the receptionist said. "Perhaps he can remember something."

But the man only shook his head. Fisher had given him ten francs.

"They didn't take a taxi, monsieur," he said. "Mrs. Stanley and the gentleman left in a car. A big Mercedes. I just put in the luggage and they drove off. I'm sorry."

"Never mind." Fisher turned away and slowly he walked back into the hotel. He couldn't quite believe it. Paula had gone with a man, leaving no message, nothing. Just walked out of the hotel and out of his life. It didn't seem possible. He was about to go back and ask the receptionist to check once more if there was a letter, and then suddenly he thought there might be something in his room. He raced up the stairs again and rushed inside. There was nothing. His bag was on the bed. There was no envelope anywhere. She had gone. Now he did feel sick. He pressed his fist against a sudden cramping in his lower gut, and fought against the pain. It was a real physical fact, a reaction of his body to the volcano bursting in his mind. He had lost her. And somebody else had come and taken her away, somebody she had never mentioned, somebody intimate enough to arrive and drive her off in his car, with her suitcases in the back.

But they had spoken on the telephone the same evening; she had been gentle and tender, patient with him when he was jealous. Jealous of Dunston taking her shopping and to lunch. *Dunston!* He grabbed the telephone and gave the number. There was a long pause while his hotel tried to find him and then reported that his key was with the desk and he'd gone out. Fisher swore. He asked to be put through to Mrs. Stanley and was suddenly confronted by a raucous Middle Western voice claiming to be her. He hung up. She wasn't there. Paula wasn't with Dunston. It had been a crazy idea. He got up slowly and went into the bathroom; he washed his

face and looked at himself. He looked ravaged, debauched by
the shock.

"You bloody fool," he said out loud, "you poor bloody fool.
Let this be a lesson to you." He had bought her a bracelet
that morning. It was gold, with lapis lazuli stones and tiny
diamonds set between the links. He had looked at rings but
lacked the courage to produce one when they met. Not till
he had got the Salt out of its hiding place and seen the last
of the Von Hessels. He was in the middle of unwrapping the
box to throw the bracelet out into the street or give it to the
chambermaid when he stopped, rocked back by the solution
which had come to him. The general. That was who she went
away with. They'd found each other. And for all he knew,
while he sat breaking into pieces, they had gone to get the
Salt.   .

"Mother," Philip Von Hessel said, "mother, where is it? I
have a right to know!"

"You have *no* right! How dare you pick up that woman
and bring her to this hotel. Have you gone mad?" He had
never seen her so angry; she was pallid with fury, her curious
yellow-ringed eyes dilated till they seemed black. She stood
in the middle of her drawing room, filled with red roses from
the management, and shouted at him. It was the first time in
his life that Philip had seen his mother lose control. "You
imbecile—you've meddled and interfered from the beginning
—now you install Bronsart's daughter in the one place in the
world . . . Oh, my God, I can't believe it of you!"

"Where is the Salt," he repeated. "Fisher told you. Where
is it?"

"You really want to know?" She snarled at him like an animal; she moved toward him, and for a moment her right hand
lifted as if she were going to hit him.

"You want to know where it is? Very well then, I'll tell you;
I'll tell you where it is. It's in the suite! It's hidden in the

suite where she is staying! Now do you see what you've done?"

"You should have told me," Philip said. "You should have trusted me."

"Trust you? You never wanted me to get it back—you've been against it from the first. Why should I trust you? This is nothing to do with you!"

"You are obsessed," he said. "You know the risk involved in finding it. Nothing is worth the ruin and disgrace of us all. Heinrich couldn't stand against you—God help him—he was like someone already dead. But I'm not afraid of you, mother. I love you, but I'm not afraid. The Salt isn't your property; it belongs to the family. You've pursued this thing in spite of my advice, but you can't go through with it alone. I brought Mrs. Stanley here because she needed help. I also promised her that when the Salt was found I'd tell her; I shall keep that promise. If it's hidden in the Louis XV suite that makes it easier."

"I see." The princess swung away from him. "I see. You want to act the nobleman, the shining knight! That's how you see yourself, isn't it? The man of honor, the good German? You wait, you fool. You wait until the truth comes out, as well it may, and that woman is a witness to it! There won't be money enough to buy her off!"

"I don't think she'll be bought," her son said quietly. "You haven't met her or you wouldn't say that. She's promised to give it back to us, if she has a legal right. And she may have one; we both know that. I won't stand by and see her cheated. When is Fisher coming?"

"I'll tell you nothing." The princess' eyes blazed at him. "Nothing! Get out of my rooms!"

"Very well." She turned her back to him, then the door closed. It was their first quarrel, and it had shaken her. She had depended upon his affection and the habit of submission to her will. Since Heinrich's death, her son had altered. He had always been mature, serious; now he had developed a direction of his own, irrespective of her wishes. He had a different code and strength of character as formidable in its way as her own. For a moment she reflected in mixed rage and pride, that he was not her son for nothing. But where was Dunston—what was he doing? It was always possible that he had reneged on their arrangement and decided to forfeit the money. But in her judgment the princess didn't think so; he was ruthless and cool-headed. Above all he was passionately greedy. For what she had offered, he would take the risk. There was nothing she could do, no outlet for her impatience; she had to wait.

Paula was getting ready to go down to lunch when she heard the knock on her door. The maids had cleaned the bedroom and brought a big bowl of yellow and white roses for the drawing room. Paula had been too tired to inspect the suite when she arrived; that morning she walked around the lovely little paneled room, looking at the period ormolu clock on the mantelpiece, and the eighteenth-century bronze candlesticks that stood on the desk. It was a quiet, sunny room, a blend of delicate autumnal coloring, dictated by the soft honey-colored wood that covered the walls. The carving and design was exquisite, the work of a master craftsman. She had never imagined that such a unique apartment could exist, even in a hotel like the Ritz. It had an atmosphere of peace and remoteness that reminded her of the country. And yet Philip Von Hessel's brother had been the last person to use it, and from the same idyllic setting he had gone out to take his own life.

She heard the first knock and then the second. She opened the door to the passageway.

"Good morning, Mrs. Stanley."

"Oh, hello, Mr. Dunston."

"Sorry to bother you, but I just wanted a word. Can I come in for a moment?" Paula opened the door and stood back.

"Yes, of course. Do."

The general was still lying on the bed when he heard the cry. It came through the open window, high-pitched above the traffic rumble from the street below. He sat up quickly. There was a second cry, but fainter, and it stopped as if something had choked it off. He stepped to the window and looked out. The window of the Louis XV suite was open; there was a clinking sound of breakage. Instinct impelled him. The muffled scream had been a woman's; the faint crash indicated some kind of violence. He wrenched open his door and with a few running strides he had reached the suite. For twenty-five years he had carried a key on his watch chain. He used it then and flung the door open.

Inside the drawing room, a man and a woman were struggling. The man was big and powerful, the windows were latched back, and he was dragging the resisting body of a woman toward them. One hand was pressed over her mouth, the other arm was locked around her, pinioning her. A small table had toppled over and a china figurine lay in pieces on the carpet. It was a scene in which the silence intensified its menace. The general didn't wait; he sprang, and with the half-forgotten reflex of his military training, his right arm swept up and crashed down on the side of the man's face, missing the vital spot in the neck which would have killed him. But the blow was enough.

Dunston's grip on Paula fell away; for a moment he reeled, blinded by the pain in his cheekbone. His vision blurred on the sudden apparition of another man. He grabbed Paula by the arms and threw her violently against the general, knocking him backwards. He heard her breathless cry as he rushed to the door to get away. His head was swimming, and there was a warm rivulet of blood dripping down the side of his face where the general's hand had sliced the skin. He pounded away down the corridor, panicked by the interruption. On the floor below, he found the safety of the service entrance; he slapped a handkerchief against his face and raced on down toward the exit. He didn't know what would happen, beyond an immediate alarm being set up inside the hotel. He'd failed, and with only minutes to go. He'd gone inside the suite, chatting amiably and started some story about meeting Fisher. She was alone and quite off guard. When he opened the windows and made a remark about the view, she actually moved nearer to make it easy for him. He had gone up to her smiling, and seen by her face that she thought he was going to try to make love to her. When he seized hold of her, that was still her impression. She had shouted "No," and tried to pull away, before he slammed his hand over her mouth to stifle a second scream, and pinioned her, dragging her across the floor. The windows had gaped in front of them, only a few yards away. He didn't dare to hit her and knock her unconscious because the assault would leave marks to prove it wasn't suicide. But they had never reached the sill. Outside the hotel Dunston collapsed into a taxi cab. His nerve had been badly shaken. Now it was recovering; he held his throbbing face and swore.

They hadn't got near the window before the intervention of the other man. It was just possible that Paula Stanley hadn't realized that his intention was to throw her out. She might still mistake the attack for an attempted rape. In the initial stages of the struggle before he got her arms pinned down, he had handled her breasts. He went back to the hotel and straight to his room. In the bathroom closet he examined his face. There was a two-inch-long opening and a fleshy bruise. It had been a hell of a blow. He found the bottle of brandy on his dressing table and swallowed a mouthful. Failure. At the best he could expect her to charge him with sexual assault, at worst with attempted murder, if she had realized the connection with the open window. There was a sofa intervening; she might have thought him dragging her toward it. He leaned on the table and steadied himself. So much for the money. There wasn't a chance now.

There was nothing he could do but get to hell out. He pulled his suitcase off the luggage stand and onto the bed, flinging back the lid. As he began packing the first of his clothes, the telephone rang. He hesitated. He could always deny it; there hadn't been witnesses. Women had been known to allege that kind of thing before and the man accused them in turn of being hysterics or acting out of pique . . . The telephone went on ringing and suddenly he picked it up.

"Oh, Christ," he said. It was Fisher on the other end.

"I've been looking everywhere for you," he said. "What the hell do you do in the mornings?"

"I've been seeing the sights," Dunston said. He held the handkerchief to his face, took it away and saw that fresh blood had stained it. He needed sticking plaster. By rights it ought to have a stitch. The man had given him a really professional karate blow—

"What's doing?" He didn't want to know, but he had to say something to Fisher.

"Plenty," the reply came. "Look, I'm going to need your help. I know where the Salt is, and I'm going to pick it up with the princess today. But there's a complication."

"Oh?" Dunston said. Every tooth was aching down the injured side of his jaw. "What's happened?"

"The general," Fisher said. "He's with Paula. When we go to get it, he'll be waiting. I don't want her hurt, if there's any trouble. I want you to come along."

"Where is the Salt?" Dunston said. His mind was far ahead of the conversation; he sucked hard on his lip, seeing again the figure looming at him as he struggled with the girl, delivering that sweeping expert blow. It was a killer stroke, aimed at the neck. There had been an impression of a tall man with white hair, now he remembered it. White hair.

"Christ," he said again, but softly, so that Fisher couldn't hear. That was who had saved Paula Stanley. Of course—he must have been hiding in the suite. . . .

"Where is it?" he repeated.

"In the Ritz. In the general's old suite where he lived during the war."

"Very ingenious," Dunston said slowly. "And I believe you're absolutely right. When you go for the Salt, you'll find both of them. Don't worry. You can count on me to come along. Just let me know the time and the room."

"I will," Fisher promised. "As soon as I've seen the princess. And not a word about the general when you meet her. I've a special reason; I don't want the police called in on this."

"Why should you?" Dunston asked. "You won't need them. I'll come along and hold your hand." He hung up. She wouldn't be able to complain. With her father hiding out with her, she wouldn't dare say anything to call attention. He took out the shirts he had packed and put them in the drawer again. She couldn't accuse him of anything, and risk the police coming around. He was safe. And Fisher had called him in. To recover the Salt. He opened the smaller drawer in the chest and took out his Smith and Wesson pistol. He loaded it and put it in his pocket. He was going to confront a dangerous war criminal, wanted by Interpol. Two birds, he said to himself, and laughed, which changed into a grimace of pain from his swollen cheek.

Two birds with one stone. He might very well earn his money and a medal at the same time.

"Don't be afraid," the general said. "I'm not going to hurt you. Look at me, Paula." She had fallen to the ground when Dunston flung her against him; he knelt beside her, an arm around her shoulders. Her face was streaked with tears; she stared up at him, and he saw the expression changing in her eyes.

"I am your father," he said quietly. "I am your father."

"Father?" It was a whisper from her; for a moment her

mouth quivered, and then she put up one hand and touched him as if to establish that he was real.

"It's you?"

"Yes, it is. Don't cry, my darling child. Let me look at you." He helped her up and for a moment they stood, the general holding her at arm's length. He leaned forward and kissed her on the forehead. Paula took a step forward and threw her arms around his neck. For a long, silent space they stood locked together.

"I can't believe it," she said. "It's really you, and you did come— That man—he suddenly attacked me—"

"I heard you cry out," the general said. "He was trying to kill you. Why?"

"Not kill, rape." She shuddered. "I know him slightly. My God, if you hadn't come in—"

"I should have killed him with that stroke," the general said. "But one slows down; one loses the old skills."

"Father, you shouldn't have come here; you shouldn't have taken the risk! Without the glasses, anyone would know you."

"It's our eyes," he said and smiled. "The mark of Cain. You're beautiful, just as I imagined you. Sit down with me and give me your hand. For twenty-seven years I have dreamed of this."

"And so have I," she said. Her eyes filled with tears. It was a handsome face, but lined and tight-skinned; the brilliant blue eyes gazed at her with tenderness and a strangely triumphant light. The hand holding hers was gripping hard.

"Smile," he commanded. "Smile for me, be happy! This is the most important day in both our lives." He raised her hand and kissed it. "Tell me the truth, am I a disappointment? An old man—feeble and white-haired? Am I what you expected?"

"I don't know," Paula said. "I never even saw a photograph; I hadn't anything to judge by. I just made up a picture of you when I was a little girl, and said, 'That is my father; that's what he looked like.' I am so happy to find you,

I can't think of anything to say. I can't express it, I'm sorry."

"I knew you'd come when Schwarz gave you my message. I knew you'd find out where the Salt was hidden. But before we come to that, my darling, I want to know about you."

"How did you ever find me?" Paula asked him. She slipped her free hand through his arm and clung. There was a fresh, barbered smell about him. Seated so close to him, she felt almost childish, as if the years and the maturity had dropped away from her. "Oh, father." She leaned her head against his shoulder. "I'm so glad we're together."

"And so am I," he said. "I saw the report of your divorce in the English newspapers. That's how I recognized you; you have a strong family likeness to my mother and my sisters. And I knew that Ridgeway was the name of the man your mother married after the war. So I sent Schwarz. He was a good man, very loyal. But even so I couldn't trust him with our secret. I had to send you the riddle because no man alive could resist the Salt. And Schwarz had seen it."

"Why didn't you just send for me?"

"I would have, if he hadn't been killed," the general said. "When I was sure that you wanted to find me. You might have been ashamed, or your mother could have prejudiced you. I didn't know what your reaction to him would be."

"Mother never talked of you at all," Paula said. "She told me you were killed on the Russian front."

"She didn't know the truth," he said. "She couldn't be trusted with it. She hated me."

"I know," Paula said. "She told me almost nothing, just that you were a general in the German army. They changed my name to Ridgeway."

"I was a general in the elite," he said quickly. "In the S.S., where the flower of our manhood served the Führer. We were gods, Paula. We ruled the earth in those days." He held her tight and smiled.

"This was my suite, during the Occupation of France. I lived like a prince—the best food and wines, charming women, people crawling for favors. They were exciting years, wonderful years. I look back on them now, and it's my present life that is the unreality. Mr. Weiss from Switzerland, working in Madrid."

"You don't regret the past?" Paula asked him. His head was lifted, and a proud smile curved his mouth. He looked down at her.

"I regret nothing except defeat," he said. "I regret what was lost, that's all. And we came so close, my child, so very close to winning everything. Now the Jews and the Communists run the world. It has no attraction for me anymore. Tell me about yourself. Your marriage—what kind of man was your husband?"

"It's not easy to describe him," Paula said. "Mother liked him because he had a snob value. But he wasn't made for marriage. All he wanted was motor racing, sex, and excitement. It was disaster for both of us."

"That doesn't matter," the general said. "Next time you will choose better."

"I'll never choose again," she said quickly. "I'm finished with marriage. Now that I've got you, I don't need another man."

"You are a woman." He reproved her gently. "Not a little girl. You must have a man to take care of you. Not an old father in sight of the grave."

"You're not to talk like that," she told him. "I mean it; now I've got you I don't need anyone else. Father, all my life I've wanted someone of my own who loved me. Mother never did, the man I married didn't, now I don't care. To hell with them all. You and I can be together. I can spend my life with you, and I shall be perfectly happy. That's why I came to find you. The Poellenberg Salt doesn't mean anything to me. It was you I wanted. And I've got you now."

"You don't know what you're saying." The general spoke briskly. He hugged her for a moment and then let her go. He lit a cigarette. "You've no idea what you are suggesting. It is quite impossible. Believe me."

"Oh, no, it isn't! We're going away together—back to Madrid if that's where you live. I'll move in with you and we'll just disappear."

"No." He shook his head. He puffed out a stream of blue smoke. "No. You can't ally yourself with me."

"Why not? What do you expect—we meet here and then you just walk out and vanish? I'm not going to let you!"

"I came to find you for a purpose," the general said. "I left Spain, where I've been safe for ten years, and came back to France, to Paris. Not to take you away with me to share my life of exile. A modest flat, a modest income, loneliness, boredom, anonymity! You think that is what I want my daughter's destiny to be?"

"It's what I want," Paula insisted. "It's what I've always wanted—to be with you!"

"You are my child," he said. "And all those years I put something away for you, when I knew that the end of our world was coming and I might well be killed or swept away. I wanted to make sure of your inheritance. I have kept one of the greatest treasures in the world to give you. And now, my darling, it is yours."

"I don't want it," she said. "I don't want the Salt. It doesn't interest me."

"Stop being foolish." He spoke sharply and got up, leaving her on the sofa staring up at him. He began to pace the floor. "The Poellenberg Salt is yours. How can you dismiss it in that way? You've never seen it! You don't know what it means! A huge fortune in gold and jewels, a work of art that could command any price in the world—you will be one of the richest women—you will be powerful, sought after— You'll marry a prince if you want one! People will fawn over you, as they did with me, anxious for a look or a word!"

"Father, please," Paula begged, trying to stop the flow. It had an ugly ring of exaggeration; there was a hard, impassioned look on his face which mocked his former gentleness. When he stared at her, he was angry, almost hostile.

"I may live like a nonentity, an exile—but you shall not! Come to Madrid and share my life—play nurse to me till I sink into the grave! If you imagine I would let you do it, then it was a great mistake for us to meet at all! No—you have a destiny. I planned it for you, and you're going to fulfill it. You're going to possess the Poellenberg Salt. I've come to give it to you."

"It doesn't belong to me," she said desperately. "It belongs to the Von Hessels. And they've discovered where it is— they're planning to get it sometime today!"

He stopped abruptly; the hand holding his half-smoked cigarette lowered slowly to his side.

"What do you mean? How can you know this?"

"Because they have a private detective working on it; he contacted me and I gave him your clue. We made a bargain. He wanted to find the Salt; I wanted to find you. They know everything about it."

"You say they know where it is hidden?"

He was stiff and watchful, completely changed. Paula shivered. The man in front of her was stern and frightening.

"Well," he said. "Answer me, Paula. Do they know where it is hidden?"

"Yes—I told you. They intend to get it today."

"I see," he said quietly. "That woman is trying to cheat me, it seems."

"They're entitled to it," Paula said. "You took it from them, father. It was in their family for hundreds of years; you looted it."

"That's what you think? You think I stole it from them?

But they would try to say this, naturally. It is a lie. The Poellenberg Salt is legally mine. And legally yours. As you will find."

"No," Paula said. "I mean this, father. As far as I'm concerned the past is done with. I'm not your judge for what you did; but the Salt is part of it. I wouldn't touch it. I don't want to be rich or famous because of it. And you've forgotten yourself. You run a risk of being recognized as long as you stay here. An old woman called Madame Brevet recognized you; I went to see her, and she spat in my face when I told her who I was. You had her son shot. We won't talk about that part of it, father, but the Poellenberg Salt *is* part of it. And if you gave it to me now, I'd give it straight to the Von Hessels. I've promised to do exactly that, if I do have any claim."

"You fool," he said slowly. "You fool, to propose such a thing. You know nothing about it. You know nothing of the truth. You'd give it back to Margaret Von Hessel?" He laughed, and it was harsh, contemptuous.

"If you refuse it, one thing I promise you. She will never get it back!"

"Oh, please, please," Paula begged. "Don't let's quarrel—father, can't you see what really matters is you and me! Money isn't important to me, I don't want any of the things you want for me, I don't care about treasure or power or anything. I only have you, in the world. And you talk about going away, leaving me—you'll break my heart if you do."

He looked down at her, and his expression slowly changed. He went over and held out his hand; she took it and he embraced her. She held him tightly, and for the first time since her childhood the prayer formed silently . . . Please, God, please, God . . . Don't let me lose him . . .

"I want you to be happy," the general said. "You are the only person I have ever loved. Thinking of you kept me alive; it gave me hope to know you were somewhere growing up, away from the ruin that followed our defeat. When you were a baby, I held you in my arms and promised you the world. I am not the world, my darling. I have nothing to offer you— don't interrupt me, let me finish this. I have no future; I am an old man and I'm safe. For me that's enough. If I brought you back with me and saw you condemned to live my life, wasting yourself, then it is my heart that would break. I should lose hope completely. I can live through you, know- ing that you are enjoying what I would have given you if we hadn't lost the war. Don't deny me this. Let me gratify my love for you. Take the Salt. At least," he said slowly, "let me show it to you and prove that it is really yours. Then if you refuse it—" He lifted her face and looked at her. There were tears in his eyes. "Don't deny me," he repeated. "I have lived for this."

"Oh, God," Paula whispered, "oh, God, what am I to do?"

At that moment the telephone rang. He held her, his grip on her tight; suddenly it relaxed and he stepped back. "An- swer it, Paula."

She lifted the receiver. "It's me," Fisher said. "Don't say anything, just listen. He's with you, isn't he?"

"Yes," she answered. "Yes, how did you know?"

"Never mind that. I'm coming up in a few minutes. Has he told you where it's hidden?"

"No," Paula said. "Why don't you just leave me alone? I don't want to see you."

"I appreciate that from the way you walked out on me," he said. "But it's not just me; the Salt is in your suite. I'm coming up with a carpenter and Princess Von Hessel. So you'd better get him out of there. I thought I'd warn you."

"Thank you," Paula said quietly. She glanced at her father, standing, listening without comprehension to the one-sided conversation. "Thank you for telling me. And I'm sorry about what happened."

"Don't give it a thought." Fisher sounded curt. "I always

knew if it came to a choice between him and me, you'd choose him." The line clicked as he rang off.

"They're coming," Paula said. "They're on their way up here! Father, you've got to go!"

"The Salt is here in this room," the general said. "I brought something to help us get it out. But now there isn't time. Who told you this?"

"The detective," she answered. "He guessed you were with me; he gave me time to warn you. Please, kiss me good-bye and go *now!* Wait, wait—where can I find you?"

"You cannot," the general said.

"But you won't disappear—you won't just leave me and disappear?"

He bent and kissed her. "The Salt," he said, "that is what matters. Soon you will see your inheritance. And it is yours. The proof is with it." He left her, and without turning to look back, he went out of the door and through to the corridor. For a moment Paula hesitated, fighting the impulse to break down and cry with the abandon of a child who finds itself deserted. Then she ran to the door of the suite and looked for him, but the corridor was empty. A few minutes later the receptionist rang to say that Prince Philip Von Hessel was on his way up.

"You've been crying," he said. She had let him in, expecting to see his mother and Fisher; she showed her surprise in finding him alone.

"What is the matter?"

"Nothing," Paula said. "I'm quite all right. I thought the others would be with you."

"What others? I came to see how you were and to ask you to have dinner with me."

"Your mother," Paula said. "And Eric Fisher. The Salt is here, hidden somewhere in this suite. They're coming to get it. I thought that knock was them."

"She never told me," Philip said slowly. "She never said a

word about it. I think it's a good thing I shall be here. You may need an ally, Mrs. Stanley, if I know my mother. We'll wait for them together. Is that what made you cry?"

"No," Paula said, "something quite different. Could I have a cigarette?"

"Of course." He lit it for her, his face grave. Uncharacteristically he touched her shoulder. "I won't ask about it," he said quietly. "But after this business is over, perhaps we could go somewhere and talk?"

"I don't know," she said. "I don't know what's going to happen. I want to run away!"

"Not now," the prince said. "You have come to the end; you will face it and for what it's worth, you know I'm here as your friend."

"Yes," she said. "I believe you are. I hear them now—that was the door opening."

The first person to come into the drawing room was Margaret Von Hessel. As she saw Paula and then her son, she stopped. She spoke over her shoulder.

"Mr. Fisher—what are these people doing here?"

He came in, followed by a man in overalls carrying a tool bag. He looked first at Paula and then, with taut suspicion, at the prince. Philip had moved close to her; he stood so close that they were side by side.

"Mrs. Stanley?" That was the princess, sharp and imperious. "Would you be good enough to leave—this does not concern you. And you"—she glared at her son—"had better accompany the lady!"

"Mrs. Stanley stays," Philip said quietly, "and so do I." There was a sound outside, and then Dunston walked into the room, one hand in his pocket, an oblong piece of plaster covering his cheek. Paula gasped and stepped back. He looked directly at her and he smiled. He spoke to Fisher.

"I think I'll make sure there's nobody else in here," he said, and before Fisher could say anything, he opened the door connecting with the bedroom and went inside. He came out again and glanced at Paula. His message was clear. Say one word about what happened and I'll set the dogs on *him*. She turned away from him, repelled and helpless before that taunting grin. The memory of his hands on her, of that vicious grip on her mouth and the force of his knee propelling her from behind made her tremble suddenly. He had recognized her father; he knew that there was nothing she could do, that even with Fisher standing a few feet away, she couldn't accuse him. He had gone away from the bedroom and moved to the window; she saw him nudge the long curtains to make sure that nobody was concealed behind them.

"Unless you and Mrs. Stanley leave, I shall call off the search," the princess spoke again.

"They stay or, at any rate, Mrs. Stanley does. I'm not interested in your son," Fisher said coldly. He didn't look at Paula. With the younger man standing so close beside her in that intimate way, he couldn't trust himself to do so.

"I'm the only one who knows where the Salt is, and I shall not do another thing about it unless Mrs. Stanley is a witness. There's a question of ownership, and she's entitled to be here."

"That is exactly my view," Prince Philip said. "Please proceed, Mr. Fisher."

"All right." Margaret Von Hessel swung around on him. "All right, we'll have it on your terms! For God's sake, get your man to work!"

The hotel carpenter came forward and Fisher said, "Try the walls. I think that's where we'll find it. Look for any woodwork that's been replaced."

"Tell me one thing," Paula said to him. "Before you start. How did you find out where it was?"

For the first time they looked directly at each other; Fisher felt the same solar plexus pain. She looked different; the habitual poise was gone. There was something distraught about her—the slight dishevelment of her hair, usually so chic and groomed, and the anxious glances around the room, to Dunston standing immovable and inscrutable, a little away from them all.

"I got it from a friend of Madame Brevet's," he said. "A neighbor who knew the family. Jacquot was a master carpenter; that was the clue. Your father picked him out from the hostages because he discovered what his trade was. And he put him to work here that night. In his own private quarters, where he could work without anyone disturbing him or knowing what was going on. And then he picked him out the next morning and had him shot to stop him from telling anyone. I was sure the general had used him to wall up the Salt or hide it, and when your mother told me he stayed in this suite at exactly that date, I knew that this was where the master carpenter had been employed. As soon as I heard what Jacquot's trade was, all I had to do was find a suitable place. It wasn't very difficult."

"Why don't we get on?" the princess snapped at him. "You've told all this to me—tell the man to begin looking!"

It took half an hour for the carpenter to find the portion of the wall which didn't ring true. He went over the surface from ground level upwards, tapping, while Paula watched him, and the princess remained in a chair, her back stiff in disdain of fatigue, one foot swinging in rhythm to the sound of the carpenter's knocking. She never once looked near her son. Then the carpenter turned around and spoke to Fisher.

"There's something wrong here. It sounds different from the rest of the room." They were to the right of the marble fireplace, about four feet from the ground. The paneling was covered with a beautiful tracery of leaves and acanthus, with a design of daffodils and ears of corn. Fisher bent over the area and ran his finger down the tracery. It was impossible to see a join. "You're sure of this?"

The man nodded; a blackened cigarette hung from one corner of his mouth. The princess had forgotten to object when he lit it.

"I'd say the wall behind this was hollow," he said. "There's nothing solid behind this wood panel. But I can't see where it's been cut—one minute, there's a torch in my bag. . . ."

The beam of light flashed on and hung over this woodwork. Fisher directed it while the man ran his fingers over the raised carved surface.

"Impossible," he muttered. "Impossible to see. Whoever took this wood out and put it back was a master craftsman."

"Yes," Fisher said quietly. "Yes, he certainly was. Can you feel anything different?"

The carpenter was kneeling with his back toward them. His fingers were curled around one large piece of fine scrolling. "Bring the light in closer. That's right. Ah! I think I've found it. There's a roughness here. Look, there it is—a hairline right along the curved piece there! And it goes on, smaller, but it's still there. This is where the wood was cut!"

There was a sound from the princess; before, she had sat silent, betraying nothing except through the pendulum swing of that one foot.

"Open it!" she commanded. "Cut it open!"

The man glanced at her over his shoulder. "I'm not going to damage this paneling, madame. It's eighteenth century and beautiful work. I'll do a good job and I'll take my time." Nobody spoke. Fisher stayed beside him, holding the torch. Slowly and with great care, he put the point of a fine saw along the carving and began to cut. The sound seemed loud out of all proportion; it was as if the watchers had stopped breathing. Paula couldn't move, transfixed by the yellow circle of light and the motion of the saw, backwards and forwards through the wood. Suddenly there was a movement. The princess was on her feet.

"Cut!" she shouted. "Cut through it and for God's sake get on!"

"Do as she says." Fisher spoke quietly. "She can pay for any damage. You can't avoid it. Hurry up, let's get the panel out."

Outside the windows a clock struck; immediately a little Ormolu and porcelain timepiece in the room began its sweet chime. There was a foot left to cut through; the wood was gaping on three sides, showing a line of blackness.

"Hah! That's it—" The carpenter dropped his saw and slowly pulled. Fisher swung the torch beam into the aperture, and there was a sudden brilliant gleam of gold. Because he was nearest, the carpenter saw it first. He shoved the panel aside, and it fell with a clatter, knocking against a table.

"Jesus Christ!"

Fisher dropped the torch and it rolled across the floor; its light went out.

"Help me," he said. "Help me to get it out."

In spite of herself, Paula moved toward them, her view masked by the figure of Margaret Von Hessel.

The two men reached into the darkness to the yellow gleam and very slowly lifted. "Get away from it," the princess rasped at them. "Get away—let me see it!"

It stood on the carpet, shining like sunlight, flashing with diamonds; the huge ruby in the base was red as a wound. Fisher stood upright. "My God," he said, "my God, look at that."

The photographs had not prepared her. They showed something priceless but inanimate. The golden ornament seemed to be alive. The leaves of the tree were visibly trembling; the nymphs and the pursuing satyrs were as mobile as gilded flesh. The beauty and the magnificence burned and glittered like a sun.

"At last," Margaret Von Hessel said, and her voice trembled, with triumph, with passion, with so many emotions that she sounded almost incoherent. "At last I have it back."

"No, Princess Von Hessel. You do not!" The words came from behind them; Fisher sprang around and then stood very still. They were all turned, looking at the man standing in the doorway. There was a gun in his hand.

Fisher didn't need Paula's anguished cry or the gasp of the old woman, who was staring, hands upraised as if to ward off an attack. The general stepped forward into the room. He took deliberate aim at Margaret Von Hessel.

"There is something else in that opening. One of you get it out. If anyone tries anything foolish, I will shoot this woman. You"—he gestured at Dunston—"you—stand with the others. I would very much like to kill you—" Fisher went to the opening; there was something in the darkness, something pale that crackled when his fingers touched it. It was an envelope, yellowed and stiff.

"Ah," the general spoke softly, "good. Now, it is all in German. Let me tell you what is in it."

"No," Margaret Von Hessel cried out, "no!"

"On the twenty-third of April, 1944, you signed the document inside that envelope. It made me the legal owner of the Poellenberg Salt. By deed of gift. Witnessed and binding, legal in any court in the world."

The gun was pointed at her; Fisher calculated that if he made a move, the general would get the first shot through her left breast. There was nothing he could do.

"Father," Paula cried out, "father, don't—"

"That is one document." The general didn't even turn his head toward her. "The second is another deed of gift, made by me for my only daughter. Giving her the Salt. That too is legal. Anywhere in the world." He spoke directly to the princess. "But that is not what you're afraid of, is it? You could fight those papers; you could use your money, and you might even win because I can't defend myself. I thought of that. I knew the end was coming, and I thought of everything. There is another paper, Paula. That is what the princess doesn't want anyone to see."

He spoke to Fisher. "Open it," he said. "Give the papers to my daughter. And move slowly; otherwise she dies." And looking into Margaret Von Hessel's face, he smiled. Fisher glanced at Dunston and quickly shook his head. He handed three folded documents to Paula; he moved very carefully as the general had suggested. He had seen men with that expression in their eyes before. He didn't want to be responsible for the princess' death.

"General Bronsart." Philip Von Hessel's voice was calm. "If you intend to shoot anyone, I suggest it is me. Please don't point your gun at my mother."

The general glanced at him. "Your courage is misplaced," he said. "Your mother would take a risk on your life; you won't do the same with hers. So long as she is in danger you won't move. None of you will. Paula, the two large documents are your proof of ownership of the Poellenberg Salt. The small piece of writing paper is the reason why no Von Hessel will ever dare dispute it. Open it and read it aloud."

She did as he told her, slowly, because her fingers were stiff and clumsy with a growing sense of fear. Dunston had been standing immobile beside the princess. His right arm was crooked slightly against his side; so long as that gun was directed at her, he couldn't move his hand toward his pocket. He was watching the general.

"It's in German," Paula said. "I can't read it."

"Destroy it!" There was a jerky movement from the princess; she took a step forward, one hand thrust out. The little black eye of the gun muzzle followed her. "Destroy it," she cried out. "I'll give you anything, anything—one million dollars—for that letter!"

"No"—the general smiled, mirthless and implacable—"no, you can't buy my silence a second time. You bought it all those years ago, and then you tried to cheat me. To cheat my daughter. The Salt belongs to her. Tell me, Prince Philip, when you offered yourself instead of your mother, did you know about that little note she wrote me? I think not." He shook his head. "I think she kept that secret to herself. Shall I tell you what is in it, Paula? It's a letter from the princess addressed to me. Delivered one night in May, 1944."

"It was the only way," the princess shrieked at them. "You found out about Heinrich's marriage; you threatened to denounce him—you threatened to destroy us all!" She turned to her son, standing white and immobile near Paula. "I told you," she went on, "I told you we have no alternative; Hitler was raving, he would have sent us all to concentration camps, seized our factories; we would have been destroyed!"

"I know this, mother," Philip Von Hessel said. "You told me."

"Ah, yes," the general said, "but that's all she told you, isn't it? That she gave me the Poellenberg Salt as the price of my silence. You knew that, didn't you, and you knew the lie told to the world that it was looted? But that's not what she is offering a million dollars to suppress. That's not what is in that letter which my daughter has. I'll tell you what it says."

"No," Margaret Von Hessel cried out once again, "it's a lie, a forgery—" She stopped suddenly, as if defeated.

"It gives the name of a village on the Franco German border, near Alsace, and the address of a small pension. That, it says in the letter, is where you will find them. 'They suspect nothing and are waiting to be brought to us.' I remember the words. I remember the bargain we made, Princess Von Hessel, you and I, when you signed away the Salt to me in exchange for my silence about your Jewish daughter-in-law, and for a further favor you requested. I granted it to you, didn't I? I kept my bargain. I had your daughter-in-law arrested and your baby grandson. I sent them to Mauthausen to the gas chambers as we'd agreed. How old was the child—eighteen months?"

There was a moment of complete silence. Time seemed suspended. Paula heard his voice and that last question, asked in a mocking tone, and thought suddenly that the ground was sliding away and she was going to faint. With a tremendous effort of will, she focused on his face and saw the burning blue eyes, blazing in triumph at the stricken woman, saw the smile on his mouth and the horrifying, unbelievable lack of remorse at what he had just confessed. Now the floor was swaying. She felt a hand come out and steady her. It wasn't the prince, who was only a few feet away. In defiance of the general and his leveled gun, it was Fisher who had come beside her.

"Mother," Philip Von Hessel said, "mother, you said he *found* her; you never said there was a child—"

"I had no choice," she answered slowly, gathering strength, straightening herself from the moment of collapse. "So long as they lived we were vulnerable. He had discovered it. So might someone else. She was a Jewess, an adventuress."

"And the child," Philip asked her, "Heinrich's son—you had him murdered, too?"

There was no answer. She gestured with one hand as if to defend herself and then decided to say nothing.

"Now, Paula"—the general spoke with exultation, with vindication—"now you know the truth. Do you still want to return the Salt to her? Look at it! Look at the beauty of it!"

"May God forgive you," Paula trembled. "I can't bear to look at the filthy bloodstained thing! The mother and the child—you murdered them, father!"

"A Jewess and a half Jew," the general said. "They were nothing to me. They were dying in millions. Inferior people, polluting the world. What were they compared to that?" In the middle of the floor the great golden Salt glittered and flashed its jeweled eyes at them.

"I wouldn't touch it," Paula cried out, "or you."

"I see," the general said. "I was afraid of this. But I have come prepared. Paula, go to the passage and bring me the bag that's near the door."

"No," she said, "no, I won't do anything for you."

He looked away from her to Fisher, who had his arm around her. "You go," he said. "Take your hands off my daughter and get the bag. Bring it to me. If you don't, I will shoot the princess."

"Steady, darling," Fisher whispered. He let go of Paula and went to the doorway. A duffel bag was just outside. He carried it inside and brought it to the general. The thought passed through his mind of diving on him and hoping that the stray bullet wouldn't hit anyone. If it had struck the princess, he wouldn't have cared. But Paula was there, white and stricken, swaying on her feet. He couldn't take the risk. "Open it," the general ordered. "Now give it to me." There was a small cylinder and a muzzle on a cable. He put the muzzle into the general's outstretched hand. "Now light it!"

His lighter flicked, there was a loud hiss, and a plume of brilliant blue white flame shot from the mouth. Immediately the room filled with a dazzling light.

"No," Margaret Von Hessel screamed, "no, no . . . oh, my God!" The fierce flame of the oxyacetylene licked at the top of the golden tree. In his right hand the general held the gun; with his left he directed the searing fire at the Salt. Already the upper branches were sliced off and lay misshapen and dripping on the floor; the metal began liquefying, as they watched, shielding their eyes against the blinding light. The shape began to blur; the figures of nymphs so nubile in their grace, were mutilated and running rivulets of gold onto the carpet; jewels fell in a glittering cascade.

Margaret Von Hessel was sobbing. There was no noise beyond her choking grief and the fierce hiss of the scorching flame as it devoured and mangled the great golden mass, now so misshapen that it had no longer any recognizable form.

"There is your Salt," the general shouted. "Look at it! Now you can have it back!"

For a brief few seconds he faced Margaret Von Hessel, and the hand holding the gun lowered. With a single movement Dunston got his hand to his pocket. He fired through the cloth, and then brought the pistol out and fired again. The general lurched and gave a cry; his gun fell. Dunston moved around and took deliberate aim at Paula. The oxy-acetylene flame swung in a brilliant arc, and a single agonized scream came from Dunston as the fire hit him. The bullet meant for Paula cracked into the wall feet away from her. For a second it seemed that the general stared at her and tried to speak. Then the dazzling light went out and he fell, hitting the ground at dead weight. Paula screamed. But louder still came the anguished cry of the princess, directed at the maimed and groaning Dunston. "You fool! Too late— you fool!"

Fisher turned the general over. The eyes were still open, the mouth ajar for the words he had never spoken. Within reach of his outstretched hand, the mutilated shapeless mass of the Poellenberg Salt wept golden tears.

"I'm leaving this afternoon." The prince looked older; there were lines under his eyes and a crease running across the fine forehead, which Paula had never seen before. He stood in the suite, very upright and dignified; she thought that outwardly, except for the look of bitter strain, he seemed completely un-moved by what had happened. Whatever their enemies said, no one could deny the Von Hessels' self-control.

"I was going to come to see you," she said. "I'm going back to England. How is your mother?" The last she had seen of the princess was when she had been supported out of the suite, suddenly a collapsed old woman in the throes of shock.

"I think she has recovered," Philip said quietly. "I haven't been to see her, I'm afraid."

"I understand how you feel," Paula said. "I'm sorry."

"I hope you will never understand," he answered. "What my mother did can never be forgiven. I shall have nothing to do with her now."

"You may change your mind," Paula said.

"Would you, if your father had not been killed?"

"No," she agreed. "I don't think I would either. I want to give you something. I won't be a moment. Please, sit down, you look terribly tired."

"Thank you," he said. He made an effort and smiled. It only emphasized the misery in his eyes. "I was worried about you, Mrs. Stanley. I hoped you weren't too upset."

Paula came back; she held an envelope. "I was," she said. "But I wasn't alone, thank God. That made it easier. I'm going to be able to forget the past. You must try to forget it, too."

"It will be very difficult," he answered. "I am a German as well as a Von Hessel. I shall have to live with it all my life. I have to live with the knowledge of what my mother did; that will be the hardest thing I have to do."

"I want you to have these," Paula said. She gave him the envelope. "The legal documents and that letter to my father. You can destroy them and nobody will ever know. Please take them."

He looked at her. "I won't thank you. I won't say anything, but you know—I'm sure you know—"

"I have to leave soon," she said. "I want to go home."

"To England? Home?"

"Yes," she said. She held out her hand. He took it, and instead of the formal kiss, he held it.

"We're going different ways," he said quietly. "But I meant what I said. Will you come to Germany?"

"No," Paula said, "no, Prince Philip. Not now. Looking for roots in Germany was like looking for my father. I'm finished with fantasy. I'm not running away anymore. I said home, and I meant it. Good-bye, and good luck."

He bowed and raised her hand to kiss it. "Good-bye, Mrs. Stanley. I wish it were *auf Wiedersehen!*"

The door closed and he was gone. Paula crossed to the telephone.

"This is Mrs. Stanley," she said. "Please send up for my bags."

The rasping sound of death was in the room. It rose and fell to the rhythm of the brigadier's labored breathing. A bright beam of afternoon sunshine poured from the window and fell over the foot of his bed. Uncountable millions of dust motes flickered in it. It was a very hot day, and the windows were open. Sounds of life interrupted the drowning rattle coming from the brigadier's flooded lungs. He had caught his last cold and suffered his last chest infection. There was nothing his wife could do now but sit beside his bed and wait for him to die. She had refused to leave him, even to let the nurse attend to him.

He was still conscious, although he lapsed into a doze which would be prolonged into death. His hand was held tightly in his wife's, and sometimes he exerted a little strength and squeezed, trying to comfort her. People had been very kind over his illness. Paula's mother had never appreciated the sterling qualities of English character until the nightmare of the general broke over their heads, and the façade they had erected around themselves was torn away by the press and television. Their friends had not deserted them. They had expected to be isolated; instead they were surrounded, comforted, and sympathized with in their dilemma with the hungry newspapers, supported upon every issue by the people they had known over the years. There was not a word of reproach or a look which could be construed as criticism. The village stood fast beside the brigadier and his wife. And then, within a month of it all, he caught pneumonia and she was going to lose him. He was propped high up in the bed, and he turned his head toward her and smiled with blue lips.

"I'm so sorry, darling," he whispered. "I can't fight anymore."

"Don't try," she begged him. "Don't use your strength—just close your eyes and sleep."

"I'll sleep in a minute," he said. "In a minute, darling." But his eyes had closed and he was drifting. The semisleep was restless; he shifted, his head rolling from side to side, and he made little anxious sounds. The rattle of phlegm in his chest was getting louder. Paula's mother lowered her head and wept. She had stayed very calm for his sake, reserving the agonies of crying for the hours spent alone in the spare bedroom. Her daughter and the man she was going to marry had come down as soon as they heard from her; they were downstairs in the drawing room. The doctor had told them it was only a matter of a few hours. Certainly not overnight. They had offered to take her away with them, but she had refused.

She appreciated her daughter's sympathy; she seemed less reserved, less hostile than Mrs. Ridgeway could remember. Not that it mattered, because when her husband died, her own life would come to an effective end. She recognized this with the dignified fatalism of her background. It had made no real difference that her daughter had come down. But it was kindly meant. The hand which she was holding tightened suddenly and then wrenched away. The brigadier's eyes were open, staring at her. There was a slight gray film over them which she had not seen before.

"I couldn't stop it," he rasped at her, choking. "I tried, my darling, but I couldn't do it . . . I killed him. I followed him from Paula's office that day and I killed him. To protect you. To stop the story from getting out—"

His wife gazed at him through her tears. She found his hand and clasped it.

"I knew you did," she said. "I knew it was you when I realized you'd slipped away to London the first time and there was no committee meeting. You did it because you loved me. And you were right. There's nothing on your conscience, except love."

"I failed," he mumbled. "All your suffering—I'd have done anything . . . You'll be all right, my darling, won't you? You'll be all right?"

"Of course," she said, "of course. I shall do just what you want me to do. And please God we will soon be together."

"He died very quickly." The brigadier was gasping, fighting for the words. "I burned my walking stick. I don't regret it, my darling. There's nothing in the world I wouldn't do for you—"

"There's nothing in the world you haven't done." His wife leaned close to him; for a moment her lips pressed against his cheek. His jaw slipped, and suddenly there was a harsh, throttled sound coming from the open mouth.

"I love you," Paula's mother whispered, "I love you, Gerald. I'll just wait to be with you."

He didn't answer and he didn't hear. There was a last choking breath and then the room was quiet. His wife put her hand over his eyes and pressed the half-closed eyelids shut. Before she went out of the room she kissed him again.

"I'm very sorry, mother. I wish there were something we could do." There were tears in Paula's eyes; Fisher had his arm around her, but when her mother came into the room, he let go. Paula had gone up to her and taken her arm. Watching them, Fisher saw the mother flinch. She didn't like being touched by Paula. He was not surprised when she disengaged herself. She had come into the room and said simply, "Your father is dead."

It was the same flat statement as the one which had brought them down from London. "Your father is dying. I thought you would like to know."

And now in the sunny room, with the two Labradors settling at her feet, she faced them both with the same stoic dignity.

"He was a wonderful man," she said. "He gave me perfect happiness." There seemed nothing more to add; she didn't appear to want confirmation or sympathy. She had sat down and was stroking one of the dogs. He saw Paula standing in the middle of the room, more forlorn and alone. than her mother. And that was when he went over to her, taking her hand.

"You're quite sure you don't want us to stay, Mrs. Ridgeway? We'd be very happy to stay with you or take you back with us."

"No thank you," she answered. She even gave him a faint polite smile. "It's very kind, but I don't want to keep you and Paula here. I would prefer to be alone. I don't want to leave this house; it was our home. He loved it."

"We'll be in touch tomorrow," Fisher said.

Mrs. Ridgeway got up and came over to them. She held out her hand and Fisher shook it. There was a brief moment when mother and daughter embraced and then Mrs. Ridgeway had stepped back.

"Thank you for coming," she said. "And I'm very happy for you, Paula. If you have anything like the joy in your life that your father and I have had together, you will be very fortunate indeed. If you don't mind, I won't come outside with you. I think I will go and lie down."

They went out of the drawing room and through the front door into the sunshine. His car was parked in the forecourt. He opened the door for Paula and then climbed in the other side. He lit a cigarette and gave it to her.

"I'm not going to say anything to you," he said, "except I

love you very much and I'm going to make you very happy."
He reached over and kissed her. "It's all over now, my darling. It's a new life for both of us." He switched on the igni-
tion and the engine throbbed. "Let's get to hell out of here."